UNEXPECTED GUESTS

There was an explosion of gunfire from the dining room, sounding like a close-up gunfight.

Matt Kincaid lurched to the side, turning as he went, hands flashing for his guns. It was instinct, animal self-preservation.

By the time he had turned, his guns—the ivory-handled Scoff and the Peacemaker—were finding their targets and starting to dance.

He found himself recognizing the enemy moments after he'd killed them.

EASY COMPANY

EASY COMPANY

IN COLTER'S HELL

COMPANY

JOHN WESLEY HOWARD

A JOVE BOOK

First Jove edition published October 1981

First printing

Printed in the United States of America

Jove books are published by Jove Publications, Inc., 200 Madison Avenue, New York, NY 10016

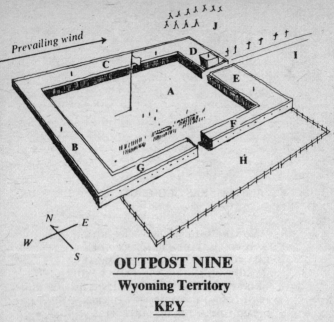

OUTPOST NINE

Wyoming Territory

KEY

A. Parade and flagstaff

B. Officers' quarters ("officers' country")

C. Enlisted men's quarters: barracks, day room, and mess

D. Kitchen, quartermaster supplies, ordnance shop, guardhouse

E. Suttler's store and other shops, tack room, and smithy

F. Stables

G. Quarters for dependents and guests; communal kitchen

H. Paddock

I. Road and telegraph line to regimental headquarters

J. Indian camp occupied by transient "friendlies"

INTERIOR   OUTSIDE

OUTPOST NUMBER NINE
(DETAIL)

Outpost Number Nine is a typical High Plains military outpost of the days following the Battle of the Little Big Horn, and is the home of Easy Company. It is not a "fort"; an official fort is the headquarters of a regiment. However, it resembles a fort in its construction.

The birdseye view shows the general layout and orientation of Outpost Number Nine; features are explained in the Key.

The detail shows a cross-section through the outpost's double walls, which ingeniously combine the functions of fortification and shelter.

The walls are constructed of sod, dug from the prairie on which Outpost Number Nine stands, and are sturdy enough to withstand an assault by anything less than artillery. The roof is of log beams covered by planking, tarpaper, and a top layer of sod. It also provides a parapet from which the outpost's defenders can fire down on an attacking force.

one _____

The dispatch rider, Private Clayton Pomeroy, rode for his life. He was a nervous gent to start with, and the band of Indians swarming after him didn't help any.

He glanced back, his face contorted by fear.

"Band" and "swarm" were dead-on, he decided.

Dead wrong, actually. He was given to exaggeration. There were only four Indians, not enough to *swarm*. But the danger appeared real enough.

He'd ridden out of regimental HQ early that morning, bound for Outpost Number Nine and Easy Company. He'd been told the mount he'd drawn could run forever.

He split the air now with curses as he realized that forever wasn't far away and that the durned horse could run so far because he ran so *slow*.

The early morning on the gently rolling High Plains of Wyoming had been pleasant enough. Spooky perhaps, with the early light filling the draws with purple shadows and creating worrisome shapes elsewhere, but pleasant and uneventful. But then, along about noon, with the high sun flattening the plains and turning them a brilliant yellow, the Indians had ridden out of a draw and gotten on his tail.

1

After the first whoops and yells they'd fallen silent. That was kind of spooky too.

Pomeroy asked his mount for more speed, but didn't get it.

He thought of emptying his Scoff at the hostiles. But he also didn't figure that would do much good. They were probably too far back, and he'd miss.

He lay over his mount's neck, deciding to let the hostiles tell him when they'd come into range. If the first slug didn't get him, then he'd know. And he'd cut loose with his Scoff and—

Damn! They'd be using rifles, the brand-new repeaters the government kept giving those bastards. They'd still be out of range.

The plains flowed under his mount's hooves, the sandy soil, the buffalo grass with its two-foot roots, bunch grass, grama grass. Perfect for a goddamn cemetery.

He figured he was about halfway to Outpost Nine. But halfway didn't count. He sure as hell hoped the message for Captain Warner Conway was important. It could be Pomeroy's epitaph.

He dipped down into a draw and his mount labored up the far side. It wouldn't be long. Maybe he should just hit the ground and make a stand. Pomeroy's Last Stand. It didn't have the same ring as another, more famous Last Stand, but he'd be just as dead.

His horse stretched out as the ground ran level for a distance. Pomeroy glanced around to see how close the hostiles were now. . . .

And almost had a heart attack!

There was one practically running up the ass end of his horse, and he was grinning.

Jesus! Merciless, cold-hearted bastards. They were toying with him. He grabbed for his Scoff.

The Indian closed fast, reached out and grabbed Pomeroy's hand. "Please. We mean no harm. Please stop."

Pomeroy stared at him, wild-eyed. His horse kept running.

"If you do not stop, then we will have to kill you," shouted the Indian.

Since his dash for safety hadn't gone as planned, Pomeroy threw on the brakes and his weary horse stumbled to a halt.

The Indian grinned again. And his three companions grinned too. Pomeroy was chilled to the marrow. "It is a nice day for

2

a hard ride," said the Indian, "but this is far enough."

Pomeroy finally noted the absence of warpaint. Could these be what were called friendlies?

"We think you must be riding for the Americans at what they call Outpost Nine. Is that right?"

"Yeah, goddammit, Outpost Nine. An' you 'bout scared me half to death. Whyn't you *say* somethin'?"

"We did, and you rode faster."

Pomeroy didn't care for the implications. "Jeez, you fellers is real lucky I didn't shoot and kill you."

"We are Cheyenne," said the Indian, as if that were sufficient rebuttal (and it probably was), "from the village of Chief Walks Bent Over."

"You're from the reservation?"

"Yes."

"How come you're off it?"

The Indian responded crossly, "We were still on it when we saw you."

"So whaddya want?"

"I am Brave Elk. And this is a gift from Walks Bent Over to the American, Kincaid, at the outpost." He handed Pomeroy a worn notebook.

"What is it?" asked Pomeroy.

"We have kept it this past year. It is from the Greasy Grass."

Pomeroy, young and new to the frontier, wondered what the hell the greasy grass was. "You're sure he'll want it?"

"We think he will. It is our gift for being a friend. Goodbye." They turned to leave.

"Hey," cried Pomeroy, "you don't know if there are any more of you fellers up front of me somewhere, do you?"

"The path to the American post is thick with danger," said Brave Elk portentously. "Ride with care." Brave Elk, like many Indians, had a nice sense of humor.

Pomeroy's eyes bulged. "You-all don't feel like ridin' along a ways, do you?"

"If we wished to ride farther, we would deliver the gift ourselves. But we must return to the land that the White Father has given the Cheyenne. He has been so good to give us land that we have always lived on . . . we do not wish to make him mad."

"Good thinkin', Brave Moose—"

"Elk."

3

"Same thing."

Brave Elk smiled thinly, held up a hand palm outward, and said in Cheyenne, "May the Great Spirit spit on you." Then he and his friends rode off.

Pomeroy's mount had been contentedly nibbling at the grass. The dispatch rider had a hard time getting him moving again.

A few hours later he spied Outpost Number Nine in the distance. It was his first visit, and he hadn't known what to expect. What surprised him was that it looked like a fort. Not some casual, token outpost—a shack in the wilderness—but a real fort.

And he was quite right. Outpost Number Nine, which squatted atop the highest rise within a mile's radius and which commanded an unimpeded field of fire with no draws or gullies for about a quarter-mile out from its walls, was indeed built like a fort.

There were high walls or ramparts, behind which guards strolled, peering out over a chest-high parapet. The walls, as he drew closer, revealed themselves as composed of sod and timber, and they appeared to form a large, square fortification, unbroken save for the eastward-facing main gate and a gate to the paddock, which he saw and identified at the southern end of the Post.

What Pomeroy didn't realize was that a "fort," in army terminology, was not a physical description but a designation. No fortification below regimental level was supposed to be called a fort. A number were, of course, but inaccurately.

Pomeroy rode through the main gate and immediately saw that all the post's housing was built right into the walls. That was what the guards walked on. While soldiers were sleeping, there were guards walking right over their heads . . . and likely *peeing* right over their heads too. Pomeroy smiled. He hoped the roofs were thick, which they were, mercifully, though not quite thick enough to withstand the winter meltdown and the spring rains.

Directly to Pomeroy's front, on the far western side of the parade, was the orderly room, Easy Company headquarters. Pomeroy rode toward it, skirting the flagpole in the center of the parade. The everpresent plains wind was making the flag at the top of the pole stand tall, but at ground level the air was calm. And right warm, thought the dispatch rider.

Pomeroy dismounted and marched into the orderly room.

First Sergeant Ben Cohen looked up from behind his desk.

"Message for Captain Conway from Regiment, Sarge," said Private Pomeroy, handing over the dispatch bag. "Also got a gift here for someone named Kincaid . . . from another someone named Walks Crooked and the Brave feller."

Upon hearing his name, the tall, raw-boned person of First Lieutenant Matt Kincaid, company adjutant, appeared from an adjoining office. "Brave Elk? From Walks Bent Over?"

"That's them, sir. They s'prised me on the way here. I almost kilt them 'fore I found out they didn't mean no harm."

"Is that so?" Matt said laconically. "I'm Kincaid. What have you got for me?"

"Just this, sir." Pomeroy handed over the worn notebook. "He said they'd had it a year. I'd be careful though, sir—handling it, I mean. Injun said it came from some greasy grass."

Matt vanished into his office with the notebook, and Sergeant Cohen took the dispatch into the CO's office to give to Captain Conway.

Cohen reappeared and went back behind his desk just as Matt was coming back out of his office. "There's no name on this book, Sergeant, but it reads like it might have belonged to Kellogg."

"Mark Kellogg? The journalist who was with Custer?"

Matt nodded.

"But they didn't do anything to him, sir, besides kill him. Didn't take his clothes like they did the rest, didn't mutilate him."

"Yes. But no one found anything that Kellogg had written, either, which was kind of unusual, seeing he was there to write." Matt weighed the book in his hand. "Maybe I'd better send it on for some kind of verification."

"If it's the real thing," said Cohen, "you'll never see it again, sir."

"No doubt. But what if it's not the real thing, just the notes of some poor, dead soldier, if indeed it came from where Brave Elk had said it did?"

"'Scuse me, sir," Pomeroy broke in, "but what's the greasy grass?"

"That's what the Indians call the Little Big Horn, soldier." Matt flashed him a quick smile, forgiving him his ignorance.

Then he asked Cohen, "What did the captain get?"

"Dunno, sir. He's readin' it now."

Captain Warner Conway had broken the seal on the envelope, removed a set of orders, read them . . . and then read them again.

Now he leaned back in his chair, a faraway look in his eyes. . . .

It had been 1872, five years earlier. Warner Conway, a captain then as now, had taken his leave back East. And as was customary when they spent his leave in the East, he and his black-haired wife, Flora, passed the time on the spacious Maryland estate of Flora's family. Most of the time, at any rate. But there were parties about the state to attend, as well as functions in the nation's capital, and there were the Washington sights to see. Tourist attractions. Warner and Flora had been out West for so long that with every passing year they felt more and more like tourists.

One such tourist attraction was the exhibit of paintings that hung in the Capitol Building, and on one afternoon, Warner and Flora Conway were part of a small crowd that stood before a large painting.

The painting was by Thomas Moran, one of several Moran canvases on display. It showed a deep, yellow-sided canyon with an apparently prodigious waterfall in the distance. The scene was awesome. And the painting was entitled *Grand Canyon of the Yellowstone*.

"Warner," murmured Flora, "do such places really exist?"

"Congress thinks they do. When they got a look at these paintings and some photographs and eyewitness reports, they—"

"Lookit them falls," said another tourist. "How high d'you suppose they are?"

Warner Conway looked at the tourist, a stout man a good deal shorter than himself, and answered, "They measured them out at three hundred and eight feet." He turned to his wife. "Flora, remember when we went to Niagara Falls? Well, these are supposed to be twice as high."

"No kiddin'?" said the stout tourist. "That a fact?"

Warner wouldn't have guessed the man's name was Flora. He and his wife exchanged smiles and decided to humor the fellow. "Yes it is," Conway said. "And beyond those falls is

6

the plateau. Enormous, almost eight thousand feet high, and filled with boiling geysers and sulphur springs and the Lord only knows what else."

"Awww," said the man, "come on."

"It's a fact," declared Warner Conway. "Back in 1807 there was a man called Colter. He'd been with the Lewis and Clark expedition, but the year before, he'd left them to go on his own, trapping and exploring. That way, I suppose he figured that if he found something great, it would be his."

"That makes sense," said the man.

"Well, he stumbled into this place, likely the first white man ever to see it. But when he came out and described what he'd seen, no one would believe him. They figured he was just spinning yarns, as Mountain Men are apt to do, the grander the better. But he told the stories so well that they became legend and this place came to be known as Colter's Hell. Then Old Gabe went on in and came back out—"

"Who's Old Gabe?"

"Jim Bridger. He came out telling of boiling springs and steaming fountains and this cliff of black glass, and they didn't believe him, either. They called his stories 'Jim Bridger's Lies.' Of the two names, I kind of prefer Colter's Hell. Anyway, that plateau's just as virgin as what's in that painting there, and it's going to remain so."

"How come?" inquired the stranger.

"Because Congress just made it a National Park."

"What the hell's a National Park? Pardon the French, ma'am."

"I'm not exactly sure," replied Warner Conway slowly. "Just a place where everything gets left alone, to live and die— the land, the trees, the animals, everything."

The man thought it over. "I dunno," he finally said. "That don't sound American to me. I mean, look at that place. A feller could make a bundle sellin' tickets to look at that, and *that's* American."

Warner Conway shook his head slowly. He had to agree that that was the American way, up until then.

"Well, somebody'll do it, you wait and see," said the man. "By the way, long as we're talkin' so much, my name's Hiram Peckinpah. You're infantry, aintcha?"

"Sort of," said Warner—the trim on his uniform was certainly light blue. He introduced himself and Flora to the pushy but pleasant fellow, and then explained the difference between regular infantry and mounted infantry.

"So you ride horses, so what? You're just like regular infantry, only lazier."

Conway was preparing a retort when Peckinpah grinned disarmingly. "I sell food, myself. An' hardware. An' hotels. An' guns. Just about everything. I'm an entry-pre-noor. I'd give yah my card, 'ceptin' it wouldn't do me no good, you being in the army. But, talkin' about food, I'm *hungry*. How about joinin' me fer dinner?"

The Conways declined.

"My treat. Mind yuh, that don't happen often."

"Thank you, no, Mr. Peckinpah—"

"Hiram."

"Hiram. But we'd rather look around some more, and then there are some places we have to visit."

After Peckinpah had hurried off, Flora said, "Funny little man."

"Funny?" Warner Conway was thinking about "the American way." "I suppose so."

"Oh, Warner. Do you think we'll ever get to go to someplace like this?"

"Maybe, someday. But I just remembered, we have to go to the Adamses for dinner. We'd better hurry."

"The Adamses? Who are they?"

"Classmate of mine. Sam. He met you a few times." He watched for a reaction, but there was none. "It's a party for a lot of my classmates. There are some I'd like to see."

"But not Sam," she said, reading his expression.

"No. Sam was always . . . envious." And again he eyed her very closely.

"Envious? Of what?" She was oblivious to his meaningful stare.

Warner Conway smiled, remembering. It was well that he could remember the fiercely competitive Sam Adams.

Conway straightened in his chair and barked, "Sergeant Cohen! Matt!"

The two men entered the office, the rangy Kincaid and the shorter, bearlike Sergeant Cohen. "What's up, sir?" asked Cohen.

"We're going to Colter's Hell."

Matt grinned, but Cohen frowned. "We? All of us?"

"You've been wanting to get off post, haven't you, Sergeant?" Conway smiled. "I figure fifty, sixty men. We've got about a week to decide. Come on, Ben, don't look so unhappy."

"Jes' thinkin' about the work, sir, to say nothing of the saddlesores. It's gonna be some move."

two ─────────────────────

In 1864, the year Montana was declared a United States Territory and Bannack City became its first capital, a small mining camp sprang up in the west central part of the territory and was named Last Chance Gulch.

The next year, when Virginia City replaced Bannack City as the capital, it was still Last Chance Gulch.

But by 1875, when Last Chance Gulch became the territorial capital, that small mining camp had grown to accommodate more than three thousand souls and had been renamed Helena.

And it was in Helena, in the Spring of 1877, that U.S. Marshal William Quaid gave his young deputy marshal, Cal Murphy, an assignment. Young Murphy, twenty-three going on fifty, had recently returned from a successful six-month manhunt.

"Do you remember the Raffertys, Cal?"

"Natcherly. I remember last year, after they rid south from here, heard they was biddin' t' turn into right serious outlaws. Got them some pards, even worse than they was, an' played hell down t' Radersburgh an' Bozeman an' Virginia City an' the mining country." He shook his head in sorrow.

10

"And we were thinking we were going to have to stop them."

"You mean *I* was gonna have to stop them. They was once my buddies." Both Murphy and the Raffertys were Irish and local boys, but while Cal was small, wiry, hard, fair and straight, Tom, Jim and Jack Rafferty were all squat, muscular, mean and crooked. "But they ain't my buddies no more, not since they went wrong," he concluded.

Marshal Quaid eyed a wall map.

"But we figured they was finished," Cal went on. "Disappeared last summer after they got down kinda close to what you might call Sioux country. Leastways, Custer woulda called it that." He grinned, showing tobacco-stained teeth. "We figgered the hostiles musta done 'em in."

"Well, they didn't," said Marshal Quaid. "Last fall, soon after you took off after the Pittman gang, they showed up again. Same stuff, down around Yellowstone City, 'Ginny City. I figure"—he regarded the map again—"that they got a hideout of some sort, south of Yellowstone City, somewhere in the mountains there."

"You don't mean Colter's Hell, do you?"

"No. Ain't no point in them going that far. All that's up there is boilin' water and geysers."

Murphy had never been to Colter's Hell, but he'd heard differently. He didn't say so, though. Wouldn't make any difference. He'd go where the trail led.

Nonetheless, he too expected to locate the Raffertys somewhat closer. "They still operatin' in the 'Ginny City area?"

"Three, four weeks ago I would have said yes, but now they've dropped out of sight again, same as last year."

"Mebbe the Indians did get 'em this time."

Marshal Quaid shook his head slowly. "It was a better bet last year. Them hostiles was nailin' everyone then. But this year's a whole different story. The Sioux Nation's just about had its back broke, Chief Joseph's on the run. Hey, if you run into that old bastard, give 'im a howdy for me."

"Will do."

Marshal Quaid's eyes narrowed as he peered into some imagined distance. "No sirree, I don't plan to wait another six months to find out the hostiles didn't get them."

"Get who?"

"The Raffertys. Who else?"

"Had me confused there for a second."

"Well, get unconfused real fast, Cal. Find those Raffertys, them or their scalps. They've done run out of rope."

Murphy had headed for Virginia City, and from there had trailed southeast, scaring up leads where none were apparent. One pestered cowpuncher had managed to remember some "fellers," and a flustered saloon gal had babbled something about a mean, heavyset gent with the initials "T.R." tattooed on his butt—courtesy of his brothers, Cal recalled—and still another gent, a hollow-eyed drifter, had tossed down a shot of rotgut and said something about Yellowstone.

By early summer, Murphy had made Yellowstone City, but the trail didn't stop there. It headed south, climbing into the mountains.

Murphy had moved real gingerly then, following the Yellowstone upstream. He figured they were somewhere close by.

But they weren't. Folks in both Emigrant and Emigrant Gulch—flanking the Yellowstone west of Emigrant Peak—had seen some men answering the descriptions, but they weren't around anymore.

"Where'd they go?"

"Upriver. We figgered they was hunters or trappers or mebbe even gummint folk. That's a gummint park up there now, y'know."

The Raffertys, government folk? That was either a big laugh or he'd made a big mistake somewhere along the line. But he had no choice, so he climbed on.

The traveling wasn't hard. There was a trail alongside the Yellowstone, just about wide enough in most spots for two wagons to squeeze by. And judging from the wear and tear on the trail, a number of wagons had done just that.

More folk were visiting the park than he'd figured on. He'd heard it was going to be popular, but not that soon.

He climbed steadily, but moved more and more slowly as the air got thinner and his horse had more trouble breathing.

Finally, as summer was beginning to crest, he reached the park. He didn't know where the boundaries were, but he saw something steaming off to the side and he figured he was there.

He continued following the river upstream as it curled east and then began to curl back around to the south. He found himself riding into a slight trench, a shallow ravine. Slopes of yellow rock began to lift away from the river's banks.

Then, at the lower end of the twenty-four-mile-long Grand Canyon, the trail left the river and climbed to run along the edge of the fourteen-hundred-foot-deep ravine, the Grand Canyon of the Yellowstone. Cal Murphy followed the trail, his wonder increasing with each careful step his horse took.

At length, something more than ten miles later, he dismounted and stood about where the painter Thomas Moran must have stood when he painted his picture. He gazed at the distant Lower Falls, their turbulent thunder audible even at that distance, and surmised, *I'll say it's going to be popular*.

But he wasn't there to sightsee. He had work to do. He grained his horse, mounted and rode on.

As the day grew late he reached the plateau proper, which the Indians called the "Summit of the World," and angled west, following a set of wagon tracks over grassy meadows and in among fir and aspen.

The place abounded with game. If he'd kept a list, he would have written bear, moose, elk, buffalo, bighorn sheep, deer, antelope, wolves, coyotes, rabbits, mice. . . .

A trumpeter swan soared overhead. Murphy thought it was a big goose. . . .

There didn't seem to be any species lacking—even livestock cattle with a Rocking K brand.

What the hell? Had he wandered back outside of the park? If not, what were these cattle doing here?

Murphy lost the track he was following, and soon after that, as it rapidly became a pitch-black, moonless night, he got lost himself.

He rode slowly through the trees. He didn't think a wild animal was apt to jump him at night, unless his horse stepped on a bear's foot or something, but maybe the animals way up here were different. And further contributing to his unrest were the odd rumblings and hisses and gurgles and murmurs—not the soothing nocturnal sounds to which he was accustomed. He rode with his right hand resting on the butt of his Colt.

At length he came out on what seemed to be an open patch of meadow. His eyes had become sufficiently accustomed to the dark to tell him that much.

He picketed his horse where it could graze, built a small fire and spread out his bedroll. It was about a half-hour between

13

the time he came out upon the meadow and the time when, squatting in front of his fire, he figured the coffee and beans were hot.

Along about then his horse began to make noises and yank at its picket rope.

Murphy drew his Colt, kicked out the fire and waited. It might be a cougar after the horse. Then again, it might be hostiles.

His eyes slowly became reaccustomed to the dark.

And then, suddenly, less than a hundred yards away, there was a huge roar and a white cloud shot up into the air, a dim, ghostly fountain, climbing and climbing. . . .

It went on for better than four minutes.

Murphy wasn't in the path of the runoff, fortunately, but he got sprinkled some, and damn!—that water wasn't cold, not by a long shot.

It was back into the trees for him, pronto, him and his horse. What in the world had he stumbled onto? Colter's Hell didn't begin to describe it.

Murphy didn't get much sleep. Besides the constant symphony of muted rumblings, gurgles and wheezes, the damned geyser kept roaring. All night. Just when he was about to drop off, whoosh! there it went again.

It got so unsettling that he began to distrust the trees he was lying among. What the hell kind of tricks did *they* do?

And then, unexpectedly, it was getting light again.

Murphy pulled himself together, dragged himself and his saddle back out of the trees, and looked around.

Whoosh! there went the geyser, and in the morning light he could appreciate its magnificence. Well, he allowed, if something was gonna keep you up all night, it might as well be spectacular. He tried to guess at the height of the geyser's plume. More than a hundred feet, sure.

"Now where the hell's that damned horse?"

He'd let the horse, already spooked, run free. He was an old friend, the horse. He wouldn't go far, just far enough to get out of harm's way should a cougar or bear come wandering by.

Murphy whistled and the horse replied, and Murphy dragged his saddle in that direction.

A half-hour later, chewing on Indian pemmican, he was

backtracking his own trail, trying to find where he'd lost the wagon track.

He rode northeast, through trees and across open meadows, over the Central Plateau (although he didn't know it was so named), eventually reaching a vast, open valley. He recognized it as one he'd crossed the previous evening. Was that where he'd lost the wagon tracks?

Cattle were grazing in the valley and Murphy saw, far off, a couple of punchers. And some kind of wagon.

Damn. He must have been following a chuckwagon.

Murphy stayed in the trees that fringed the valley and began to work his way east. By noon the trees had curled around northerly to encounter the Yellowstone. He rode down the river, which was placid, thinking he'd come upon something he'd seen the day before and get his bearings.

He heard a roaring up ahead and was puzzled. He hadn't seen anything familiar yet, but here he was at the falls again.

As it turned out, though, they weren't the same falls. These were the Upper Falls, half the height of the Lower. And he remembered having seen them a mile or so off when he'd turned away from the river.

So that's where he was.

Just then, movement caught his eye. Approaching him, working its way upstream, was a mule train of nine wagons drawn by three ten-mule teams. They were still some distance off, and Murphy dismounted and moved deeper into cover.

Mules made sense, he thought as he waited. Oxen might have been surer and stronger, but oxen were grazed and there wasn't a hell of a lot of graze on the way up the trail. Mules were grained.

But what were they hauling? And where?

And what kind of National Park was this? It was busier than a goddamned beehive.

The mule train passed him, the three teams driven by three ornery-looking teamsters, one of whom seemed vaguely familiar. Murphy waited until they were a quarter-mile beyond him, then rode out on their trail.

After a short distance, two of the mule teams were turned west. The third team, with the three remaining wagons, continued on along the Yellowstone. Murphy followed them.

At the point where the river opened up into the magnificent

Yellowstone Lake, the mule team drew the three wagons across the river, which was just a stream at this point, and continued on along the east shore of the lake. Murphy waited until the three-wagon train was out of sight and then he too crossed the river and rode after them.

Murphy thought the last of the three wagons was loaded with rough-hewn timber. But where could they be hauling it, and why?

An amusing thought then crossed his mind. Was it possible that the Raffertys took up freighting in the summer? He tried to remember whether any of the Raffertys he'd known had ever plied an honest trade, such as freighting.

But he couldn't remember. It was a silly idea, anyway.

He rode on.

three ────────────────────

The cavalry detachment, a forty-man troop commanded by First Lieutenant Marcus Grady, left Fort Ellis early one morning and rode a few miles west to Bozeman to meet the team of surveyors.

The team was made up of several civilians, including a woman, and several officers from the Corps of Topographical Engineers. They'd stayed the night in a comfortable Bozeman hotel, both out of deference to the woman and in order to store up cozy memories for the rugged days and nights that lay ahead.

The survey team's leader, Captain Bryce Forsythe, greeted the cavalry with, "Are Montana mornings always this nice?"

"In summer, like as not they are, sir."

"Forget the *sir*, Lieutenant. I don't take this rank seriously. It's more in the nature of a diploma. The name's Bryce Forsythe."

"Marcus Grady," replied the Lieutenant. "As I was saying, the summer mornings are like this, clear, cool and dry, and it'll stay clear and dry all day long. There's the rare storm, but they mostly stay in the mountains. Spring's different, though;

17

you damn near drown from the rains and the runoff. And in winter you might as well be posted to Alaska."

"And the park?"

"Now? It'll be cold at night. Hope you brought your woolies."

"I'm wearing them. Shall we be off?"

They trailed south until they hit the Yellowstone, and then rode upstream.

It was slow going. Not only were the surveyors not expert horsemen, but they were further slowed by two mule-drawn wagons packed with supplies and equipment. And the cavalry had their two wagons. They were planning on a lengthy stay.

Besides Captain Forsythe, the survey team included Lieutenants Klepper, Magnuson, Bossy, Peters and Sawyer, all second lieutenants and all products of West Point, which meant that their topographical expertise was buttressed by a firm knowledge of civil engineering, for whatever good that might do (but no one escaped West Point without it). The civilians—Armstrong, Dandridge, Maxwell, Webley and Miss Mills—had been culled from the geology departments of various universities, topography being the graphic representation of geological realities. Though none had ever been west of the Mississippi (army or civilian) they had read much about the West, especially Colter's Hell, and were anxious to see it.

The cavalry detachment included second Lieutenant Foster, a fiery young man with designs on out-Custering Custer—stopping short, of course, of Custer's sudden demise—and Master Sergeant Jack Faulkner, the troop's first sergeant, plus sergeants Boatwright and Fuller and various corporals and many troopers. And it also included, inevitably, a generous measure of *esprit de corps*. They were cav—"yellow legs"—and proud of it.

"You've been to Yellowstone before?" inquired Lieutenant Grady of Captain Forsythe.

"Nope. You?"

"No," replied Grady, frowning. "How about the rest of your group?"

"None of them, either. We're pretty excited."

Grady nodded. If they stayed by the river they shouldn't get lost. "This the first time the place has been surveyed?"

"Lord, no."

"I mean *really* surveyed."

Forsythe grinned. "This is about the last time."

"Pardon?"

"Do you know anything about the surveying work that's been done up to now? All over the West?"

"No."

"Well then, you might as well learn, so you'll know what we're doing—and this is a good time to start your education."

"Yeah. Guess so."

Lieutenant Foster, riding just behind, overheard Forsythe and dropped back, not wishing to let any knowledge dilute his fighting temper.

"Now," said Forsythe, "before 1848 there'd been several explorations of the West. You're familiar with them, of course."

"No, not really."

"Lewis and Clark, 1804 to '06, Zebulon Pike in '06 and '07, Stephen Long in 1820, Iremont from '42 through '45, James Abert in '45 and '46, and Emory in '46 and '47 . . ."

"The names are familiar," allowed Grady.

"I should hope so," said Forsythe, thus getting on Grady's bad side.

"Were you once a professor?"

"I've taught, yes. Why?"

"No reason."

"Well, in any case, despite all the explorations nothing was really down on paper, in detail. So along comes the California Gold Rush in 1848, and the folks back in Washington suddenly realize they don't know what the West really looks like. They decide to organize some surveys. And since the army was about the only outfit capable of conducting such surveys, the War Department soon became the basic clearinghouse for all cartographical information. Cartographical means—"

"I know what it means," said Grady crossly. "Maps."

"Good, good. So, during the fifties, the surveying began. And most of it was done by officers of the Corps of Topographical Engineers. There were a few civilian mapmakers, and some of them took advantage of late reports from the West, but for the most part the maps were drawn by officers of the Corps."

Grady nodded, wondering how long his education was going to take.

"The first map of the West was by Lieutenant Gouverneur K. Warren of the Corps. That was in '57, and that was a great map."

"How come a lieutenant gouverneur was part of the Corps? I'm not familiar with that rank."

Like all good teachers, Forsythe ignored a question he couldn't answer. "The next map was Edward Freyhold's revision of the Warren map. That was in '68, and it too was splendid."

"Ahhh," said Grady.

"And Freyhold's map benefited somewhat from the most recent surveys, which had been undertaken after the War. The government's first priority was to get the railroad across the country. Consequently there was the Fortieth Parallel Survey in '67 and '68. That team was headed by Clarence King, and it surveyed a wide swath on either side of what became the Union Pacific railroad. The second great survey—"

"How many *were* there?" Grady cut in.

"Four. The second was the Wheeler survey in 1869, headed by Lieutenant George Wheeler of the Corps. Wheeler, who was under the command of the CO of the Department of California, just charted Nevada to start with, but later on . . ." Forsythe saw that Grady's attention was beginning to flag.

"Well anyway, hurrying along . . . the third was the Hayden survey. Ferdinand Vandeveer Hayden. That began in '67 as a purely geological survey under the auspices of the General Land Office, Department of Interior, but in '68 it came under the direct supervision of the Interior Secretary and was called the Geological Survey of the Territories, namely Colorado, Wyoming and New Mexico. But then—"

"Excuse me, sir," interrupted Grady, "but I've really got to pee." He ordered a halt and announced a ten-minute break.

As soon as that was done, though, and he was back in the saddle, Forsythe picked up where he'd left off.

"But then, in '71, the Hayden survey enlarged its work to include topographical work, and in '71 and '72 they did intensive work in and around Yellowstone Park."

"So *they're* the ones."

"What ones?"

"The ones that found this place."

"And the fourth federal survey," said Forsythe in a rush,

"was by Major John Wesley Powell, who did the Green and Colorado rivers in 1869."

"What?" Grady managed, weakly.

"Just wanted to get through all four surveys before you lost interest." He smiled encouragement. "But to answer your question, no, they didn't find this place. Colter did first, then Bridger, and then there were some more random, individual visits. But it wasn't until '70 that the first real expedition went in to look around. That was the Washburn-Langford-Doane Expedition of 1870—"

A shot rang out from the far side of the Yellowstone, and a trooper toppled from his mount.

The rest of the troop jumped from theirs, and for a while, as the civilians and Topographical Corps hugged the ground, a fairly lively firefight raged over the rushing Yellowstone.

None of the troopers could see a damned thing save for muzzle flashes and an occasional feather.

"Hostiles," muttered Lieutenant Grady. "We're lucky. They never do shoot worth a damn."

"Shoulda brung the Gatling," said First Sergeant Jack Faulkner at his elbow. "We could really clear them out."

Grady nodded. Maybe so, but they were prepared to unpack the wagons and pack the equipment in by horse if the trail got too bad. They would have had trouble doing that with the Gatling, which, with all its equipment, weighed damned near half a ton.

"Want me to charge 'em, sir?" called out Lieutenant Foster from down the line.

Right, thought Grady. Good idea. Drown or get washed downstream or get picked off as easily as Reno's men did, getting back across the Little Big Horn and up the bluff. "Not yet, Mr. Foster," he replied, loud and clear.

Then he raised his voice again. "Sergeant Boatwright? Sergeant Fuller? Take some men, and one of you work up the river and the other down. Cross over and we'll pincer them. When you hit 'em, I'll charge Mr. Foster at their front."

A lot of men started volunteering for the flanking details, but no sooner had the sergeants started to edge along the river with their men than the firing stopped.

"Must've heard me say you were coming, Mr. Foster," commented Grady, loudly enough for the frustrated second

21

lieutenant to hear. "Tell you what, Mr. Foster. Cross over with Spotted Calf and try to figure out who the hell that was. And," he shouted to the rest, "let me have a report, who's been hit and how bad."

It turned out the first man hit was the only man hit, and he just had a shoulder wound.

Lieutenant Foster, after almost losing two men struggling across the rapids and back, reported that the attackers had probably been Blackfoot.

"They came a far piece to shoot us up," observed Grady. "Are you sure about that? Blackfoot?"

"No," replied Spotted Calf, the unit's Crow scout.

Sergeant Faulkner got the column reorganized and they rode on.

Captain Forsythe reclaimed his position beside Lieutenant Grady, and Grady gave him a smile, a tough, veteran fighter's smile.

"The Washburn-Langford-Doane Expedition," Forsythe reminded him. "Henry Washburn was the Surveyor General of Montana. He and Nathaniel Pitt Langford organized the expedition. And Lieutenant Gustavus Doane provided the military escort."

Grady's eyes glazed over.

"They were authorized by Congress to investigate the area and report. Which they did. Investigated, that is. And they were overwhelmed by the incredible sights they beheld. At first they thought that each member of the expedition should claim a particular wonder for himself and then charge admission to see it, but a Montana lawyer named Hedges came up with the National Park suggestion. And they all agreed. I would guess there was some argument, but in the end they all agreed.

"When the expedition broke up, they went across the country arguing for a National Park. Langford sort of took the lead, talking up a storm, but it wasn't until the Hayden survey of '71 and '72 got back that the idea took hold. And then only because Hayden had taken this painter, Thomas Moran, and this photographer, Jackson, along, and when they got back with their pictures, their proof, Congress made it a park and made Langford the superintendent."

There was silence for a while, broken only by the steady clip-clopping of the horses.

"That's it?" asked Grady. "You're through?"

"Isn't that enough?" Forsythe asked.

"So what are you, the Forsythe survey?"

"Oh no. We're the Hayden survey. Still. Or again. Ferdinand should be along later."

"And what are you going to be doing? It's already been surveyed once, according to you."

"Oh. Of course. That's what I started out to tell you, isn't it, what *our* job is? Well, the first survey was somewhat superficial, not surprisingly. We intend to be more thorough. For instance, we know where the boundaries are, or should be, but we have yet to get them fixed precisely on a map, in true and accurate relation to the actual topography. Here, look at this map. Here are the boundaries, but the details of those boundaries have yet to be plotted. And then, also, we'll be drawing a better overall map of the park, showing where everything is located, and finally, perhaps most important, we'll be deciding where the roads shall be."

Grady frowned. "Roads?"

"Well certainly, roads. The government expects a lot of visitors, and they won't be allowed to ride around willy-nilly. There will be roads along which tours of the park will be conducted. Our job is to plot those roads."

"That shouldn't be hard."

"I don't expect so," Forsythe replied. "And you can be of great assistance in deciding where your headquarters will be."

"My what?"

"Didn't they tell you? They plan to station a cavalry detachment up here to patrol the park."

"The cav is going to patrol the park?"

"For now. I imagine that eventually some separate department will be created. You know how the government works."

"Yeah. Slow." He'd been a first lieutenant for almost five years. "You mean a whole department just for this park?"

"This and all the rest."

"What 'rest'?" Grady asked.

"This is just the first of many such parks, Lieutenant, you mark my words. Just the first."

"So that's it. Survey the park and map road locations?"

"Of course. What did you expect? And then, if we have time, there's been some difficulty with the land south of the park. South or southwest, that is."

"Well, which?"

"That's the problem. No one's certain about the actual location of the Tetons and Jackson Hole, whether it's south of Yellowstone or southwest."

"Oh," said Grady, but no more. He didn't plan to get the garrulous captain started again. In fact, he planned to keep his distance the rest of the way.

At the end of a week the cavalry and the surveyors began the climb to overlook the Grand Canyon of the Yellowstone. They climbed into the night, carefully but steadily. At about midnight they called a halt and bedded down. In the distance they could hear the sound of rushing water.

At dawn they saw that the sound of water belonged to the grand Lower Falls, cascading into tumult and mist some several miles farther up the Grand Canyon. They gazed with awe.

The steep, sloping walls of the 1,400-foot-deep canyon were predominantly yellow. The color ranged from pale lemon in the sun to bright orange in the parts that were shaded. There were also specks of red, brown, pink and white, reflecting the mineral compounds in the rock, and those flecks of color were ever-changing as the rock crumbled. But the dominant color was yellow.

"That should tell you why it's called Yellowstone Park," said Captain Forsythe.

Grady didn't need to be told. "This has always been called 'yellow rock' country," he said. "Rock, stone, what's the difference?"

"Philistine," muttered Captain Forsythe, finally fed up with casting his pearls before swine.

four _____

A small herd of pronghorn antelope grazed contentedly on the same vast plateau meadow that Deputy Marshal Cal Murphy had carefully circled. Not far from the pronghorns was the Yellowstone River, winding placidly towards the Upper Falls.

The grass the antelope munched on was tall and yellow. They did not chew far down the stalk, and the dent they made in the meadow's natural cover was minimal. Their eating habits also held true for most of the plateau's ruminants: deer, antelope and buffalo. They all tended to "top off" the grass, accounting in part for the abundance of the grass generally known as buffalo grass.

But that grass, that abundance, which alone had maintained half a continent, man and beast, from Mexico to Canada, faced a new danger as times changed. Cattle, while they didn't normally graze as close and ruinously as sheep, could be made to overgraze any stretch of ground and ruin it, turning it into sagebrush desert. And that was happening.

But not on the Yellowstone Plateau, not yet, even though a large number of cattle were spread over that meadow, the closest not two hundred yards from the pronghorns. There seemed to be an awful lot of cattle, all bearing the Rocking K brand, but considering the vast size of Yellowstone, their numbers were well within the capacity of the park.

No, it wasn't the cattle that the pronghorns and the rest had to fear. Rather it was copper-skinned men who slithered through the grass downwind from them.

They were a mixed bunch of Utes from the west, Utes and Horse Utes, also known as Bannock. They were tough fighters who, though related to the primitive Paiute and peaceful Hopi farther south, had adopted much of the Siouxan High Plains culture. What they hadn't acquired, though, was the friendship of the Sioux and the other members of the Lakota Confederacy, which included the Utes' closest neighbors, the Arapaho. For all those Confederacy members, the Utes were the favorite enemy, and a coup counted among the Utes was prized above all others.

Naturally the reverse was also true, and an Arapaho, for instance, trod carefully indeed when he smelled Ute.

At the moment, though, the Utes were thinking of their bellies, not honors. They'd trailed eastward from the reservation to gather meat, to kill and feast and carry the rest back to their people. And they were a few moments away from doing just that. Only if a large group of Arapaho suddenly materialized would their purpose be shaken.

Or so they thought.

Red Adair looked like he was falling asleep. He sat motionless on his short-legged, deep-chested roan cow pony as the pony stood almost shoulder-deep in grass, its head buried in it, munching. Red's torso was kind of curled as he slumped back against the saddle, one leg hooked up on the saddlehorn and his Stetson tilted down over his eyes.

But beneath that tilted Stetson, Red's eyes were alert, studying the terrain constantly. Wolves creeping up on the cattle were no joke.

His slitted eyes were rimmed with red. He'd been losing a lot of sleep with all the night riding. There were too damned many predators up there, including Indians.

Red took out paper and tobacco and rolled himself a cigarette.

The only break they had, there in that particular valley, was that it wasn't a grizzly hangout. Those beasts preferred the slightly higher country in the northern part of the greater Yellowstone Plateau. Unfortunately, Red and his buddies had to herd the cattle right by that grizzly country both coming and going—they hailed from the southwest, in Idaho, but not far from where Montana, Wyoming and Idaho came together—and that was no great pleasure.

Red drew on the cigarette and then, briefly, the smoke got in his eyes and hung around beneath the brim of the Stetson before curling away. When it was gone he blinked the tears away . . . and suddenly squinted all the harder. His eyes weren't telescopic, but they were damned good, and that grass rustling way over yonder just wasn't acting natural.

He fixed his gaze on the spot and finally saw a blade of grass that looked very much like a feather.

Damned Injuns!

Red looked around. About three hundred yards away, on either side of him, were two other punchers, both as motionless and as much a part of the landscape as Red. Red knew they glanced his way as often as he glanced theirs. He took his Colt out and held it in front of him, pointing straight up. He jabbed the sky with it until he received answering jabs from both men.

The jabs meant Indians. Anything else they simply took care of alone, but Indians called for concerted movement.

Once the signal had been returned, Red slowly pointed his piece toward the foe.

Then he pulled gently on the reins, raising the cow pony's head. Tufts of grass poked from the pony's mouth and he looked a bit annoyed. But he was well trained, and a knee-nudge had him practically tiptoeing toward the Utes.

The Utes, squirming through the grass, had their heads close to the ground. And the sounds coming from the ground confused them.

First there was a light rattle, which might mean that the sharp-hooved pronghorns were running. Then there was a heavier rumble, which was puzzling, but which might mean something was going wrong. A Ute stuck his head up.

Very much was going wrong.

Bearing down on the Utes at a hard gallop were the three cowpunchers.

The first Ute sprang to his feet and shrieked a warning. The

Utes had been carrying bows and arrows for hunting, but guns for protection, and now the first Ute tossed his bow aside and raised his carbine. The first rider was too close to miss.

But that worked both ways. Red Adair, seeing the carbine come up, rose up in the saddle and steadied his Colt. He couldn't miss either. And he didn't. And the .45 slug did the rest.

That slug was a blunt-nosed bullet propelled by such an explosion of black powder that at fifty yards the slug still had an energy of 528 *joules*, or a 390-foot-pound force, which was eight times that needed to down an average man. And the Utes were smaller than average, everybody knew that.

But it was suddenly apparent that there were more than just a few less-than-average-sized Utes in that hunting party. They seemed to be springing up all over the meadow and were waving guns and yipping like it was turkey-shoot time. Red dove from the saddle and his buddies did likewise.

There was a lively exchange of gunfire. But the Utes quickly realized that the Americans were too good with their guns, making up for the unequal numbers. And it wasn't long before Red and his friends were having trouble finding targets.

And now it was they who were down low and hearing noises from the ground. They looked up in time to see the Utes riding off along the Yellowstone, heading south toward the lake.

They poked through the grass and found three bodies.

"What kind are these, Red?"

"Can't you tell them apart yet, Stack?"

"'Rapaho?" guessed Stackpole.

"Naw. These are from prac'ly down home. Utes. Bannock, mebbe. They don't live so far away from us."

"What are they doing here?"

"Huntin'. Messin' up our land. And they'd likely take a cow if we didn't get to 'em first."

"Hell's bells, Red, iffen it ain't the Crow, it's the 'Rapaho, and if it ain't them, it's the Utes. Makes a feller kinda jumpy."

"Good, Benny. You stay jumpy. You'll keep your scalp a little longer." He glanced at Stackpole. "Now what's wrong?"

"I dunno about this, Red. If these Injuns was only huntin'—"

"*Only?* I tol' yuh, Stack, if they don't git enough deer they'll take cows. They don't care. They used to be all over the place, but we chased them out, and they're gonna stay chased, or stay the hell out of our way. They kin hunt someplace else—"

"Red."

"—South of here is real fine—"

"Red!"

"What?"

"We got some more visitors."

"What? Awww, Jesus Christ Almighty, what the hell's *this*? You ride an' get the boss, Stack. This looks like *real* trouble."

The surveyors and their cavalry escort had climbed past the Lower Falls and the Upper Falls and had followed the winding river upstream until they came to the vast valley meadow.

"When do we get to the sensational stuff, sir?" called a trooper.

"Weren't the falls good enough for you?"

"Aw, you know what I mean, sir. All them steam things and the bubblin' pools of hot water."

Forsythe, alongside, glanced at a rough map. "Up ahead there's supposed to be some kind of mud volcano, whatever that is. But aside from that, most of the main sights are spread around west and northwest of here."

"Hold your water, Trooper," Grady yelled back. "We're not there yet." Then he asked Forsythe, "Are we in the park yet?"

Forsythe gave him a strange look. "We entered the park yesterday, before we left Montana. This is Wyoming. You *do* know it's Wyoming, don't you?"

Grady gave him that look right back.

Forsythe handed him the map. "Look. This may not be that clear, or that accurate—which is why we're here—but this is the Yellowstone up here"—he pointed to the top of the map—"and this dotted line is the park boundary, approximately, and this line is the territorial boundary. As you can see, the park overlaps a little bit into Montana and Idaho."

"Is it supposed to?"

"Yes. Now, the river loops around this way to the right, around these mountains, and this is where the Lower Falls are . . . and the Upper Falls . . . and here we are, almost in the middle of the park."

Grady looked the map over. "Then if we marched straight west and then cut north through what looks like a pass, we'd be right back where we started, just coming into the park."

"Right! You're doing fine."

"Dammit, Captain, why didn't you tell me we were in the park already?"

"You seemed to be unavailable much of the time."

Grady nodded impatiently. "Yeah, yeah, but you asked me where I might set up a post, didn't you? And this here, according to you"—he was jabbing at the map—"will be the main entrance."

Captain Forsythe sighed. "For now it seems most sensible."

"Well then, that's probably where I'd set up a main post, right at the entrance."

Forsythe studied the map. "That's odd," he mused. "There are some hot springs right around there. We could have looked." He raised his eyes to Grady. "Well, Lieutenant, why don't we do just that?"

"Do what?"

"March west, and then north through that pass, back to the entrance. It'll give us an opportunity to survey that particular stretch, see if it's suitable for a road, and then we'll set up camp at the entrance. No sense building something here if that's where the army post is going to be."

To Grady it seemed odd that the authorities in Washington should leave it up to him, an obscure lieutenant, to decide where to locate the permanent post. But then Washington was full of odd, uninformed authorities. He shrugged. "Then that's where the post will be. Let's do it."

Forsythe said, "Good," and let it go at that. He was quite prepared to overrule his junior at any time but, as it happened, he too had belatedly decided that the park entrance was where the post should be.

"Lieutenant." The Crow scout, Spotted Calf, rode up. "There is shooting."

Lieutenant Grady hadn't heard anything and he was inclined to doubt the scout. But then he glanced at Sergeant Faulkner. Jack could hear sounds almost before they happened. The first sergeant nodded.

"Whereabouts?"

"South."

"Then let's take a look. Get your men ready, Mr. Foster. Could be anything. Hunters perhaps. But most likely hostiles. Spotted Calf, what kind of hostiles are we apt to find up here?"

"Ute. Arapaho."

"They're new to me," said Grady. "What do they look like?"

30

"All Indians look the same," replied the scout.

"Now you're catching on," said Grady, grinning.

They moved out smartly, riding in a column of fours but ready to spread out into a thirty-man skirmish line, with ten in reserve to guard the surveyors and the wagons.

Various species of wildlife scattered before them, but suddenly they were having to pick their way through cattle, which didn't scatter. "Cattle? What the hell's going on here?"

"Rocking K brand, sir!" called a trooper.

Grady frowned. That didn't mean anything to him.

At length they spied three cowpunchers in the distance. Soon after sighting them, they saw one of the three riding like hell to the west.

The cavalry slowed their approach. Grady was still hoping it was some kind of big mistake.

By the time they reached Red Adair and Benny, a larger group was fast approaching from the west. Lieutenant Grady halted his men and sat there silent, waiting for the western group to arrive and for Forsythe and the surveyors to catch up. The silence got to Red.

"Air too thin up here for you fellers t' say nothin'?"

Grady smiled warmly at him and then, almost out of habit, called down the line, "Just simmer down, Mr. Foster."

The group of six riders from the west and the surveyors reached the meeting at about the same time. There was one man among the cattlemen who was the clear leader. He rode a horse at least a hand taller than all the other mounts and seemed less a working cowhand. He lost no time in snarling, "What the bloody hell's the effin' infantry doing here?"

"We're cav, goddammit!" squealed a trooper, taking the bait.

"All the same," the man observed coolly.

Grady couldn't quite place the accent, Canadian, possibly. "Not quite," he said mildly, "but I might ask you the same question. What are *you* doing here? This is a park. It's federal land."

"Nonsense. The park's over there, where those steamholes are. This here is for grazing cattle."

Forsythe was scowling fiercely at his map, but Grady guessed that the cattleman knew exactly where he was and what he was doing. He'd found good graze and would defy the army to prevent him from using it. The boundaries of the park may have been vague, but not that vague. "You may have to move your cattle out of the park," said Grady calmly.

"The hell we will!" shouted a shorter, grizzled type sitting his mount by the side of the previous speaker. The man on the tall horse seemed content to let him rant.

"We found this graze, me an' my men. We drove the Injuns out an' we're keepin' them out. We've done all the work makin' this goddamn place safe for the likes of you. Now if you're thinkin' we're jes' gonna stand by while some old ladies in Washington decide to make a playpen outa this land—well, mister, you're badly mistook."

"Your name?" Grady inquired.

"Ain't none of your goddamn business."

"That's all right," said Lieutenant Grady mildly. "'Asshole' will do."

The moment he said that, pieces were cocked all along the cavalry line, and the surveyors went goggle-eyed with fear.

"Kreutzer," said the man on the tall horse. "Roman Kreutzer."

"Lieutenant Grady, U.S. Cavalry. These people are federal surveyors. They're going to be surveying and mapping, putting a fix on this place, especially its boundaries. I have an idea you already know where the boundaries are, Kreutzer, but just in case you don't, the surveyors will point 'em out to you. And those boundaries will be official, legal and permanent. As I said, you may have to move your cattle, possibly a considerable way, but I'll be getting back to you about that."

Kreutzer glared at him. "At the moment you've got us, Lieutenant. I've only eight up against your forty, but this isn't my full crew, not by a long shot. I have damn near forty more, and if you think you're going to push us around just like that, well, I'd think twice. So before you get back to us, you'd best carefully consider what you're getting back to us *with*."

Grady was already considering it. He didn't believe Kreutzer's manpower claim, but if his home spread was of any size, a twenty-five-man crew wouldn't be unusual. And twenty-five tough punchers would shape up as a formidable foe.

"An' besides, Lieutenant," said Kreutzer's alter ego, the one sitting beside him, "we ain't the only ones up here. There're hunters an' trappers an' Injuns an' even sightseers."

Grady blinked.

"That's right. They's a dude settin' up shop west of here,

buildin' himself a ho-tel and the whole works, runnin' tours through all them godawful steamy things."

The park was beginning to sound right crowded to Lieutenant Grady. And Captain Forsythe was scowling even more fiercely.

"What's that fellow's name?" asked Grady.

"Peckinpah. Hear tell he's a real nice feller, but he's got some tramps what were passin' through, and they ain't so nice. I think he hired them, got 'em workin' for him."

"Then we'll be seeing about him too," said Lieutenant Grady. "Now, what was all that shooting about?"

"Shooting?" wondered Kreutzer.

"That was us, sir," Red Adair spoke up. "Caught us some Injuns sneakin' up on the cattle. Killed us some. Utes." He appeared quite righteous, possibly for his boss's benefit. "They're lying around over there. I figgered if the army wants 'em buried, they can dig the holes. Otherwise"— he grinned— "they ain't gonna hurt the grass none."

Kreutzer and Lieutenant Grady then sat on their horses staring at each other for perhaps a full five minutes. Their horses were of equal height, their eyes level.

Finally, Kreutzer reined his horse around, muttering, "Let's move these cows to a different graze before the blood spooks them," and then he and his four companions rode back the way they'd come.

Red Adair, Benny and Stackpole set about nudging the cattle west.

Grady ordered a burial detail formed, stipulating shallow graves. "If they're dug up, they're dug up. Hell, like as not the Utes'll come back and stick 'em up on platforms. Hope they don't do it right here, though."

Lieutenant Foster rode up then, and asked eagerly, "What do you think, sir—shall we take 'em?"

"Kreutzer and his punchers? No. Give them a chance to think things over. He may not have the forty more men he says he has, but he likely has a handful. Taking them might not be that easy. Put them and the hostiles together, along with this Peckinpah gent, if he should want to make some trouble . . ." The prospects were a trifle daunting. "Lucky we've got some mounted infantry coming to side us. We—"

"What!" Foster fairly screamed. "There're effin' *blue legs* headed this way?"

33

"'Fraid so." He heard the muttering among his men. "I'm no happier about it than you are. We'll likely have to take care of them as well as the surveyors. But Division couldn't spare any more cav, not at the moment. They'll be shakin' some more cav free soon, but until then we'll just have to put up with the infantry."

"They wouldn't send no one what's gonna rank you, would they, sir?" asked Sergeant Faulkner.

"I hope not. I've got five years as first officer and I should rank anything below captain. And I shouldn't think one of those fat dragoon captains would want to make the trip up here."

five ⸺⸺⸺⸺⸺⸺⸺

"Do you really want to go, sir?" asked Sergeant Cohen with a hint of desperation. If the captain didn't go, then possibly Cohen wouldn't have to go.

"You're damned right, Sergeant. Ever since Flora heard about this...hell, ever since she saw that painting in Washington, she's wanted to go."

"But do *you* want to go, sir?"

Captain Conway laughed. "As a matter of fact I do. But even if I decided to stay, Flora'd go without me. And I wouldn't let her go without you along. What about Maggie?"

"She's kind of enthusiastic too, sir, I'm sorry to say," Cohen said morosely. His wife was not only Catholic, counterbalancing his Jewishness, but Irish, and the Irish often had too damned much imagination, too much romantic energy. It was tiring just being around it. "'Specially since you've got the Bainbridges going."

"What's that got to do with Maggie?"

"Maggie's the best—hell, the only—midwife around, sir, and the Bainbridge woman's expecting."

Captain Conway looked alarmed. "But not for a while."

"Yeah, but she's got a history of miscarriages, sir. Three, to be exact. They're real worried."

"I know, I know." He pawed through papers on his desk. "I had a letter here somewhere. . . ."

"Did you see his request, sir?"

"Hm? Whose request?"

"Bainbridge, sir. Transfer request, for medical reasons."

Captain Conway was still rummaging. "Ah, here it is. What's that? Bainbridge's request?" He eyed the paper he'd found, reading it over.

"Is that it, sir?"

"This? No, this is just a letter. The request is here." He reached out and handed a sheet to Cohen. "Turned down, naturally. Didn't you warn him, Sergeant?"

"Told him, sir."

"I can't approve and forward a transfer request on the grounds of his wife's medical problems. Didn't you explain that he can't be transferred for *his* convenience—"

"Sure did, sir, several times."

"—but only for the convenience of the service. Why is that concept so hard to understand?"

"He understands that, sir. He just doesn't realize how hard and fast a rule it is."

"That's too bad. Maybe this'll convince him. Nonetheless, I think Mary will be just as well off with us in Yellowstone, with Maggie there, and Sergeant Rothausen, who knows something about babies. Even Flora might pitch in."

Cohen really couldn't see the captain's lady, well-born and genteel, midwifing anyone. Besides which, she and the captain were childless. It might cause some tension. "Quite possibly, sir, quite possibly."

"Good, good. Now, you have our manpower requirements in order, don't you?"

"Yessir. Everyone's got the word. There'll be you goin', me, our wives, Matt Kincaid, Mr. Branch and First Platoon; Mr. Weaver, his wife and Second Platoon; Amy Breckenridge, Sergeant Wilson and Supply; Dutch Rothausen and one cook. Which leaves Mr. Carpenter, Sergeant Chubb and Third Platoon to hold down the fort, and they'll keep half the mess crew, the kid in Supply, Bradshaw here to help Carpenter with the paperwork. What about wranglers, sir, and the blacksmith?"

"Decide later. But we're going to have quite a crew, aren't we?"

"Yessir. Them cav are gonna be surprised."

"Oh. That's another reason I'm going. I don't want Matt up there outranked by some wild-eyed cavalry officer. You know them, they all think they're Custer reincarnate these days. I wonder where they were when old George needed them? Anyway, I don't think there's a cavalry captain alive that's got time-in-grade on me."

"Or a looie that's got it on Matt. He got his bar a couple of days after you got your tracks."

"Do tell, Sergeant. Matt and I have discussed those high points of our youth many a time, over numerous bottles of Kentucky bourbon. But that's behind us, Sergeant, way behind us. For now, well, let's go look at some maps and figure out our route."

"Now there, sir, is a real problem," said Ben Cohen, leading the captain out into the orderly room. "I've been giving it a lot of thought and—"

"Where's Matt?"

"Mess, I believe, sir," said the company clerk, Corporal Bradshaw, from his corner of the room. "He said he had to recover from an affair of the heart, sir."

"Heartbroken? Matt?" It was a new one for the captain.

Cohen shook his head. "That's Matt's way of sayin' he found himself a gal last night and they drank themselves silly havin' fun and things. And now he's hung over."

"That's marvelous, Sergeant. Let's go rag him."

"Now Captain, sir, that's sure tempting, but it ain't real nice. Four Eyes, send a runner to fetch Matt, but tell him to be gentle."

"Right, Sarge, I'll go myself," Bradshaw said, pushing his spectacles up on the bridge of his nose, and off he went.

An hour earlier, Lieutenant Matt Kincaid had surrounded a steaming cup of Sergeant Dutch Rothausen's strongest and vilest coffee. Now he'd pulled back some and was regarding the cup, his fourth, with a mounting sense of distrust. He turned to address the cook.

"Dutch, some of the men claim you spike this stuff with a bit of something that keeps the coffee flavor up and *their* flavor down, if you get my drift."

"You can drift all you want, sir, but I don't have the fuzziest notion of what you're talking about." The mountainous mess sergeant, Dutch Rothausen, appeared most benign, which was dangerous.

"Saltpeter," growled Matt. "Ring a bell?"

"Perish the notion," said Dutch, and he attempted to pirouette back into the kitchen, a grotesque movement that almost upset three tables.

Matt, smiling as he tried to focus on the kitchen doors, then heard Rothausen's scandalized voice. "Private Bauer! What are you putting in the coffee?"

Matt had been joking about the saltpeter, but Dutch's performance made him edge a little farther away from his cup.

"Ah, sir, there you are!"

Matt swung his head slowly around to regard the approaching shape of Corporal Bradshaw. Bradshaw was ill-equipped for almost everything. That, he decided, was what saltpeter did. "Yes?"

"The captain, sir. I think he's planning the trip, figuring out the route. He needs you."

"Trip?" Matt showed confusion.

Bradshaw giggled until Matt's gloomy stare got to be too much. "Didn't you know, sir? You're going."

"I know, Corporal. I was funning you."

"Yessir. I knew that, sir."

"Good. And as long as you're out roaming around, why don't you take a ride over to the friendlies' village and drag Windy back. Make sure he puts his clothes on first, and leaves the Cheyenne wench behind."

Bradshaw grinned.

"Or why don't you just pick up with her where he left off?"

Bradshaw's eyes opened wide, and he hustled from the mess.

"Glad we're not leaving today."

Captain Conway looked up from the maps spread out on Cohen's desk and said, "You are in a bad way, aren't you?"

"Felt worse," said Matt. "Wish I could remember when . . ."

"Have you thought about our route?"

"Not yet." Matt scratched his head. "Anyone seen my dog?"

"Your dog?"

"Yeah. That dog I found has kind of taken a liking to me."

"He's taken a liking to the mess," corrected Sergeant Cohen. "I was just there."

"He's around," said Captain Conway, curt and impatient. "Now look here, Matt. If we head northwest, pick up the North Platte Wagon Road and follow it and the Sweetwater to around St. Mary's Station, where we can pick up Bridger's Trail north, then jump off where the Wind River runs into the Big Horn, and follow that to where it runs into a mess of mountains . . . I'd be willing to guess we couldn't get our wagons up that way, but the alternative's to go all the way around and come down from the north. If it were just men and horses . . ."

"The wagons and dependents do pose a problem, sir."

"Now don't you start in on me, Matt. I've decided who's going and who's staying."

Matt read Cohen's look. "So you have, sir. Sergeant Cohen, have you been warming up your Percheron?"

"Yep. He's gonna race Dutch's Clydesdale."

Matt looked back down at the maps. "You're sure these maps are true maps, sir?"

"Of course I'm not, Matt, but they're the only ones we have. And the only ones available. This old one here is Warren's '57 map, but these are the '68 Corps of Engineers map, Freyhold's revisions of Warren's maps. They're supposed to be the most dependable, most up to date. Even this other one here, *Rand McNally's Business Atlas*, it just came out but it's about the same as Freyhold's. Probably just copied Freyhold's and added a few late discoveries. I—"

Corporal Bradshaw burst in. "Jeez, sir," he squealed at Matt, "you almost got me scalped."

The would-be scalper, Windy Mandalian, entered moments later, obviously fuming.

Have to pour some of Dutch's soothing coffee down that man, thought Matt.

Windy was dark and hook-nosed, with high cheekbones. He was supposed to be the issue of an Armenian furrier and a French Canadian lady, but there were those who alleged that there had to be some Cree on the French Canadian side. There were also those in the lower ranks who said there was no such thing as an Armenian, but they didn't say that to Windy.

"Ever been up to Yellowstone Park, Windy?" asked Matt.

Windy frowned and shrugged.

"Colter's Hell? Bridger's country?"

39

Windy's face cleared and he nodded.

"Then take a look at these maps. How the hell are we going to get there with wagons and dependents?"

Windy made a grunting sound and then bent over the maps. After a few minutes he said, "The maps are wrong."

"What?"

"No problem getting there."

"What about here?" said the Captain. "These mountains?"

Windy nodded. "That way is problems," he allowed, "but that ain't the way to go." He scratched his head. "You got some Idaho maps?"

"Got more maps than you can shake a stick at," said Sergeant Cohen, sifting through several. "Here you go."

Windy took it, spread it out and studied it. "Here," he said, pointing to where Idaho bordered Wyoming. "Far as I can tell, they've got the lay of the land right, only they've got Wyoming's borders too far east. The Tetons here, an' Jackson Lake, which they've got just over the border into Idaho, is actually in Wyoming, directly south of Yellowstone. All we gotta do is go west, under the Wind River Mountains, hit Fort Aspen, then angle up past Fort Bonneville toward the Tetons and Jackson Hole. There's this high valley, got a big lake, Jackson Lake. Go around the lake an' head north an' you're right there, in Yellowstone."

"How much longer is it that way?"

"It's the *only* way, Captain. Fifty miles or so longer, but a whole lot easier."

"Wonder why they didn't send men up out of Aspen or Bonneville."

"Last time I seen them, Captain, there was only a handful in each."

"I see. Well then, I guess that's the way we'll go." There was no argument. "Funny name," he murmured, "Tetons . . ."

"Means 'tits,' Cap'n," said Windy. "French trappers called 'em *Les Trois Tetons*, The Three Tits."

"Uhhh, that may be accurate, Windy," said the captain, "but should you translate in polite company, 'breasts' is somewhat more genteel, though not by much."

"Some others what used 'em as landmarks," Windy went on, "called 'em the Pilot Knobs. The Indians call 'em the Pinnacles or—what was that word we figgered out, Matt?"

"Oh. That one." Matt and Windy had discussed the area

some months previously. "Hoary... Hoary-headed Fathers."

"That's not much better than 'tits,'" Conway muttered. "How long does it take an Indian to say that hoary-thing?"

"'Bout as long as it takes 'im to climb the mountains."

"And Jackson," said Matt, getting his two cents in, "comes from the Mountain Man, Dave Jackson."

"Very good, Matt," said Captain Conway dryly. "You can point out the sights along the way. We'll leave in the morning."

"That means I've got to find George by then," said Matt.

"Who's George?"

"My new dog, my hound, faithless bastard. Named him George Armstrong. He should like it up there."

It occurred to Captain Conway that Matt Kincaid was not taking the mission very seriously.

"I think the exercise will do you good," said Flora Conway several hours later, running the tip of a forefinger from one of her husband's nipples to the other.

"What—that tickles—what do you mean?" Warner Conway, though, knew exactly what she meant. Middle age and life on the windy Plains had begun to exact its toll. There was a slight sag to his abdomen and a bulging at the hips—neither visible in uniform nor, as then, lying down—and spiders had begun to work overtime on his weathered face. But his vanity had also begun to work overtime. "I haven't lost much—if anything at all."

"Show me," said Flora, and she giggled. Flora's demeanor in bed, beside Warner, was in sharp contrast to her public presence. To the men of Easy she was a queen, darkly beautiful, warm and solicitous, and they revered her. To Warner, however, she was often hot and wanton....

"You're shameless," he accused her.

"Yes," she moaned.

Not surprisingly, Warner revered her too. But at the moment his thoughts were elsewhere.

"A life outdoors," he reasoned, pinching a bit of his own excess flesh, "on the Plains, in the saddle, there's a price—"

"Any time you want to climb into the saddle," husked Flora.

"Flora! Have you nothing else on your mind?"

"Nothing!"

Well, Warner did. He used to look like Matt Kincaid. Tall, rawboned and, he admitted, even better looking. But now he

41

was a bit bigger all over, was more commanding than ever, even tended to look distinguished, and he didn't like it one bit. Old men looked distinguished, not army officers in their prime. Hell, Matt didn't look distinguished.

"Do you think I look distinguished?"

"Ohhh, yessss . . ."

"Don't you think I look more . . . vigorous . . . than distinguished?"

"You're not acting vigorous," said Flora a trifle huffily. "Warner, quit worrying about promotion. You'll get it sooner or later."

"I wasn't worrying about that. What made you think so?"

"You always do. As soon as we get to bed you start talking about not being promoted. You're beginning to make *me* feel guilty."

He grinned. "If only they gave medals for . . . you know what."

"No I don't. I've forgotten. Show me."

But now that she'd reminded him, he was thinking about his many years in rank. Damn President Hayes and Congress eighteen ways to hell. They could sign up and pay thousands of raw recruits, but pay one more cent to those already in the Army? Not on your life. Serve them right if he retired . . . if only he could afford to.

A sudden ruckus out on the parade brought Conway bolt upright. Something awful was happening.

"Stop that bastard!" he heard. "Sonofabitch got a whole goddamn leg."

It sounded like Sergeant Rothausen. What the hell was Dutch doing fighting? *Who* was he fighting?

Conway was half out of bed when he heard, above the furor, another familiar voice.

"George! Goddammit, George, c'mere! Good, George, good dog, bring Uncle Matt the bone. . . ." There was silence for a while. Then, "Not much left, Dutch."

"You're gonna have to keep that mongrel tied up, sir," cried Dutch. "Effin' mutt eats like a goddamned elephant. Big as one, too."

"Elephants don't eat meat, Dutch," said Matt reasonably.

"Then he eats as much as . . . as . . . as Ben Cohen."

"Oh. That much, huh?"

There was a loud noise from the NCO quarters, but finally

all the noises subsided and Warner did too.

"Is Matt taking George with us?" asked Flora.

"Yes," growled Warner. "I think he's gonna ride him."

"Talk about *riding* . . ."

Warner frowned, but then appeared struck with inspiration. "Flora . . . Mrs. Conway . . . why don't we . . ." He took a dark, erect nipple gently between thumb and forefinger. "Why don't we . . ."

"Oh yes!" cried Flora. "Good idea." And she threw herself around until her nightgown had gone flying and she was on her hands and knees, looking back at Warner over her shoulder.

"You can't be serious."

"Don't be a spoilsport, Warner."

"You know it's hard on my back."

"Oh pooh! Just lean over and rest your itty-bitty tummy and your manly chest on my back. You were just saying how fit you were, that you hadn't lost anything—"

"I never had *this* to lose."

"Tut-tut. There, see how relaxing that is?"

Comfortable rather than relaxing, thought Warner. "All right, darling," he said mischievously, "now what?"

"What do you think?"

The moon rose that night at midnight. And along about 2:00 A.M., when it was high, George started baying. Matt decided that there was some kind of blood in George that he hadn't guessed at. He prowled out onto the parade, took hold of George and led him back to his own quarters.

The only trouble was, George had gotten the coyotes going, and the coyotes, not knowing George had retired, kept their howling up all night long.

"I don't like it," growled Private Malone, deep in his sack. "Don't like it one bit." Malone's Irishness inclined him toward a belief in omens and portents.

"Don't like it one bit."

"Shut the hell up, Malone," came out of the darkness.

"In my good time, boys, in my own good time, 'less you'd be wantin' me t' step all over your face."

There were no more complaints.

"Aye, don't like it one bit."

43

six ━━━━━━━━━━━━━━━━

The column rode out of Outpost Number Nine at eight o'clock the next morning. It was an impressive procession.

Windy led the way, followed by Captain Conway and Sergeant Cohen, Lieutenant Kincaid and Lieutenant Branch, Sergeant Olsen, First Platoon, and completing that section, three Delaware scouts.

Next came three ambulances, the lightly sprung wagons that women favored. They carried Flora Conway, Maggie Cohen and various dependent womenfolk, including the pregnant Mary Bainbridge.

After them came Sergeant Rothausen and the mess wagon, Sergeant Wilson and the supply wagon, and two more wagons packed with arms and random equipment. Each of those wagons dragged ammunition caissons.

Then came Lieutenant Weaver, Sergeant Breckenridge and Second Platoon.

There had been some debate, but it had finally been decided that the post sutler, Pop Evans, one of the rare honest sutlers, should be left behind. Supply Sergeant Wilson, through an agreement with Pops, would act as temporary sutler, supplying such items as tobacco, candy, uniform replacements and accessories, and possibly even some 3.2 beer.

Private Fitzpatrick of Second Platoon watched the supply wagons wobble along ahead of him. "Wonder if Supply's brung any beer from the sutler's?"

"Who the hell gives a damn?" said his companion, Private Fallon. "That three-pernt-two's like drinkin' warm piss."

"Better'n nothin'."

"Not by half, it ain't."

Bringing up the rear of the column was Private Basco, the remount orderly, with the remuda of reserve mounts, about forty horses, all bay geldings. Two young boys from town, Clay and Jeff, worked as wranglers. Matt had been instrumental in landing the jobs for the boys.

Finally, rounding out the column, was George. He ranged up and down the length of the procession. Matt guessed the big brindle pup had a lot of staghound in him, but a lot of something else too. Something else that was *big*.

"Aren't you afraid he's going to get tired out, Matt?" asked Warner Conway peevishly after his horse had made an abrupt adjustment to the dog's passage.

"I hope so," said Matt. George had pushed him halfway off his bed the previous night. Maybe the dog wasn't such a good idea.

But George finally did get tired, and went to sleep on the wagon seat next to Sergeant Rothausen.

"Dog never bites the hand that feeds him," Matt reassured the Sergeant, but Dutch looked as if he thought there could always be a first time.

They made forty miles that day, which was not bad, considering the wagons. They pitched camp near the North Fork of the Platte River, and the next morning forded the river and proceeded west.

The column was moving at a slow, easy gallop down a slight incline when there was a loud gunshot from somewhere in the ranks.

Captain Conway, Matt and the rest of the command up front twisted in their saddles to scan the column. Their eyes searched for the offender and soon converged on Private Malone, who still held a smoking revolver.

"What the hell are you doing, soldier?" barked Matt.

"Sorry, sir," said Malone happily. "Jes' tryin' out me new Scoff. Jes' drew it, sir. It'd be hardly fittin' if it didn't perform when it was needed."

"You might give us a bit of warning, soldier. Anybody else want to see if their guns work?"

No one did.

Matt decided to give his own guns, the regulation Schofield Smith & Wesson and the extra Peacemaker, a light cleaning. Both guns, worn in regulation cross-draw fashion, were ivory-handled, Matt Kincaid's sole affectation.

It wasn't an idle affectation, however, since it served notice that the owner of the guns held them in some esteem, nor was it an inexpensive affectation. A pair of engraved, ivory-handled Peacemakers in embossed holsters cost a man one hundred dollars. Of course, Matt's guns weren't matched or engraved, nor were his holsters embossed, save for the US on the flap, but the flap had been cut away for a faster draw.

"Kee-rist!" said someone back in line, and it sounded like Malone again.

"Lieutenant Kincaid, sir—"

Matt twisted around. Yep, it was Malone.

"This here asshole, sir, he's sayin' the Scoff is a Rooshan gun."

"Who's saying that?"

"Parker here, sir."

"Who told you that, Parker?"

"No one in pertickler, sir, I jes' heard it."

"Well, don't you worry about that."

"It ain't true, sir?"

"That the Scoff's a Russian gun? No it's not. One hundred percent American."

"Hoo boy," said Private Parker, "wait'll I find that lyin' sack o' shit."

Matt decided he'd have a word with Parker later on.

Lieutenant Branch, the young second lieutenant riding beside Matt, couldn't resist comment. "Imagine that, thinking it's a Russian gun."

Matt looked at him. Where did they all come from, this seemingly endless stream of second lieutenants? Or more to the point, perhaps, where did they all go? Outpost Nine and Easy Company seemed to be just a short layover for most of them. A few were killed, but most just stayed around long enough to learn how not to get in the way of their men, and then they were gone.

"Well," said Matt, "the men are sometimes easily confused, and I didn't see any point in confusing them, but the gun is called the 'Russian gun'—or was."

"Well, I'll be damned."

"Didn't they mention that at the Point?"

"Ummm, I didn't go to the Point, sir."

"Ah."

"It *is* a Smith & Wesson, is it not, sir?"

"No one's listening, Cliff, call me Matt. And yes, it is a Smith & Wesson, which is why I called it one hundred percent American. But its history explains a lot regarding sidearms out West here. Now, Smith & Wesson has always made a damn good weapon. And in '69 or '70, 'round about then, they made a move into really heavy-caliber revolvers, turning out a .44-caliber they called the American. It was a decent gun. Not great but decent. At about that same time, the Russians decided to equip their cavalry and artillery with a modern revolver, and in '69 they sent a purchasing commission to the States. They saw the S&W American and thought it was pretty impressive, but they weren't going to buy any without some modifications they had in mind."

Matt looked around to make sure George was somewhere in sight. He whistled, and Sergeant Rothausen answered with a distant roar, "He's back here eatin', goddammit."

"What you have to understand," continued Matt, "was that up to that point ammunition was a matter of guesswork and past experience. There were no real rules governing ammo, no precise measurements, close fit, nothing like that. Just so the bullet came out the end it was supposed to come out of. Now, you know how the cartridge is usually a shade thicker than the bullet, or it seems so? Well, it used to be a lot more. The American, for instance, had a pretty exact .44-caliber cartridge, but the bullet itself was not a good fit in the barrel. Kind of rattled around, which made accuracy fall off after fifty yards. That doesn't mean much if you're only standing ten or twenty yards away, and a lot of folks don't care, but the Russians did care, they wanted more. The original American bullet weighed about half an ounce, but when the Russians got through redesigning, it weighed almost a tenth of an ounce more. Actually, about seven or eight hundredths of an ounce."

"How do you know all this stuff, Matt?"

"Because I've made it my business to know, Cliff," snapped Matt. "Now this new bullet wasn't longer but thicker, and it was a snug fit in the barrel. So both cartridge *and* bullet were about .44 caliber. I'll tell you, Cliff, the new ammunition was a revelation to the industry. The bullet may have taken more powder, which raised the muzzle velocity considerably, about one hundred feet per second faster, but the big thing was that the accuracy improved enormously. Suddenly it was some weapon."

"So why didn't Smith & Wesson clean up?"

"I'm getting to that. Now the Russians were satisfied with the accuracy, but they wanted, and got, a few more modifications—a kind of lump at the top rear of the handle that kept the gun from sliding during recoil, another finger-rest under the trigger guard, and the barrel shortened from eight inches to six and a half. And then the Russians were happy."

"So?"

Matt grinned. "So they placed an order for two hundred and fifteen thousand, seven hundred and four pistols."

Cliff Branch grinned along with Matt. "And that kept them so busy that Colt was able to lock up the Western market."

"Smith & Wesson were making pistols like crazy, but not many were showing up out here. Not that they didn't take a shot at it. And this Scoff we carry is a variation on the Russian design. There were a few variations, but this is the best known, and probably the best. A Lieutenant Colonel George Schofield designed the variations. He changed the barrel catch somehow, and the ejector mechanism, and it's now .45 caliber . . . but there was another problem not connected with the gun itself. Though Schofield was an artillery officer, he was associated with the Ninth and Tenth Cavalry units."

"The niggers?"

Matt frowned. "Yes, the colored outfits down south of us. For some reason the brass in charge of placing gun orders held that against him. For no good reason, as far as I know. Those two cav units are good fighting outfits, Mr. Branch"—suddenly it was Mr. Branch, the significance of which was not lost on Cliff Branch, who was no fool— "in case you hadn't been so informed."

"I hadn't. But now I know."

"In any event, only nine thousand Scoffs were produced,

but I understand Jesse James carries one, and there's a fellow I came across back in Dodge City recently, an assistant town marshal, runs a faro game besides, really cleans up. A real fast gun. Named Earp. But anyway, he's fond of these Scoffs too."

Three days and 120 miles later, Easy Company rode into Fort Aspen, at the southern base of the Wind River Mountains. There seemed to be more civilians than there were soldiers, probably because there was reportedly gold in the nearby mountains. But Windy had been right, Fort Aspen was manned by only a small detachment of men, disenchanted cavalry who thought they'd been stuck out there and forgotten.

But the posting had its bright side. There really was "gold in them thar hills," and of Fort Aspen's twenty-five troopers, seven had found some, which solved the problem of desertion, a dilemma for most Western commands. Why desert when the army was underwriting your prospecting?

"Mind if I hang around here for a while, sir?" asked Private Malone. "Me and Stretch? We'll be catchin' you on the way back."

Matt Kincaid barely smiled. Gold fever was nothing to joke about. He hoped there wouldn't be any men missing in the morning.

They made camp just outside the fort, and the next morning . . .

Private Basco, the remount orderly, looked down at the body of Jeff Perkins and at the boy's bloody head.

Tears welled up in Basco's eyes. He'd liked the kid. What the hell would they tell Mother Perkins?

Sergeant Olsen got there. "What's the trouble?" He looked around and frowned. "Are these all the horses?"

"Injuns got 'em. Snuck off what they could. Got Jeff here too. He must've been out at the far end."

Olsen hadn't seen the boy, half-hidden in the grass, but now he did. "Hell . . . he was a nice kid."

"Real nice."

Olsen hustled back toward the camp, letting out a roar. Basco and Clay Manson, the other young wrangler, began to push the remaining horses after him.

A number of the horses had been tethered closer to the camp, and by the time Olsen arrived, Matt Kincaid and First

Platoon's first squad were saddling up. Matt knew there was trouble. Olsen didn't yell and run like that for fun. All Matt wanted to know was what kind of trouble and where. Sergeant Olsen told him.

A man was sent for the Fort Aspen CO, a first lieutenant.

The officer showed up quickly, riding a white horse. The man's name was Quarry and he was aching for some action. "Do you want us to go after them?" he asked. "I know you've got business elsewhere."

"You can ride along if you like," Matt cut in, "but it's our show. Who were they and where'd they go?"

"Well, hell," began Quarry, momentarily confused, "I *suppose* they were Shoshone or Utes. See that butte way off there to the southwest? That's Pilot Butte. If the trail heads that way, well, I hear the Shoshone sometimes camp there by the creek, Big Sandy Creek."

Chivington and the Sand Creek massacre flashed through Matt's mind. Matt wasn't Chivington, and it wasn't the same creek, not even the same territory, but if Matt caught those bastards . . . and he *would* catch them. . . .

"Maybe I should let Mr. Branch go, Matt," said Captain Conway, sensing the rage that Matt was trying to control.

"I can handle it, sir," said Matt through clenched teeth.

"Did you . . . know the boy?"

"Got him the job, know his mother. *Windy!*"

There was a hoot from out where the horses had been stolen; Windy was looking the ground over. Matt and the squad rode out to him.

"Came from the east," said Windy, "headin' southwest. Mebbe a war party comin' home."

"Move it out," growled Matt, and they did—Matt, the white-horsed Quarry and the squad thundering off after Windy.

Windy shouted at Matt that the Indians had probably hit early in the night since they were moving slowly. They probably weren't expecting pursuit, or not right away.

They soon came to a road. At Hamilton, some forty miles east of Fort Aspen, the North Platte Wagon Road forked. One road, the old Oregon Trail, continued on through Fort Aspen, and the other road angled to the southwest. It was that second road they came to. And since the Indians had followed that road, they did too.

Pilot Butte was growing larger. Just about smack-dab in the middle of the South Pass, thought Matt.

"They're startin' to run, Matt," cried Windy, pointing at the ground. "Ponies are stretchin' out."

"They've seen us?"

"Or they've seen somethin' up ahead that they're hurryin' to get to."

Matt hoped the Indians had stopped to attack someone else. It would be a mistake they'd pay for, the greedy bastards.

They heard gunfire in the distance and their pulses quickened.

They topped a rise and came to a quick halt.

There was a fight going on up ahead, but all they could see were Indians. Who the hell were the Indians attacking?

"They're fightin' each other, Matt," said Windy, shaking his head, "which means . . . what the hell *does* it mean?"

"We weren't chasing Shoshone? Or Utes?"

"Don't look that way. The ones we were chasin' came on these others . . . what look like they're villaged here. Which means *our* hostiles is likely either Arapaho or Cheyenne."

"What the hell?"

"War party, like I said, only I had 'em comin' back instead of goin'. They're after coups. Shoshone coups are good, but Utes are best. I'd bet them's Utes under attack."

Matt was tempted to wait out the fight, then kill whoever was left. Windy read the temptation.

"We got no argument with Utes, Matt."

"Not yet, we don't."

"And I figger the Utes will either kill 'em or drive 'em off."

"No," decided Matt, "I don't think so. *We'll* take 'em. You ready, Lieutenant?"

Quarry nodded and bared his teeth.

"Then let's go get 'em . . . and don't shoot until they see us."

They never did see the army.

"Cheyenne," called Windy, before he dropped back.

The Cheyenne didn't know Matt and his men were coming until they were there. One moment the Cheyenne were shooting at the distant enemy, indeed their favorite enemy, as it later turned out, and the next moment they were fighting for their lives, smashed from the rear.

The fight was over quickly. Matt and his men were dealing

with them at point-blank pistol range. There were twelve in the Cheyenne war party, and twelve died.

With the sudden appearance of the army the distant Utes had held their fire to await developments. The Americans were not their enemies, at least not just then. And the ranking Ute, War Dog, thought he recognized the American riding the spirited white horse.

Abruptly there was total silence on the South Pass prairie.

Matt glanced at the massive Pilot Butte, standing sentinel over the South Pass. Too bad such objects couldn't speak. This one must have seen a lot.

Windy finally caught up, not that he'd been trying to awfully hard—he fought well, but only when he had to—and signaled the distant Indians their peaceful intentions.

War Dog thought it a mite strange. The Americans had just slaughtered the Cheyenne and now they said they were peaceful. He supposed there would be an explanation; the Americans *always* had an explanation. He rode forth.

Matt, Windy and Quarry rode to meet him.

"I know him," said Quarry. "That's War Dog."

Windy muttered, "I said they was Utes. Cheyenne go crazy fer Ute scalps."

War Dog spoke first to Lieutenant Quarry, thinking the white-horsed cavalry officer the leader. Quarry, through Windy, deferred to Matt.

Matt explained what had happened. Then he said that they were headed for Yellowstone, the Summit of the World, beyond the Pinnacles, the Hoary-headed Fathers.

"Good hunting grounds," replied War Dog.

Not for long, thought Matt, but he only said, "Why are you not on the reservation?"

"We need food," said War Dog and, as Windy translated, gave Matt a man-to-man look that requested understanding.

Matt didn't mind their leaving the reservation to hunt. He didn't even like the idea of reservations. In that respect he resembled George Armstrong Custer, who'd once written, "If I were an Indian, I would greatly prefer to cast my lot among those of my people who adhered to the free open plains, rather than submit to the confined limits of a reservation." But Matt, who knew that Custer quote, also knew that was not army policy, but quite the opposite. So he said, "That is not good. The White Father does not like his red children to leave the lands that have been given him."

Matt felt vaguely like a traitor. At the same time, though, such warnings helped keep the red man off balance, which was good if they fought as well as the Utes.

War Dog had heard it before. Windy, however, invested the translation with some of Matt's ambivalence. Matt, unaware of that, thought the war chief took the warning rather well. But Matt had his suspicions.

He didn't say anything then, however, or until after they'd rounded up their own horses, presented the Utes with the Cheyenne ponies, and were riding back toward Fort Aspen.

"Just what did you tell that bugger, ol' scout?"

Windy looked blank.

"Don't play dumb, Windy. When you translated me, did you tell him, 'Hunt all you want. The tall American officer doesn't mind?'"

Windy appeared offended. "You didn't see him dancing with joy."

"Didn't see him very upset, either."

"Indians don't show much," grumbled Windy. "You know that."

Matt glared at him.

"Tall, handsome officer," sneered Windy.

Matt muttered to himself. He had a feeling that his own ignorance of the many tribal dialects, combined with the Indians' renowned stoicism, had convenienced Windy on more than one occasion. Hell, there was the time Windy almost had him married to a chief's daughter in exchange for some hostages. He and the chief had stared woodenly at each other while Windy pledged heaven and earth, and Matt's troth as well.

"Your scout," said Lieutenant Quarry with a smile, "suggested a small amount of ambivalence on your part regarding confinement to reservations. I believe also that you were compared, not unfavorably, to the well-known Long Hair."

Matt stared at Windy aghast, and the look Windy gave Quarry wasn't much better.

"Custer?" squawked Matt. "Windy! You didn't!"

Windy eyed Quarry. "You talk Ute, huh?"

"Them and the Shoshone, they're the ones I deal with most. I made it a point to familiarize myself with the language."

"Why didn't you say so?"

"Didn't want to interfere. Wasn't the commanding officer."

"You still ain't," grumped Windy.

Quarry grinned. "I didn't say I disagreed with the sentiments as expressed. I might have said the same myself, though possibly I would have stopped short of likening myself to a military hero. But I also had presumed that Lieutenant Kincaid had some idea of what you were saying, that the two of you understood one another."

"We do," confirmed Matt, adding, however, "Even more so now. Windy, you bastard, you keep doing that to me. Just once give a straight translation both ways, all right?"

"You're the boss," Windy agreed.

"Sometimes I wonder," said Matt.

Back at Fort Aspen a burial service was conducted for Jeff Perkins, and the young wrangler was lowered to his final rest. Then, after trading with the cavalry for some fresh mounts, which introduced a few sorrels and chestnuts to the otherwise bay-hued remuda, Easy rode on.

"See you on the way back," Matt called out to Lieutenant Quarry. "We'll trade back then, if you need 'em."

Quarry made a dismissive gesture and called, "Just make it back."

Some ways along the trail Sergeant Cohen remarked, "They didn't seem bad . . . for cavalry."

"Probably because they're off by themselves," guessed Captain Conway. "Sometimes takes the starch out. They're happy to see anyone."

With the late start they only made about twenty miles that day. But the next day they made the Green River, so ably plotted by Major Powell of the fourth federal survey, and followed it upstream.

Captain Conway referred to his map. "So far, so good," he said. "River's right where the map says it's supposed to be. What's your plan, Windy?"

"Foller it up, cut through McDougall's Gap an' up to Fort Bonneville, then on up, kind of follerin' the Divide till we kin catch the Gros Ventres Creek, and that'll take us right down into the valley—Jackson's Valley, right there underneath them big tits." He grinned.

"Which reminds me, Captain," said Matt, "how's Flora taking it so far?"

Captain Conway puffed up like a blowfish. "What do you mean, *reminds you?*" Flora Conway was certainly blessed with a noble bosom, but it could not be used as an excuse for conversation.

Matt stifled a laugh. "Just a figure of speech, sir. Sorry."

"Well, she's taking it nobly, considering that she's now thinking it's the biggest mistake she ever made."

"Oh? I've always found those ambulances rather comfortable."

"Not for two or three hundred miles you haven't."

"You may have a point, sir. What about you, Sergeant? Any complaints?"

"From Maggie? I dunno, sir." Cohen scowled. "Maggie may be hurtin', but I'm so busy complainin' myself, I wouldn't hear her even if she was screamin'."

"Some combat outfit we've got, sir," remarked Matt.

Captain Conway nodded, saying, "And there are some who might say it was quite typical of the Army of the West."

"Beg pardon, sir? Who would say a thing like that?"

"Come on, Matt, we don't have to kid each other."

"Perhaps you are alluding," said Matt delicately, "to rumors concerning General Crook this past year?"

"Everyone knows about Crook," said Captain Conway, "or almost everyone. But I got this letter from a man I know, a Captain Sam Adams."

"A friend?"

"Not really. He was at the Point with me, and we saw a bit of each other afterward. He was quite smitten by Flora."

"Aha!"

"Smitten, no more. But for a while we saw quite a bit of him. Then I heard that somehow he'd managed to get into medical school. I don't know how many strings he must have pulled."

"He left the army?"

"No he didn't, and he's still in the army. Thank God he's only a captain. Anyway, I had occasion to write him, and he replied. Now, you couldn't call it a nasty letter, but he did make some snide remarks concerning the level of generalship west of the Missouri. Said it often seemed the frontier was being tamed by a bunch of clowns."

Matt sometimes thought the same thing, but he never said

it, much less put it down on paper.

"He mentioned, at considerable length, the Powder River Expedition of '65."

"Now just a minute, sir. That was supposed to be a great success."

"New information has apparently come to light. Or gotten as far as Captain Sam Adams."

"The expedition cost about forty million dollars, which, back in '65, *meant* something, Matt. And it is now considered one of the greatest fiascoes of American military history."

Matt rubbed his hands together gleefully. "Yes, go on."

"The idea was for three columns to converge on the Powder River country and kill the hostiles. Connor marched north from Fort Laramie, Sully west from the Missouri, and Cole and Walker up, northwest I guess, from the Black Hills."

"Is that the same Sully that said the red scoria up around the Little Missouri looked like hell with the fires out?"

"The same. Possibly he was a better poet than a general. In any case, Connor, heading north, did have some success, routed a lot of hostiles, but he ran out of ammo and couldn't follow up his victories, so he just rode down the Tongue to meet up with Sully and Colonels Cole and Walker.

"Sully, however, had been diverted, sent north of the Missouri by some imbecile, where he marched around for two months without spotting a single hostile."

"I thought he had some great battles."

"Apparently not. But maybe he did. But that's where *he* was. As for Cole and Walker—first, they didn't know a damn thing about fighting Indians. Second, they didn't have any guides that knew anything either. And third, their troops were men that had signed up for the War and didn't want to go fight any Indians. Walker actually had to bring his cannon to bear on his own men before they'd budge.

"But off they finally went, north, supposedly in search of hostiles—as it turned out, nearly eighteen *thousand* hostiles—but their reconnaissance was so poor that they actually passed through all eighteen thousand—a couple of thousand lodges on the Powder River, that was on one side, and Sitting Bull, Black Moon and the Hunkpapa on the Little Missouri, on the other side—all eighteen thousand, passed right between them and didn't even know they were there."

Matt grinned.

"Of course, you've got to give credit, or blame, where it's due. The Sioux reconnaissance was just as bad. They didn't know the army was passing by."

"I've got an idea, sir, on that score, that the Indian vigilance isn't all it's cracked up to be. A lot of hostiles haven't known the army was around until the cav was riding into their villages."

"Quite so, quite so. But in any case, Cole and Walker's column finally reached the Lower Powder. But then they wandered into the Badlands and got lost.

"Then they got attacked by the Sioux. And then they began to starve, and their horses began to starve. There's no graze in the Badlands. Finally they found their way back to the Powder and started back up it, probably trying to get out of that country as fast as possible. Ran into about two thousand Sioux and Cheyenne. Both were surprised. Heavy losses on both sides.

"In time they did hook up with Connor's column, but by then they'd been out of rations for two weeks, had been slaughtering packmules for food and looked like tramps. That was the glorious Powder River Expedition of 1865."

Matt judged by the captain's brooding silence that he'd concluded.

"Is that all of it?" he asked.

"Isn't that enough? Actually there's more, but that's all Captain Adams wrote. I think he got a case of writer's cramp along about then."

"Well," said Matt, "it's interesting. The 'clown' theory, that is."

"And probably true. Never did care for Sam Adams."

seven _____

"Glory be, so this is Colter's Hell," exclaimed Malone. "So where are all the steam baths?"

It wasn't Colter's Hell at all, and Private Malone was soon disabused of his notion. But his mistake was understandable, because what confronted him that morning were the magnificent Tetons.

They had ridden into the Jackson Hole basin the night before, well after dark, so the mountains came as a surprise, though they'd had a hint of them the previous evening.

The floor of the basin was 6,500 feet high in itself, but the tallest peaks were more than 13,000. There were no foothills, so the mountains shot straight up for more than a mile above the basin floor. Of rugged, durable granite, they had resisted erosion much more effectively than the lava plateaus of the nearby Yellowstone.

"What's this river?" asked Lieutenant Branch, pointing to the river beside which they were camped.

"Well," said Windy, "Mr. Clark, of that expedition, tried to name it the Lewis River, but folks kind of insisted on calling it the *Shoshoneah*, the way it'd always been called."

"That's an Indian word, I guess. What does it mean?"

"Snake."

"This is the Snake?"

"Sure is. Starts here, fed by the lake an' by all the little streams outa the Yellowstone an' the Tetons, and about a thousand miles northwest from here it joins up with the Columbia. Nice little ride if you feel up to it."

"All right," said Sergeant Cohen, cantankerous as only a stiff and sore first sergeant could be, "if you folks have finished yer sightseein', we'll be movin' out."

They rode north, circled the lake and began the final, gradual ascent to the Yellowstone Plateau. They'd already climbed more than fifteen hundred feet and had less than a thousand to go. Shouldn't be hard.

Matt rode off to give George his morning run.

Captain Conway watched them go, envying the younger man his energy . . . and his tough backside.

Private Bainbridge grabbed an opportunity and rode forward from the rear of the column to flank the wagon carrying his pregnant wife.

"How's the baby, Mary?" asked Bainbridge.

"Lordy sakes, Charles," said Mary, "he was all right a half-hour ago, he's all right now."

"Maybe he's a she," said Amy Breckenridge, sitting beside Mary and handling the reins—they'd tried to give them a driver, but Amy, stronger than half of the men along, wouldn't hear of it.

"I know," said Mary, "but I can't say 'he or she' every time. I call him 'he' for Charles"—she smiled at her husband—"but when I'm talking to myself, and to the baby, she's a 'she'." She wrapped her arms around her stomach and then frowned up at her husband. "Have you heard anything yet?"

"About what?"

"The *transfer*, what else?"

"Mmmm, yes, I have. Actually, I knew before we left the post."

"And?"

"It's no good. It was turned down. Again."

"Why? They're not short on men, not anymore . . . or not that short."

"Turns out it's not that. Seems your condition's not a good

59

enough reason. Seems like the reason has to be something that benefits the army, not us."

"Why, that's . . . that's stupid."

"No it ain't, honey," said Amy, Sergeant Breckenridge's wife. "If it was up to Breck and me, he'd be stationed somewhere in Tennessee. And half the men out here would be stationed somewhere near their homes."

"So?" said Mary, unwilling to understand. "What's wrong with that?"

"There's a job to be done out here, that's what's wrong."

"Well, I don't care. I want my baby. The army's . . . the army's trying to murder her."

"Mary!" cried Charles.

"There, there, Mary," said Amy, "y'all don't know what you're sayin'."

"Oh? What do you know about children? You've never had any babies."

Amy reached out and took a firm hold on Mary's arm. "Now you listen, honey. It ain't because I never wanted any . . . an' I still got time . . . but there are other women around you that are very sensitive about not having children. They may not say nothin', but they're swelled up with regret. So you just be thankful you're carryin' one . . . and just watch your tongue, you hear?"

Mary stared at her, wide-eyed, thinking of Flora Conway and Maggie Cohen. "I never thought of that," she said softly.

"Sure you have, honey," said Amy, releasing her arm and giving her a tight smile. "You just haven't thought about it a *lot*. But believe me, they have."

An hour later, during a rest stop, Amy went up to the first wagon and conferred with Maggie Cohen. And a little after that, Flora Conway climbed up onto the second wagon to join Mary Bainbridge. She grabbed the reins.

"That Maggie Cohen!" she exclaimed. "What a stubborn, pigheaded fool that woman can be. I've been telling her, and that driver we had, that I know perfectly well how to handle a team. Why, I was practically born in a carriage." She smiled at Mary, as if the same fate might await Mary's baby. "But now that we have the chance, do you think Maggie will let me handle the reins? No. Not even once. I hope you have more confidence in me."

Mary didn't see that she had much choice. "Don't you have a driver anymore?"

"Well, to tell the truth, I suggested to Sergeant Cohen that he either supply us with a driver who washes occasionally or we drive it ourselves."

"My husband Charles is clean."

"I'll bet he is."

"He washes all the time. He knows I like it."

"He's a good man."

"But he can't get a transfer." Bitterness crept into Mary's voice.

"Goodness, why should he want to do that?" This was one matter the full particulars of which had not been explained to Flora Conway; she'd only heard that poor Mary was unhappy.

Mary realized she'd already violated Amy's commandment to watch her tongue, but now she was committed. She explained about the difficult pregnancies she'd already had, the miscarriages, and the need for better medical help than was available at Outpost Nine. "I thought you knew all about it," said Mary.

"No I didn't," said Flora, stiff-faced. "They think they're protecting me. They think I must be too distraught about not having children of my own to be able to...handle such a situation...or sympathize with you." Her face lost some of its stiffness. "But I do sympathize. And Libby Custer had no children either, but at least I still have my man. Who am I to complain? And God must have His reasons. But Warner Conway had better have some reasons too," she said ambiguously and with sudden animation. "Just wait until tonight."

They'd ridden along the eastern shore of Jackson Lake to its northernmost tip, which was, according to Windy, just a few miles short of Yellowstone Park.

They found appropriate terrain along the banks of a small river and continued north. Captain Conway hoped to reach the plateau by nightfall, but they didn't, and camped instead at the confluence of three streams.

They were, in fact, within the boundaries of Yellowstone Park at that point, but were not yet out on the plateau.

Tents were pitched for the officers and those men with women along, and Sergeant Rothausen summoned them to beans, sourdough bread and coffee.

Captain Conway stayed up for a while afterward with Matt,

Lieutenants Branch and Weaver and Sergeant Cohen, going over the maps they had and tentatively planning how they would contact the cavalry.

"We could start shootin'," suggested Cohen, not entirely in jest. "That might draw 'em."

"And use up ammunition we might be needing later," said Captain Conway.

"Needing?" Cohen knew they were hauling enough for an all-out war. What was the captain expecting?

"When was the last time you had to fight off marauding hostiles, Sergeant?" asked Captain Conway, smiling.

Cohen's eyes became slits. "Very funny, sir," he growled.

"Better safe than sorry," said Lieutenant Branch fatuously.

Cohen shot him a withering look. "I'm already sorry."

The meeting broke up with nothing decided, and Captain Conway slipped into his tent, fully expecting to find Flora sleeping peacefully. To his surprise, a match flared and a lamp was lit.

"Trouble sleeping?"

"Why won't you transfer Private Bainbridge?"

"What?" he said weakly.

"You heard me."

"I can't."

"She's lost babies before, and she'll lose this one if she doesn't have top medical attention."

"I know," he grumbled, struggling with his boots.

"Don't you care?"

"Of course I care. But I can't make exceptions. And even if I could, it would probably be rejected at a higher level."

"Not if you really pushed."

"Well no, maybe not if I really pushed." He crawled under the blanket and reached out, but she dodged the hand. "But I'm not going to *really* push."

"Why not?"

"I told you, I won't make an exception. I'm doing what I can."

"Oh? And what's that? Nothing."

"Flora . . ."

"Don't 'Flora' me. And please keep your hands to yourself."

Captain Conway took a deep breath. "The point is, babies are not a part of the army. The rules don't cover the unborn.

62

The army provides support for wives, and for children that already exist, but that's it. Babies complicate things. The army doesn't encourage them. Hell, the army doesn't even want the enlisted ranks getting married, much less having kids, you know that."

Warner Conway could hardly believe he was having this conversation with his wife. They'd always steered so far clear of the subject of children that neither of them knew who was responsible for their childlessness. And neither wanted to know.

"This has happened before with the Bainbridges," he went on. "It may have been due to faulty medical attention, maybe not. We don't know. We do know that it's nothing new. Now if a baby is that important to them, whey didn't he leave the army and live where she could have proper care? This isn't his first hitch, you know."

"Maybe he can't afford to leave the army. Maybe he wants to make it a career."

"Well," said Warner Conway, "things can't always be what we want them to be." He regarded his wife steadily, and perhaps a bit sadly. "You should know that. We both know it."

Warner Conway leaned over and blew out the lamp, then lay back down, arms by his sides.

Several silent minutes later a hand touched his, and he rolled toward her and they clung to each other.

Easy Company was up with the crack of dawn.

Matt thought the captain and his lady looked a bit dreamy-eyed, but he gave it no further thought. Instead he struck his tent and folded and stowed it before Cohen had a chance to assign the task to anyone.

In short order the men were fed and mounted, and the procession got under way.

After a few miles Matt left the column and struck out on his own, giving George his morning run. Matt pretended it was a chore, but he really enjoyed riding after his hound.

George was picking up scents all over the place, dodging every which way. Matt's horse couldn't keep up, and he decided that, first, he was going to get a different mount, and second, if George didn't take care, he'd galumph straight into a bear's den.

He heard George start to bay.

Hell, thought Matt, if the captain hears that, he'll think he's back in Maryland, riding to hounds.

The baying continued and Matt decided to stop and wait for George to tire and return.

But George didn't return, or not for a while, not until Matt began to worry, thinking of those bears again. But then he saw the big dog emerge from some firs and look around.

George saw him, but stayed where he was. Matt whistled, but still the dog didn't budge. Instead, after a few moments, he turned away and disappeared back into the trees and soon resumed his howling. This time, however, it seemed to Matt that there was a mournful edge to the sound.

Matt nudged his horse and walked him toward where the dog had vanished. He took out the Scoff and held it down by his side. No telling what George had found.

He walked his horse through the trees for about five minutes. He saw the dog. But it wasn't until Matt was almost upon him that he saw the body at the dog's feet.

Matt dismounted carefully, scanning the surrounding ground, forest and brush. Anything might have killed him—cougar, bear—and might still be around.

But when Matt bent over the body he saw that neither bear nor cougar had downed him, nor had it happened recently. Maggots were crawling in the chest cavity where the bullet had come out and were starting on the eyes. It didn't smell good, either.

Matt had come upon it upwind, so he hadn't smelled it until he was there. He wondered how George had picked up the scent. "Don't mind your howling, George," he said to the dog, who'd taken to whimpering. "I'd howl too if I'd come on this."

He stared down at the small, wiry body. And he thought about luck. Someone didn't figure the body to be found, that was for sure, but what were the chances of the body not only being found in recognizable condition, but found by someone who could recognize him? You had to think of that as a long shot. Sheer luck.

Matt's lips compressed into a thin line.

Maybe so, thought Matt, maybe it was sheer luck, but where was Lady Luck when Deputy Marshal Cal Murphy needed her?

He'd met Murphy in Denver, in the company of Marshal Long, who worked out of that city. Murphy'd just caught some men. He was obviously young, but he was supposed to be good.

Not good enough, apparently. And no longer young.

Luck. Matt shook his head. If he had his way, luck would be running out on whoever had gunned young Murphy.

Matt rode back to the column, told the captain what he'd found, and asked for Windy and a squad.

On the way back to the body, Matt explained, "I don't figure anybody shot him somewhere else and carried him there. It's too far out of the way. He had to be riding when he was shot, either chasing someone or running from someone. And they just left him there. Took his badge and identification and left him."

"Badge?"

"He was a deputy marshal."

"So what do you want *us* to do, sir?" asked Corporal Miller. "Bury the gent? You said he was rotting, right?"

"No burying," said Matt. "I'm hoping that the man who killed him shot him from the saddle and Murphy's horse took off. Or the killer simply didn't bother with the horse. Sometimes you don't hang on to things that'll tie you to a killing, that'll hang you."

They pulled up a ways short of the body. Upwind, they couldn't smell it. Windy went forward and examined the area around the body. In time he returned.

"Looks like he was trailin' someone when he got shot off. And it was right here, Matt, you was right. Horse hung around for a while, long enough to leave some droppin's, then took off slow, back the way it come."

"Spooked?"

"Nope. I tol' yah, he was movin' slow."

"All right, lead the way."

Windy tracked the horse, partially from an occasional sign, partially from guesswork.

"Hell, I can't see a thing, Windy," said Matt.

"Me neither. Tryin' to figger like a horse."

Great, thought Matt. If Windy could figure like a horse, it might mean he wasn't any smarter than one, which wasn't very smart. But if he couldn't, they'd come up empty. One way or another, someone lost.

"I give up," said Windy.

"But you figure this is the right general direction?"

"Yeah, Matt, but hell, he coulda kept walkin' and grazin' and he'd be all the way to Montana by now, back home in Helena for all we know."

Matt grunted, then said, "Malone, Dobbs, Holzer, Rottweiler, you four spread out to the right, about twenty yards apart. The rest of you to the left, same distance. We'll go straight ahead...."

He waited, thinking he should have brought George, until they'd gotten spread, and then signaled them forward.

They rode at an easy pace for about fifteen minutes, then—

"Sir!"

The far right. Rottweiler. Matt and the rest converged on the native-born German private.

Murphy's horse had gotten its reins hung up. And something had killed it.

"Looks like a cat got him," said Windy.

Matt pictured the animal struggling to get free, eyeballs rolling, while its killer stalked it....

He shook himself, leaped from his horse, and retrieved the saddle from what was left of the carcass.

"How about *him*, sir?" asked Malone. "Want us to bury him?" Since they hadn't bothered with the marshal...

Matt stared him down. It wasn't funny. But hell, nothing bothered Malone. "Let's get back before they start worrying," Matt said.

"What do you think, Matt?" asked Captain Conway.

"He was chasing someone, got caught himself."

"Why were you so intent on finding his horse?"

"Personal possessions. They'd stripped him, taken his badge. I had to find something to go on, to look for. Maybe I wouldn't have if I'd never met him. But if we hadn't found the horse, I'd have sent to Helena to try to get a description of his horse and his saddle, stuff like that."

"I still don't understand."

"This is a National Park, sir. Federal land. For the time being, we're the law."

Captain Conway looked suddenly deflated. "Oh Christ," he said. "I'm sorry, Matt, my head's been in the clouds. You're right, you're absolutely right."

Matt smiled. "You got a good night's sleep for a change, huh, sir?" he inquired mischievously.

Captain Conway replied archly, "*Au contraire*, my friend, *au* bloody *contraire*."

Matt laughed and dropped back to ride with Mr. Branch.

Just as they had entered the park by what would someday be recognized as the South Entrance, they now came upon a cascade of water that would come to be known as Lewis Falls.

Beyond the falls was a lake. Scouting turned up another lake to the left and a third to the right.

"Yellowstone Lake's supposed to be about as big as an ocean," said Captain Conway. "Guess these aren't it." He squinted at his map. "But if we're here, according to this, then the lake's not far off."

It wasn't. A couple of hours later they reached the banks of Lake Yellowstone.

The surface of the water was abundant with fowl. And the depths were doubtless teeming with fish.

"We eat!" cried someone.

"Sergeant," said Captain Conway to Ben Cohen, who was now riding beside him, "you'd better break the news gently to the men that this is a park."

"Meaning?"

"Meaning it's a game refuge. Part of our job is to prevent hunting and trapping within the park."

"That means goddamn beans and sourdough, sir."

"It wouldn't set a very good example for us to shoot up all the wildlife, would it, Sergeant?" But the Captain noted his friend's misery. "That doesn't mean we can't send hunting expeditions beyond the park's limits. And there may be some cattle ranches within reach that can sell us some beef."

That cheered Cohen a fraction. "I'll tell the men, sir," he said, and turned and rode back along the column.

Warner Conway heard him begin, "All right, listen up, you men. . . ."

According to Captain Conway's map and Windy's memory, the largest portion of the park lay west and north of the lake. They sent scouts in those directions as they proceeded along the western shore of the lake.

By nightfall they'd covered half the distance to where the lake fed the river, but as yet their scouts had turned up nothing. No cavalry, at any rate. But . . .

"American meat," reported one of the Delawares.

"What the hell's he talking about?" demanded Sergeant Cohen.

"He said cattle are over there," interpreted Windy.

"He wasn't supposed to go *that* far," said Captain Conway. He eyed his map distrustfully. "Unless this map is wrong."

Windy babbled at the Delaware and the Delaware babbled back. "He didn't," said Windy.

Captain Conway hoped morning would bring an explanation.

Sergeant Rothausen announced grub time, and under the curious eyes of many edible wild animals and overlooking a lake lousy with fish and fowl, the men dolefully fell to eating their hardtack and beans, the latter cheerily referred to as "musical fruit."

"Now I know what Colter meant by 'hell,'" said Private Malone, resigned to farting halfway through the night.

Daybreak brought a white light and a mist rising off the Lake. The men stamped around.

"Christ, I damn near froze to death."

"You're over seven thousand feet up, soldier, it's supposed to be cold."

"No one tol' me."

"No one tells you when to take a crap, neither," said Corporal Wilson, rolling from his blanket fully dressed.

"Yeah, well, I'm gonna find me one of them steamin' potholes and sit in it."

"Better be careful, soldier," advised Captain Conway, overhearing the complaints.

"Sir?"

"A lot of those holes are boiling."

"There ya go, Red," cried Private Shanks. "We'll have ourselves some o' your home-grown mountain oysters!"

That took the edge off everyone's appetites, but since breakfast was dehydrated potatoes, done up as pancakes, it didn't matter that much. "Desecrated spuds is desecrated spuds!"

"That's *dessicated*, you peabrain."

"That's what ah said, bunghole!"

Captain Conway tried to haul Flora from their tent, but Flora wouldn't budge. "Are the men quite finished with their . . . ribaldry, Warner?" she asked sweetly.

"You watch. Soon as you stick your head out, they'll turn into choirboys."

"I'll bet. Foul-mouthed choirboys."

Conway grinned. Flora had heard enough in her life, or his army career, to turn a teamster's ears beet-red. But she never quit pretending to be shocked.

They both left the tent to partake of morning grub.

The sentries had come in from their night guard, and all were gathered near the lakeside.

"I'll be damned," said someone. "*Horses*. You fellers sure you know how to ride them?"

A weird remark, for sure, and eyes searched for its author.

A soldier sat just beyond the outer ring, sipping some of Rothausen's coffee, an unfamiliar soldier. He wore forage blues, but then they spotted the yellow trim, faded and a little dirty.

"Holy smokes! Effin' cav!"

"Good for you," drawled the trooper. "You're pretty sharp." The mockery rang loud and clear. "But them's some picket guards ya got. You're lucky you ain't dead."

The officers and NCOs of Easy were a cool lot. They weren't about to fault their guards for letting a uniformed trooper creep past them in the half-light of morning.

"Y'all got some officer with you, a second lieutenant, maybe? I'd kinda like to report to someone."

The officers of Easy stood up. "Over here, Corporal," said Captain Conway quietly.

For a moment the cavalry corporal's face looked bright and cheery, but then he spotted Conway's tracks and Kincaid's silver bar, and his face fell. "Oh shit," he muttered.

"What's that, Trooper?" Matt's query was rapped out so sharply that some pronghorns took off through the nearby woods.

The corporal mumbled to himself and then approached the officers. He almost gave his usual lackadaisical salute, but caught himself in time and made it a proper one.

Captain Conway returned the salute and asked, "What's your name and why are you here, Corporal?"

"Corporal Trask, sir. We been watchin' for you, me and my boys. My CO thought you'd be showin' soon."

"Who's your CO?"

"Grady, sir, Lieutenant Grady."

"Where's your troop, Corporal?"

The corporal waved northerly, slightly to the west. "Back where the Yellowstone comes into the park, sir."

"Show me." Conway waved his map at the corporal.

The corporal looked at the map, got himself oriented, and then pointed to the north entrance.

"Why there?"

"'Cause that's where they figger the permanent cavalry post will be, sir."

Conway and Kincaid exchanged looks.

"What's the best way?"

"Two, sir. This way, which is some shorter and will take you by that cliff of black glass, or this way, down the Yellerstone and on around, which is longer, but—"

"Is that where the falls are, the big falls?"

"Yessir. Figgered you mighta heard about them."

"We'll go that way," Conway decided with no hesitation.

They broke camp.

By midday, Captain Conway was commenting, "So this is where the Yellowstone River starts."

"Nope," said Windy. "Starts further up in the mountains at the south end of the lake."

Captain Conway glared at him. "We were just *at* the south end."

"The other south end, Captain, south*east*. Sorry."

Conway decided irritably that before this trip was over, he would, just for the hell of it, go to the real headwaters of the Yellowstone.

A couple of hours later they were all standing at the rim of the Grand Canyon of the Yellowstone, staring back at the spectacular falls.

"Did Moran do it up right, Captain?"

"He certainly did, Matt," answered Flora Conway. "We feel like we've been here before."

Corporal Trask and three troopers waited down the trail for Easy to wind up its sightseeing. They were careful to keep some distance between themselves and the infantry.

"Goodamn tourists, seems like, Corp," one of the troopers said.

"Ain't no better. I don't think the lieutenant figgered they'd be bringin' women. They're treatin' it like a goldurned picnic."

"Might as well, Corp. They wouldn't be any good for any

fightin'. They wouldn't know what hit 'em."

They had a good laugh over that.

The light was fading when Easy rode into the camp of Lieutenant Grady and his cavalry troop.

Grady's expression, upon discerning Captain Conway's rank, wasn't much better than Corporal Trask's had been. And his salute was a whole lot worse. "Welcome to Yellowstone...sir."

Captain Conway smiled coldly and introduced his officers. In doing so he managed to get Matt Kincaid's time-in-grade on record, and Grady's face fell further. Might as well get the chain of command down cold right away, thought Conway, ignoring the cavalry lieutenant's discomfiture.

Grady fought back, though. He said, after a critical glance at the wagons and dependents, "You understand, sir, that yours is only a temporary assignment. There'll be more cavalry arriving to take up permanent station as soon as they can be shaken loose."

Time for a bit of give, thought Conway. "We understand that, Lieutenant, and we will try not to interfere with what you perceive as your duties. We are here to support." He smiled, but then added, "We are not, however, here to be dominated. We should be able to work something out."

Grady eyed him uneasily, as if he wasn't sure.

At which point Matt spied Lieutenant Foster, he of the Custer ambitions. Mr. Foster was giving it his best shot, wearing fringed buckskins, a large white Stetson, a red scarf, and floppy boots that were much too large for him, reminiscent of Custer's Civil War "uniform."

Foster noticed Matt's amused expression and he bristled.

He bristled even more when Matt loudly drawled, "I hope your horse isn't named Vic. Or Dandy..."

A look of chagrin pierced Grady's face. He did not at all care for the idea of having an officer under his command draw derision upon himself or his unit. He was going to have to take Foster aside and tone him down.

Grady had also taken a second look at Matt Kincaid, and he was rapidly adjusting his first impression.

At the same time that Grady, Matt, and Lieutenant Foster were engaged in their interplay, Easy's lower, cruder ranks, most of them experienced fighters, were locking stares with the loathsome yellow legs, and both were giving as good as they got.

And soon epithets were being mouthed, if not spoken.

Private Malone, reading lips, read an especially offensive epithet and dismounted calmly. He walked toward the cavalry troop and said something.

Matt was suddenly alarmed. He knew that when Malone got worked up, his brogue got thicker and less intelligible, and what Malone had just said was almost gobbledygook. Clearly, Malone was about to explode. "Private Mal—"

Too late. Malone had wandered, grinning, into the cavalry's unsuspecting ranks and suddenly buried a fist almost up to his elbow in a large trooper's gut.

As Malone disappeared under a swarm of cavalry, Easy's men leaped from their horses and surged forward.

Captain Conway opened his mouth to roar a command, but then he closed it again without a peep.

Grady, too, had been about to try restoring order, but when he saw Conway close his mouth, he did too.

Matt had to smile. There was a feisty side to his captain that not everyone got a chance to see.

There was also a feisty side to Easy's enlisted men that the cavalry hadn't counted on. Furthermore, Easy had Grady's troop outnumbered by half. True, in the name of fair sport, Lieutenant Weaver, bringing up the rear with his platoon, managed to hold back many of his men, but some slipped free.

And Malone had risen from the pile and was giving a good account of himself, as usual.

The air was suddenly rent by three quick sixgun blasts.

It brought an instantaneous halt to the proceedings.

Matt Kincaid holstered his gun and ordered, "Back off, men."

They did so. Easy's enlisted men rarely argued with their officers, and never in the presence of outsiders.

"You waited long enough, Lieutenant," said Captain Conway.

Matt didn't blink an eye.

"I think both sides have had sufficient time to measure each other," said Conway. "Wouldn't you agree, Lieutenant?"

Grady, who'd been bothered by the way the fight was going, had to agree.

"You should understand," Conway blithely continued, "it's

been a long trip, and at times boring." He let this sink in, then went on, "Well, Lieutenant, what is your idea of how we should proceed?" He wanted the lieutenant to feel, as much as possible, on equal footing.

"Well, sir, my priorities, as I understand them, are to protect the surveying team on their excursions, patrol the park to see that the intent of Congress is served, and to build a permanent post to accommodate the park's eventual patrol, which will, I further understand, be drawn from the cavalry. I—"

"You mentioned that before, about the cavalry patrolling."

"Ah. I guess so." Grady'd not yet gotten over the fight. "But I figure the post will initially just be solid stockade walls. We'll need that. But inside, tents will do for now."

"Sounds reasonable. What about this 'intent of Congress'?"

"The park will remain untouched, a refuge, its boundaries firmly enforced."

"Good. We agree. But the park's boundaries are rather extensive, are they not?"

Grady looked rueful. "I daresay there's enough ground for several troops to cover. And before we can keep others out, we have to convince those already here to leave."

"We had a report of some cows. Is that possible?"

"Some! A whole bloody herd, run by some fellows who seem determined to stay. Of course, can't say I blame them. Except for the Indians, they were pretty much the first ones here, and they did a lot to make it as peaceful as it is."

"Yes, that's an old argument, and not without merit. They earned it, they should keep it. But the idea of National Parks is a *new* argument. What do you say we discuss this later, Lieutenant, after we've eaten and gotten settled?"

"I haven't even mentioned the fellow that may or may not be setting up a hotel on park grounds," Grady went on.

"May or may not?" Conway said, puzzled.

"Have to wait for the surveyors to take a look."

"Ah. Well, later, Lieutenant, later..."

eight

Dawn found the men of Easy Company and the cavalry detachment up and hustling, Easy because they'd heard there were some weird sights nearby that they could see if they hurried, the cavalry from sheer competitiveness. The result was that when Easy's men trotted off before breakfast to look at the hot, sulfurous springs, the cavalry had nothing to do but polish leather and curry horses.

The men of Easy Company were impressed, of course, by the steaming, smoking springs, but while some accepted them as nature's oddities, others looked upon them as nature's conveniences. Malone had laughed when Dobbs, hearing there were hot springs nearby, had grabbed soap and a towel and toilet articles.

No was was laughing later, though, when Dobbs lathered up and gave himself the first good shave he'd had in almost two weeks.

Meanwhile, Captain Conway and Lieutenant Grady reached agreement. With considerations of manpower, priorities, and park familiarization in mind, it was decided that the cavalry would escort the surveyors and patrol the park while Easy built the stockade.

"I think we're getting the short end, sir," said Sergeant Cohen.

Captain Conway smiled thinly. "I know we are. But you have to admit, they do know the park better than we do. It's an intelligent division of labor. We could blend the two groups, but they'd just end up fighting each other."

"Jeez. They go off riding and we bust our humps building a stockade. I dunno, Captain." Cohen shook his head in mock disgust. "You sure drive a hard bargain."

Unfortunately the cavalry's lower ranks also regarded it as something of a victory, and said so. And they barely got out of there alive.

Some time later, Mr. Branch, a rare gleam in his eye, asked Kincaid, "Did you see that lady surveyor, Matt?"

"I not only saw her, Cliff, I met her."

"Awww, you didn't."

Matt tried to suggest circumspectly that his meeting a lady wasn't tantamount to bedding her. But such was Matt's reputation in such matters that Mr. Branch wasn't buying Matt's disclaimer.

"Oh, hell, Cliff," said Matt, shrugging, "I'd put her away in a flash, except she's not my type."

"She's not?"

"No. I like them a little meatier."

"She didn't look skinny to me."

She wasn't, dammit, she was just right. "Matter of taste," Matt said, which would make Mr. Branch think he liked fat women.

"You probably should meet my sister," Branch said.

Not in a million years, Matt thought.

Matt saw Sergeant Cohen assembling some four-man work crews. Since the captain and Flora had gone to gawk at the springs, Matt figured he'd best oversee operations. He wandered close.

"I want solid, straight timber," said Sergeant Cohen, "at least twenty feet long. But don't bring me back nothin' that after twenty feet tapers down to itty-bitty points. And—"

"Sergeant," Matt interrupted him, "where are you sending these men?"

Cohen waved toward the closest stand of trees, which was

to the west. Then he waved south and east.

Matt shook his head and pointed north.

Cohen looked that way and said, "Beggin' your pardon, sir. If they cut there, they not only have to haul it, but they have to haul it uphill. This way they can maybe even float 'em down the river."

Matt shook his head some more. "Outside the park, Sergeant. I may be wrong, but my understanding is that *nothing* gets destroyed inside the park. No animals, no trees, nothing."

"Can we get a second opinion on that, sir?"

"Nope."

"What about that fella that's buildin' a hotel?"

"*Ser*-geant."

"Hell, sir, I ain't arguin', I was just suggesting an . . . an anomaly."

A complete hush fell over the assemblage, except for a giggle from someone who thought Cohen had said something dirty.

"A what?"

Cohen's jaw thrust out. "Anomaly, sir. Deviation from the general rule."

Oh Christ, thought Matt, Cohen's discovered another word. He remembered when the sergeant ran "behooved" by him so many times he was hearing it in his sleep.

Matt knew better than to say anything then, in front of the men, but he planned to take Cohen aside and tell him that it would *behoove* him to keep Maggie Cohen out of dictionaries. She obviously did not have a flawless feel for army lingo. Anomaly was not the sort of word that had your ordinary soldier snapping to attention. But for the moment Matt merely remarked, "I plan to look into that hotel. All right, Sergeant, carry on . . . but outside the park."

"Yes, *sir*!"

Matt walked off unhappily. Ben Cohen only yelled like that when he was pissed.

"Hey, Matt, where you going?" Windy fell into stride next to him.

Matt stopped. Where *was* he going? He stared at Windy. "I think I'm going back to my tent."

"Catch a few winks, huh?"

"And do some paperwork. I'm still company adjutant, dammit. Brought some work along. And a book. Tactics. You should take a look."

Windy looked like he'd rather kiss a cougar. "See you later."

Windy went whistling after his nag, found the horse contentedly cropping grass, and explained to him that they were going to have to take a little hike. "Nothin' to it, Reb, we'll jes' mosey along."

Windy had a deal with his horse. He could use some saddle other than the slotted McClellan, which was easy on the horse but posed a constant threat to the rider's testicles, in exchange for which Windy wouldn't push Reb too hard.

They'd known each other for a good while. Reb was nearly twenty, which sounded old, but Windy sometimes got hoarse explaining that old for some horses wasn't old for others. Some of the meanest buckers were well into their twenties. But if they still weren't convinced, Windy'd let them climb aboard. Reb would still put anyone but Windy way up where they had no right being. The first buck was a warmup, but the second was an explosion that sent them soaring. Never needed more than two.

Windy rode south, heading for a gap in the hills.

An hour later he was staring up at a huge cliff face of black obsidian. "Well, hell, ol' Gabe wasn't lyin' after all," he said.

If anyone else had been along, Windy would have said Jim Bridger, but to Windy alone he was "ol' Gabe."

Reb pricked his ears.

"You hearin' things, hoss? I don't hear nothin'."

Windy rode on.

The two cavalry detachments had ridden the same way a while earlier. The surveyors had already surveyed the route through the mountains, past the Cliff of Black Glass and as far as one of the major geyser basins, and they had tentatively charted a road along that route. Thus they and their escort kept right up with the cav detachment, whose function was patrol.

Once out onto the Central Plateau, though, the two groups split, the surveyors proceeding straight ahead, plotting a route south to where they knew there were more geyser basins, and the cavalry patrol angling west, from whence all the cattle seemed to come.

Now the surveyors moved slowly, driving Lieutenant Foster, who was commanding the detachment, nearly crazy. Grady had kept Foster with the surveyors for almost the entire previous week, for some reason unwilling to turn him loose on the park.

"How are you this morning, Lieutenant? Spirits improved any?"

Since it was Miss Mills doing the asking, he did indeed feel a bit perkier. Nice-looking woman, well educated, about his own age. A bit too independent, perhaps, unusual for a woman, but...

"Speck better, ma'am, thank you." She rode well, too. "Don't look like they're keepin' you busy."

"Once we start breaking up into smaller groups I'll be busy," she said. "And if you don't mind, seeing as how I'm no older than you, please don't call me ma'am. It sounds so...elderly. My name's Clara."

"In that case," said Foster, "you'd better call me Peter—errr, Pete...Clara."

"Mind if I ride with you, Pete?"

"My pleasure."

She wore britches and rode like a man. Pete Foster couldn't decide whether that was good or bad, so he grinned and said foolishly, "You like to hang out in saloons, too, Clara?"

Clara might have taken offense—she was a lady through and through—if she hadn't been certain that Foster was not intentionally trying to insult her.

"I'm not a man, Peter," she said evenly. "Can't you tell that? I'm only wearing pants and riding like this because it's more comfortable and because I thought we were far enough away from polite society."

"I'm sorry, Clara, I wasn't thinking."

"Just to be on the safe side, don't think of me as a woman, think of me as a scientist."

"Well, reckon that's not a good idea, either." Foster could be engaging when he forgot about himself and his Custer image.

About that time, Captain Forsythe and a few of his surveyors had rightly concluded that the lay of the land, as it pertained to laying a road, was leading them away from where they thought the geysers were, bending to the west.

Ted Armstrong spoke to Lieutenant Klepper, who then spoke to Captain Forsythe.

"Then why don't we pinpoint where the geysers are exactly, and then figure out the best way back from there," Forsythe said.

Consequently they turned and rode directly south through sparsely wooded forests of fir and occasional meadows until they reached the area where many of the eruptions were concentrated.

The steaming geysers and sulfurous fountains, bubbling and gurgling, and the frequent subterranean rumbling (they'd surmised that not far below lived active lava that shifted around heavily and noisily and that leaked its incredible heat in occasional belches of steam to the surface above) all lent a persuasive note to the old myth of Colter's Hell.

They poked around the various basins, plotting their dimensions. There was one particular geyser that, while it was not the tallest or the most powerful, was the most regular in its eruptions. Every sixty-five minutes, like clockwork, it sent a plume of steam and hot water rocketing a hundred and fifty feet into the air. On the earlier maps it was noted but had been given no name, but by the time Congress had instituted Yellowstone as a National Park, it had earned the appellation that was to become a watchword for reliability: Old Faithful.

Meanwhile, the cavalry patrol had drifted slowly west, poking here and there, generally in pursuit of stray cows.

"So far they're all Rocking K," reported Sergeant Fuller. "You'd think they'd keep them bunched, what with all the wolves and cats."

"They probably do try to keep them bunched," said Lieutenant Grady. "But some are bound to stray regardless. In fact they probably count on some wandering off and getting killed. Keeps the predators away from the main herd."

The Crow scout, Spotted Calf, rode up then in a state of mild excitement. "Arapaho," he said.

The Crow were enemies of all members of the Lakota Confederacy, and while Spotted Calf had spent years with the American soldiers, the old antagonism was still in his blood.

"Well, let's send them packing," said Lieutenant Grady. "That's what we're here for."

The twenty-man patrol fanned out, a four-man squad taking up the point while two other groups of four ranged right and left, with the remaining eight bringing up the rear in reserve. Grady rode in the center of the formation, Sergeant Fuller by his side.

They came out on open ground and discovered about a dozen Arapaho in the process of chasing a pair of buffalo, sinking a multitude of arrows into the powerful, dumb beasts.

The Arapaho were beyond effective range, but Grady ordered a burst of gunfire anyway, just to get their attention.

The shots got the Arapahos' attention, all right, and bows were slung over shoulders, arrows tucked away, and rifles brought out. Grady and his men found themselves charging into a blanket of fire. Slugs whistling by told them they were well within range. They threw on the brakes and hit the ground, kneeling to send shots skimming over the tall grass.

The Arapaho wasted no time on a fight they would either lose or barely survive. It was not the Indian way to fight against superior numbers. They'd done what they'd intended, unhorsed the Americans, and now they turned their ponies and rode south.

Grady had his men mount again and they chased after the Arapaho, pursuing at a pace that would bring the Indian ponies to their knees before the larger, stronger army horses gave out.

Interestingly enough, unknown to both the Arapaho and the army, there was still another interested party to the action. He was atop a big horse and up ahead of the Arapaho. He was yelling his head off.

It appeared that a sharp turn to the side would have taken him to safety, but he followed the natural contours of the land, as did the Arapaho, and as did the cavalry.

Both cavalry men and cavalry mounts fell easily into the spirit of the chase. It had been a while since they'd had a good run. And so uncomplicated was the chase that it became a kind of race, and the cavalry began to bunch up, casting aside any tactical considerations.

As they raced along the bottom of a slight, tree-bordered depression, they suddenly took withering fire from those trees.

Men and horses went tumbling, and more men and horses crashed into and over them.

Those who survived the first fusillade hit the ground, one way or another, and scrambled for cover.

There wasn't, as it turned out, a hell of a lot of cover to be had. Nine men tucked themselves away behind three dead horses; the rest either hid behind low outcroppings of volcanic ash or hid behind their own horses, which were trained to lie down in place and, if the firefight got hot, give their lives for their riders.

The men behind the horses had the better of it from the standpoint of protection. Volcanic ash was soft and easily eroded into fantastic shapes by wind and rain. Needless to say, lead slugs did a faster job than either wind or rain.

When Lieutenant Grady had gathered his wits, he cried, "Sing out, let me hear you."

Eighteen men responded. Considering what they'd run into, that was damn good. Many might be wounded, but they were alive.

An efficient and devastating ambush. And a mysterious one too. Who the hell had ambushed them? Certainly not the Arapaho they were chasing. And if the bushwhackers were other Arapaho, or some other manner of hostile, how could they have known that the cavalry would surprise the Arapaho and chase them, and that the chase would lead here?

Too unlikely.

Had to be an accident. Good luck for some bastards who reacted swiftly and ruthlessly when the opportunity presented itself, and bad, bad luck for the cavalry.

"I figure we've got two dead, Sergeant, or too bad hurt to sing out. That your count?" Grady asked.

"Yep."

"Hostiles?"

Sergeant Fuller shook his head. "Shootin' too goddamn good and smart for hostiles. Figger it's them effin' cowpunchers, seein' more army arrive and figgerin' they'd better hit now if they're gonna hit a-tall." His head poked up and he scanned the distant trees, some hundred yards up the gentle slope. A shot sent his head back down.

"Hell, when they saw where we was ridin', they prob'ly pissed for joy. Damn, if we hadn't got so goddamned bunched . . ."

"No sense crying about that now, Sergeant. Let's think about how we're going to get out of here."

They thought about it for nearly an hour . . . and came up empty.

The men were getting cramped and cranky. They'd be able to sneak away when it got dark, but those bastards up the hill could sneak around too, then. And hell, where were they gonna sneak to without any horses?

It was a rotten situation.

It was well past noon when Lieutenant Grady and Sergeant Fuller agreed they'd have to try to send someone for help.

"Anyone know where the horses went?"

"Saw some headin' back along the trail, prob'ly ain't gone far."

"Anybody want to make a run for it?" It wasn't something that Lieutenant Grady would order anyone to do. If there were no volunteers he'd take a crack at it himself.

There were eight volunteers. Grady chose one.

He got about thirty yards. The fourth shot got him. He hit the ground and lay still . . . but then suddenly started wriggling toward a hole in the ground. Slugs created little spouts of dust all around him, but he made the hole safely. Or part of him did. His legs hung out. And the firing continued.

"Those mean sons of bitches. They're shootin' for Lenny's legs deliberate."

"Maybe so," muttered Grady, "but he's lucky to be alive. Lucky and smart. He cheated them. Waited till they'd lifted their eyes from their sights before he started crawling. That's why they're shooting, 'cause he beat them."

Kind of a triumph, true, but it was small solace to the beleaguered detachment.

But just then a sound washed over them, bringing instant relief if not joy. The piercing notes of a bugler sounding the charge.

"Thank bloody Christ," cried Lieutenant Grady. "Foster's here!"

nine ————————————————

Windy hadn't ridden much farther along before he too heard the gunfire that Reb had heard. "Better take a look, hoss."

He kicked Reb up to an easy, ground-eating lope.

In time he reached the open ground where the Arapaho had been chasing the buffalo. He saw the two critters wandering around, grazing, looking like pincushions.

He'd begun to smile when he heard the first fusillade from the ambush. "Somethin's sure happenin'," he muttered to Reb, and he started after the cavalry.

Five minutes later he crept to where he could see the cavalry detachment pinned down.

He wasted no time crawling back to his horse, mounting, and heading back the way he'd come.

A half-hour later, Reb staggered into the army camp, where the first logs were just then being raised on end.

The men saw Windy and the condition of Reb, and the logs fell back down as they ran to surround him.

Matt came out of his tent.

"Cav," said Windy. "Pinned down, can't fight their way out nohow."

Matt called for First Platoon and then he, Mr. Branch, Sergeant Olsen, and some thirty men went scrambling. "Grab another horse, Windy, and Reb"—not the beat nag but Reb McBride, the bugler—"you grab a horse too."

"Natcherly, suh," drawled McBride, who was Southern to his toes.

Less than two minutes later First Platoon, most of them still wearing only undershirts, if that much, rode out of camp. Windy, struggling with an unusually spirited animal, led the way, with Kincaid, Branch, and Olsen hard on his heels.

They hardly gave a second glance to the Cliff of Black Glass, which most of them had not yet seen. Nor did they pause when they nearly rode right through a large geyser basin. Their eyes may have popped, but they didn't slow down.

Less than a half-hour later, as the sound of gunfire grew louder, Matt yelled, "How're they laid out?"

"Cav straight ahead!" Windy shouted. "Hostiles up a slope to the right!" Windy had assumed it was a hostile attack.

Matt yelled orders, sending Mr. Branch, Sergeant Olsen, and two squads to the right to come along the top of the slope right by the trees. He led the remaining squad, straight ahead toward the embattled cavalry. "Soon as we see 'em, Reb, sound the charge."

Reb McBride readied the bugle.

Then they were over a slight rise and the cavalry was in sight. McBride sounded the charge that Grady heard, and First Platoon, with Matt and Mr. Branch up to the right, started laying leather to their horses.

Matt freed his pistols and angled his body forward and to the right slightly, bringing both guns to that side of his mount's bobbing neck. He pointed them up the slope at the distant trees, shouted, "Let 'em have it!" and started squeezing off rounds. The rest of his squad followed suit.

They were firing blind, but were taking the heat off the cavalry and providing cover for Mr. Branch and the two squads skirting the trees.

But Branch and his men were having trouble with the terrain.

Matt saw that and sent his mount charging up the hill. His squad followed, and the cavalry rose up from cover and began to scramble up the hill.

Matt and his men crashed into the trees, thrashed through them, and soon were on the other side, back out in the open, having found no one.

Several horsemen were rapidly vanishing to the northwest.

"Holzer!" roared Matt, and pointed.

Private Wolfgang Holzer snatched his rifle and left his still-moving horse in a single motion, stumbled to his knees, snapped his rifle up, froze . . . and squeezed off a round.

One of the distant riders toppled from his horse. His companions left him.

Matt thought that if he'd had all his sharpshooters from the other two squads, they might have gotten the whole damn bunch. "Corporal Wilson," he called, "take a squad down there and bring him back."

Then Matt turned toward the trees.

Branch, Olsen, and the two other squads were the first to appear. Olsen looked around in surprise. Matt nodded grimly. "I know. If I'd known the trees were just a long, narrow stand, I could have sent you around back. Could have caught 'em all."

"Who were they, sir? Hostiles?"

Matt shook his head. "Awful white-lookin' hostiles, from what I could see. We'll know in a little while."

Lieutenant Grady and the surviving cavalry came out of the trees.

"Had you in a right nasty hole, didn't they, Lieutenant?" Matt said.

Grady was slightly mortified at having to be rescued by the infantry, but he was a man about it. "Sure seemed like it," he allowed. "How'd you get here?"

"Windy was out nosing around."

"Windy?"

"Our scout."

At this point Windy rode up, complaining loudly. "Dammit, Matt, don't never let me grab this horse again." He scowled at the spirited bay, whose ears were pricked, alert. "Look at him, he's still lookin' for trouble. If there'd been any real shootin', he woulda run me right into the middle."

Grady looked puzzled and Matt smiled. "Windy's managed to develop a streak of cowardice in his own horse. Not this one, though. Whenever Reb gets close to heavy fighting, he runs slower and slower, no matter how loud Windy tells him to hurry up."

"I didn't train him that way," groused Windy. "It's just that the older he gets, the smarter he gets."

Corporal Wilson and his squad returned, hauling a human

carcass. "Wolfie's too goddamn good, sir. Nailed him square. He was dead by the time we got there."

"Let's have a look at him."

A grimy, unshaven white man was laid out.

"Anyone recognize him?"

No one did. But many agreed with the trooper who declared, "He's gotta be one of them goddamn Rocking K punchers. They know they better do somethin' now or get the hell outa the park."

"If you don't mind, Lieutenant Kincaid—" began Grady.

"Matt."

"Matt. If you don't mind, I'll take care of this body."

Matt agreed. "Be my guest. Olsen, round the men up and let's get back. We've still got a stockade to build."

Sergeant Olsen started issuing orders.

"Matt."

Matt Kincaid turned back to face Lieutenant Grady.

"Thanks," said Grady.

Matt nodded acknowledgment. Then he said, more for the troopers than for Grady, "Just remember, we don't wear these guns for decorations and we don't keep horses for pets. Any time you need help, don't be afraid to holler. Now have you got any dead or wounded you want us to haul back to camp? I sense you have something you want to take care of."

Grady glanced around to make sure his men had "overheard" properly, and then he accepted Matt's offer of transport.

Private Malone found himself staring at a familiar face. It took a few moments before he realized that it was the large trooper in whose stomach he'd buried his fist. Malone suddenly grinned.

And the trooper, unable to help himself, grinned back.

The surveyors had spent a few hours charting the various geyser basins before they discovered something just as extraordinary as the geysers but far less natural. Up the eastern slope of the basins, someone had clearly begun to construct a building. A foundation of hewn logs had been laid, and now only the superstructure had to be raised.

"It's recent," said Captain Forsythe.

"How recent?" asked Lieutenant Foster.

Abe Webley, a civilian surveyor, said, "So recent we may have interrupted them."

86

"That recent, huh?"

"No way of knowing for sure, of course."

They could have asked the man standing up in the trees ringing the basin, if they'd known he was there.

"I think we'd better call it a day," said Captain Forsythe. "I'm rather anxious to inform Captain Conway of this construction."

"Cavalry's in charge of patrolling the park," Foster reminded him heatedly.

"Don't worry, Lieutenant Grady will be informed."

Lieutenant Grady? What the hell's wrong with *me*? thought Mr. Foster, incensed.

Clara Mills saw his expression, read his thoughts, and smiled.

They worked their way back north, keeping to open ground.

"It looks as if we may end up charting that roundabout route after all," said Captain Forsythe, not unhappily, just stating a fact.

The terrain opened up somewhat. The grazed appearance of the grass and occasional droppings indicated that cattle came through there frequently.

Captain Forsythe shook his head. "Those cattle will have to go."

"This is inside the park still, is it, sir?" asked Lieutenant Foster.

"Oh, definitely."

There was a distant rumbling.

"Sounds like a whole flock of geysers going off somewhere," said one of the surveyors. "What a wonderland this is."

"Yeah, well," grumbled Mr. Foster, "sounds more like artillery to me."

"Really, Lieutenant," said another surveyor, "what would artillery be doing up here?"

Foster happened to glance west, toward the open ridge, and saw a line of horned heads suddenly come bobbing into view.

"A goddamn stampede!" he roared. "Run for it!"

He himself sent his horse toward the onrushing cattle, angling to the side, trying to find the flank of the stampede. His men rode with him as the surveyors fled for their lives.

Foster hadn't quite found the flank when the tide of cattle was upon him. He wrenched his horse around and ran with them, firing over the heads of the leaders as he tried to turn them. His men did the same.

The cattle started to turn, but not soon enough. The long-legged beasts, nearly as fast as horses, overtook a number of the surveyors and Foster saw horses stumbling and some going down, while others were caught up in the tide.

He cursed and continued to attack the flanks.

He saw a puncher fighting his way forward through the running cows, adding his gun and horse to the cavalry's efforts.

And then there were more punchers, and the stampede was finally turned, headed toward the trees, where it finally came to a milling, snorting halt.

Foster rode back to count the dead and injured.

None were dead, but several of the civilian surveyors, not used to riding horses, much less running before stampedes, were badly injured, one critically.

"Oh my God," cried Clara Mills, a decent horsewoman and one of the few civilians to escape.

Foster was relieved to find her safe.

One of the punchers rode up. Once he'd determined that no one was dead, he growled, "What the hell you sons of bitches doin' here, anyways?"

"We're working, goddammit!" cried Lieutenant Foster. "What'd you stampede 'em for? What were you trying to do, kill us? Scare us away? Who the hell are you, mister?"

"The name's Red Adair," the puncher answered tightly, "and we didn't stampede nothin'. Don't know how they got started."

Foster sensed that the cowboy knew more than he was telling, but he was too angry to press the issue beyond saying, "We ought to skin you bastards alive! You're going to pay for this, goddammit!"

Lieutenant Grady, after Matt had left with the ambush victim, took his men and Holzer's dead victim, and rode northwest. He had a fair idea where the Rocking K made camp.

An hour later the cavalry detachment came in sight of the Rocking K chuckwagon. A number of men, possibly as many as ten, were standing around. The rest of the crew were out with the cattle—some, at that very moment, were helping to turn a stampede.

Lieutenant Grady recognized Roman Kreutzer, the Rocking

K's owner; he was squatting beside another man, the grizzled gent of indeterminate years who had ranted in support of the Rocking K at their previous meeting. Both men stood as Grady rode toward them.

"Kreutzer."

"Lieutenant. You've met my foreman, Sam Billings. What can we do for you?" While the words seemed friendly enough, the tone was carefully neutral.

Grady scanned the faces of the punchers. He had fourteen men of his own, outnumbering the Rocking K contingent, but he intended nothing in the way of a fight.

His hard gaze returned to Kreutzer and Billings. "We've got someone for you."

A couple of troopers rode forward, as prearranged, and the corpse was dumped on the ground before Kreutzer and Billings.

Billings rolled the man faceup, and he and Kreutzer stared down into the dead eyes.

"A warning," said Lieutenant Grady. "The last one."

Kreutzer and Billings raised their eyes and stared back at him, betraying not a flicker of expression. An electric tension crackled through the assemblage. Punchers tensed, as did the troopers.

The cattleman and his foreman uttered not a word.

Grady began to back his horse away. His men did likewise.

At a safe distance, Grady turned his horse and rode away. His men peeled off, one by one, and rode after him.

At length they vanished over a rise.

Kreutzer took a deep breath. "I was beginning to get stiff," he said. "That officer was pushing hard."

Sam Billings nodded agreement. Then he and Kreutzer looked back down at the body.

"Who the hell do you suppose this is?" wondered Billings.

That night, back at the army base camp, was a time for licking wounds and for endless speculation.

"That man Maxwell, is he going to live?" asked Captain Conway of Captain Forsythe.

"I think your doctor is going to pull him through."

Matt Kincaid, overhearing, asked, "Doctor?"

"Rothausen. Your first sergeant thought he might be able to take care of it."

"Don't get your hopes up, Captain. Rothausen might stand

muster as a field surgeon, but in real life he's our mess sergeant. A cook."

"Oh." Captain Forsythe didn't know what to make of that. "I trust, if worse comes to worse, that we shall not be finding friend Maxwell on our plates come supper."

Matt's stomach did a turn and Conway looked thoughtful.

"Actually, Fred Maxwell's injuries do not seem to be as critical as they first appeared," said Forsythe. "He may have a cracked skull, but unless there are internal injuries, extensive breaks are the most Rothausen will face, with Maxwell and three others. I presume he knows how to set a break."

"Will he be able to work?" asked Conway.

"Good Lord, no. Even if he had a mind to, which he doesn't, he'd have to be carried, and Fred's no lightweight. And as for the others, I'm afraid that as far as the civilian contingent goes, their idea of an incapacitating injury is anything worse than a mosquito bite...save for Miss Mills. She seems cut from hardier cloth."

"Cut very nicely too," said Matt Kincaid.

"Matt, you dog," said Captain Conway in admiration.

"I only said she was good looking."

"No woman is safe with Matt Kincaid around," Captain Conway explained to Captain Forsythe.

Matt groaned while Forsythe commented, "I can believe that, Warner. I've seen the looks that woman has given him."

"What woman?" demanded Matt. He hadn't seen any looks from Clara Mills.

"Why, the woman that's been keeping Warner company."

There was a moment's pause, and then Matt squawked, "Flora?" and started to laugh as Captain Conway's eyes grew round with shock.

"That'll teach you, Captain," gurgled Matt Kincaid, and Warner Conway slowly, very slowly, came to see the humor of it.

"Hereafter, Matt," he finally said, "I'll leave your affairs to you alone." He turned back to Captain Forsythe. "Do you have enough whole people to continue your survey?"

"Oh yes. I could do it alone, with the time—a lifetime— but this will slow us considerably. I don't suppose there are any among you with surveying skills."

"Not to my knowledge."

Lieutenants Grady and Foster joined the group then, Foster busily twirling the chamber of his Peacemaker.

"Lieutenant Grady," Conway addressed the stern-visaged officer, "have you made any headway?"

Grady shook his head. "We've talked it over several times, and it's still the same. It was probably the punchers that waylaid us and stampeded the herd at Pete and the surveyors, but there's no hard evidence. And it could be someone else."

"Meaning?"

"Two things. There's this gent that's building some hotel way over west . . . and who might be the one building stuff near the geysers. Or the trouble might be simply outlaws. This place up here is a real natural hideaway if you were an outlaw, or a bunch of outlaws, looking for one."

Matt suddenly remembered Deputy Marshal Cal Murphy. The poor man had slipped his mind. "You may have hold of a live one there, Marcus."

"What do you mean?"

Matt told him about finding the body of Deputy Marshal Cal Murphy. "Chances are he'd trailed some outlaws up here."

"That'd sure account for his being here," said Grady, "but despite my having made the suggestion, I also have to say that I haven't seen any sign of any outlaws, unless it was them shooting at us. But why should they attack us? If we don't know they're around, what's the point?"

"I can see how you can go around in circles on this," said Captain Conway. "What about this hotelkeeper, or whatever he is?"

"Hiram? Haven't actually seen much of him. As I say, he's far west. Maybe outside the park boundaries. But then again he may also be responsible for the building going on inside the park, by the geysers and such. No way of knowing without asking him."

"And he'd answer truthfully?"

"I think so. He's a businessman, but he seems like a nice sort, a harmless type."

"Does he know this is a park?"

"He'd better. I told him so. Of course, I'm not sure he knows what a park is. I'm not sure *I* know what a park is. Getting so I'm afraid to piss."

"Carry an empty canteen," said Matt. "Empty it over the boundaries."

"Matt," groaned Captain Conway, "you can be so god-damned crude sometimes."

"Just don't get your canteens mixed."

"Matt!"

Kincaid asked, "Is this Hiram character there all by himself?"

"Peckinpah," said Grady. "Hiram Peckinpah. No, I don't guess so, but I haven't seen anyone else."

The name "Hiram Peckinpah" had brought a light into Captain Conway's eyes. He searched his memory, then said, "I think perhaps I'll go have a talk with this Peckinpah tomorrow morning."

ten _____

"The horses are gone!"

Again? What kind of mission was this? It was jinxed!

Captain Warner Conway, half-dressed and looking down at his still-slumbering wife, felt like undressing and crawling back under the covers. Everything was happening to them, everything but some good old-fashioned fighting. They'd already been horse-thieved once, the cavalry had been run over by a stampede, they'd been involved in a range war and made to build a stockade that the Engineer Corps and common labor should be building...

It was very frustrating.

Of course, Flora thought it was just fine. Lots of peaceful sightseeing, a second honeymoon. "Hell," he muttered, "for her it's just like vacationing back home." Tripping gaily about, hiding under her parasol, visiting friends, checking the sights...

That was it! Peckinpah. Up on Capitol Hill, beneath the dome, where the Moran paintings were hung. Could this be the same pushy gent, the all-around 'entry-pre-noor'?

"Where'd they go?" someone said outside the tent, and he resumed dressing.

"How the hell would I know? You think they told me? You think I talk horse talk?"

"You oughta. You're sure a horse's ass."

Captain Conway waited for the sound of scuffling. There was none. Puzzling.

When he stepped outside and saw that it was Dobbs and Malone, he understood. Those two men called each other everything under the sun and loved it.

Corporal Wilson was standing nearby and scowling at both men. He saluted Captain Conway. "Sorry, sir. Hope they didn't wake you."

"I was awake. Which one is the horse's ass?"

Dobbs snapped to. "I am, sir!" he shouted.

Captain Conway flinched a little at the vehemence of the reply. "What happened?"

"These two," said Corporal Wilson, "and Rottweiler and Parker were standing watch last night over the horses. The cav watch their own, real close, like to make believe they're real buddies with the beasts, like to damn near sleep with 'em—"

"Yes, yes, I'm familiar with cavalry."

"For some reason *we* got assigned to watch the extra horses, the ones the surveyors use, besides our own. We kept 'em separate."

"Why?"

"Dunno, sir. I guess 'cause they ain't ours and no one wanted them getting mixed up." He brightened, looking past Conway. "Mr. Weaver gimme the orders, sir."

"For a different reason," said Mr. Weaver at the captain's elbow, making Conway start. "Many were damaged in the stampede, came up limping, mostly minor cuts and bruises, but I thought it best to keep them segregated."

"You mean to say someone stole all our gimpy horses?"

Weaver nodded. "Don't suppose they could tell in the dark, sir."

Captain Conway heaved a sigh. All this before breakfast. "All right, then, how'd the horses get stolen?"

"I didn't know I was supposed to be watchin' them, sir."

"You mean you heard them being stolen and you didn't do anything?"

"I figgered..." Stretch Dobbs almost got a hernia trying to think of something convincing. "I mean, I heard them *movin'...*."

And figured it wasn't any of his business, Captain Conway concluded. Dobbs was a good fighter, and as strong as a horse, but also just about as bright as one.

"So, Mr. Weaver," Conway said, "what are we doing about the missing horses?"

"Just found out they were missing, sir. I—"

"Excuse me, Captain," said Lieutenant Grady, coming up. "Just heard about the horses. Why don't you let us look for them? We have to patrol anyway. And I understand you're taking the surveyors with you."

"Mmm, I think we'd better find out just where this Peckinpah is building his hotel. I'll need the surveyors for that. So yes, you go ahead and look for the horses. Shouldn't be a problem. They're damn near all lame."

"Will you have enough men left to finish the stockade, sir?"

"Are you volunteering manpower, Lieutenant?"

"Errr, no. I was just concerned."

"Thank you for your concern, Lieutenant. We'll finish it today. I didn't study all that goddamn civil engineering for nothing." He eyed Grady. "Are you a Point man, Grady?"

"Yes indeed, sir, but I wasn't any good at engineering. In fact, I was plumb lousy."

"Then I guess it's lucky you aren't building this, isn't it?"

Grady decided it was time to get the hell out of there. These were unusual infantry. Hot-tempered, hard-riding, disciplined fighters who didn't back down from anyone. And apparently it started at the top, with Conway and Kincaid. He admired it, but didn't feel like testing it anymore. "Yessir, it certainly is." He started backing off. "So, by your leave, sir"—he saluted— "I'd best go do what I can do. I'll be back soon . . . with the horses."

Confident bastard, thought Conway, also hoping Grady wouldn't send the imbecilic Foster.

He didn't. Grady trailed after the horses himself, following Spotted Calf. Mr. Foster was sent to check the illegal construction near the geyser basin, to make sure no one was doing any building or, if they were, to get their identities.

Captain Conway went looking for Sergeant Cohen, and found him.

"I'll just take one squad, Sergeant, that should leave you plenty of muscle. You know how to put this stockade together?"

"I ain't a civil engineer, sir," said Cohen, "but I guess I can put up a goddamn wall. Two, if I have to."

"Better make it four. Two-sided stockades don't make much

sense." He grinned at his first sergeant. "And make sure it opens, or faces, slightly northeast."

"I was figgerin' straight east, sir, like it's usually done."

Conway shook his head. "There's no slope straight east. The only runoff we have is to the northeast."

"There ain't gonna be no rain, sir, leastways not enough to matter."

"Not now, maybe, but come Spring..."

Cohen nodded grumpily. He hated making dumb mistakes. And it meant he'd have to shift around what they'd already started. Why hadn't the captain gotten smart a couple of days sooner?

Cohen organized the work crews and construction resumed.

A couple of hours later, Matt Kincaid and Mr. Branch were passing time with the ladies—Flora, Maggie, Amy, Mary Bainbridge, and Clara Mills, excused from that day's surveying trip—when Private Bainbridge stopped by to see his wife.

"Off down the river again," he said, "to find us some big, healthy, and probably immovable logs." He grinned. "How's my girl?"

Mary sort of purred.

"Ben keeping you boys jumping?" asked Matt.

"Sure is, sir. We had to take down what we'd already put up. But I don't mind, it's good exercise. And down the river there're some real interesting rocks."

Clara Mills' look sharpened. "Rocks? Mind if I come along?"

"Can you handle an ax, ma'am?" joked Bainbridge. "I don't mind your coming, if it's all right with the lieutenant."

"Don't ask me, ask your wife. Maybe she won't want you gallivanting off with another woman."

Clara Mills made fists and glared at Matt, but Mary Bainbridge just purred some more. "Oh, I don't mind," she said. "Charles can handle himself. Besides, I may just go walking, and who knows what handsome devil I'll find out there."

Clara Mills was still glaring at Matt. "You're in trouble, Matt Kincaid," she said with as much seriousness as she could muster. "She may not mind but, oh, wait'll I tell Mr. Foster."

Lieutenant Branch suddenly looked stricken while Matt laughed.

●   ●   ●

A while later, down the river, Private Bainbridge pointed at a distant rock shelf and said, "See that, ma'am. That's—"

"I know what that is, Private," interrupted Clara Mills. "You just go about your business. Forget about me."

Bainbridge did. He was married and this woman meant nothing to him. He could forget her like she'd never been forgotten before.

Clara Mills, in the meantime, regretted her testiness. She knew why she was edgy. While far from old, she was no longer a kid, and she was involved in what was generally thought of as "man's work," half the time wearing britches and work clothes and grubbing in dirt. As a result she was doubly sensitive about her femininity, her desirability. She resented being called "ma'am" by men no younger than herself.

The attention that Foster and Branch paid her was nice, but they were soldiers, what her friends liked to call "men without women." She should have married when she had the chance, darn it.

"What the hell do you think you're doing, Private? Put that rock right back."

"This ain't the park, Sarge."

Private Bainbridge had spotted a gold nugget and slipped it in his pocket. They'd been told they couldn't touch a thing in the park, but—

"I ain't so sure about that, Bainbridge," said Sergeant Breckenridge, the Tennessee mountain man who'd gone with the detail because he loved felling trees. "This might still be the park."

"Then what're we cuttin' trees here fer, Sarge?"

Breckenridge's jaw tensed. He was simply going to have to stand on his authority. "Now you listen up, chowderhead—"

"Don't bother, Sarge," said Bainbridge. "It's not worth anything. It's pyrites. Just looks like gold. Fool's gold."

"Who're you callin' a fool?" snarled Bainbridge.

"That's what it's called, dammit," protested Bainbridge, not wishing to get hit but not backing down.

Eventually Breckenridge smoothed things over and told Bainbridge he could keep the pyrites. Bainbridge threw it away.

A short time later Clara Mills asked Bainbridge, "How'd you know that was pyrites? I mean, that that was its name?"

"Huh? Oh, school."

"College?"

"Yeah. Just for a while, though. Things happened. I was going to be an engineer at first. But then I got interested in geology. And *then* I got interested in Mary and, well, school didn't seem so important and I got married and then I figured I could check out all the rocks out here where they were, instead of in a classroom. At least that's what I told myself. And that's how come I joined the army, to look at all the land out here, all the rocks. Pretty dumb, huh?"

"Has it worked out?"

"Not really, I guess. I said it was a dumb idea. Back where I'm stationed, Outpost Nine, there don't seem to be many rocks, just kind of sandy soil, which it seems I'm digging holes in half the time. But besides that, Mary and her miscarriages have had me kind of distracted. I'd just signed up for a second hitch when she miscarried the first time. We figured it was just an accident, but since then . . . Maybe I'll go back to school when this hitch is up."

"But by then you'll have a family."

"Maybe." But his eyes told her he expected a miscarriage this time too. "I'll figure something out. If she miscarries again I'll go to med school."

"You can afford to?"

Obviously not. He was dreaming.

"At school," she pursued, "did you take any surveying?"

"Oh sure. Basic surveying. When you're going to be an engineer, that's one of the first courses they teach. At least at my school it was."

"Would you like to give us a hand? With the surveying?"

"Sure. But you're a civilian."

"But the Engineer Corps isn't. Let me speak to Captain Forsythe."

"If you're finished gabbin', Charlie," called Sergeant Bainbridge, "give us a hand. It's grub time. Let's get these logs hauled back and get us some eats."

"Beans, Sarge? You're hurryin' back for beans?"

"Maybe not. Holzer and them went out huntin'. Things're gonna start lookin' up."

"I'll bet," grumbled Private Bainbridge.

By the time they got back to camp, the various teams, construction and logging, had all broken for grub.

"Beans," said Sergeant Breckenridge dully.

"Surprise, surprise," said Sergeant Rothausen.

"I thought Holzer and them went huntin'."

"So did I. I ain't heard no shots, though. Either they rode a hell of a way or the animals heard 'em comin'."

Private Bainbridge grabbed a plate and then headed for the tent where he'd last seen Mary.

She wasn't there. Just Maggie Cohen and Amy Breckenridge and George Armstrong, the brindle hound sleeping off his midday meal.

Maggie Cohen told him that Mary'd said she wanted to go for a walk.

"By herself?"

"No harm in that, is there?" asked Maggie. "I shouldn't imagine she'd go very far. She doesn't seem the type."

She wasn't. But not much had run true to form until then . . . and wouldn't.

Ben Cohen had gobbled his beans and gone wandering. The saddle soreness had vanished and he was his old gruff self. And not a little frustrated.

Back at Outpost Nine he often observed that he was about the only one there who never got to do any riding, never got to see the countryside, was always stuck on post.

The long ride to Yellowstone had shut him up for a while, but now he was thinking again that he was the only one that never got off post, or in this case away from camp. Here he was in one of nature's wonderlands and what had he seen? Aside from a waterfall and a couple of smelly little hot springs, not a damn thing.

He'd heard talk of the Cliff of Black Glass. He wondered how far south along the trail it was. He decided to take a look. He'd walk as far as he could. If nothing else, the exercise would do him good.

Mary Bainbridge, bulging somewhat at the waistline, had not been nearly so ambitious as Sergeant Cohen, but she'd ended up walking a good deal farther than she'd planned.

She was a good walker, normally, and the belly was not yet too much of a problem. The last month was when it would seem to explode, when it would get to be a real chore hauling herself from one place to another. Of course, she didn't know that from her own experience. She'd never made it that far. She crossed her fingers.

She was well up in the gap to the south, out of sight of the camp. The men had said there was something that looked like a huge mirror of black glass up that way, and that the shards of black rock were just as sharp as broken glass. She'd kept an eye out for that, not wanting to step on any, but so far she hadn't seen any. No big black mirror. Nothing.

She was tired, and feeling less adventurous. It was time to turn around.

But then, up the slope to the right, she saw movement.

Startled, her first emotion was fear. Hostiles? Or some savage, ravening beast?

But then the movement revealed itself as the play of a trio of bear cubs, cinnamon-hued, tubby, energetic brown bear cubs.

She climbed toward them slowly, not wishing to frighten them.

She lost track of time and where she was going and how long she'd climbed. The cubs were so much like playful little...children.

The first trio of cubs ran off, disappointing Mary, but then, elsewhere, more popped up. They saw her, but didn't seem frightened. But then they too were gone.

She'd heard stories of ferocious bears, but now those stories seemed preposterous.

Her eye caught movement at the treeline not far above her. She smiled in anticipation and began to climb quietly toward the trees.

She'd gone about half the distance when suddenly, from behind her, there came a thunderous roar.

She spun, chilled to the marrow, and saw, below her by some hundred yards, a huge shape rising out of the grass. It was the other, bad half of Yellowstone's bear population, a grizzly.

The grizzly roared again and started toward her. Her scream rent the air and she started backing away up the hill.

Her scream was heard back in camp, faint but clear, and everyone froze, puzzled.

Then, ears primed, they heard the bear's resonant roar and a second piercing shriek, and they all started charging south out of camp, up into the gap. They had a long way to run, though. They would have been better advised to saddle up some horses, but they didn't.

Ben Cohen didn't think the Cliff of Black Glass really existed. He'd climbed as far as he felt like climbing, but hadn't seen a thing. He paused, giving thought to his next move.

But then his bowels made up his mind for him.

A creature of some fastidiousness, not often finding himself in the field and lacking casual toilet habits, he looked around for an appropriate spot to dump, far from prying eyes and far from any straying feet.

Up the slope.

He climbed and climbed, until he came to a suitably high and dense stand of shrubs and grass.

He entered the small stand, took off his harness, his shirt, his gunbelt, and put them carefully aside. Then, standing there with just his head and shoulders showing, he undid his trousers. With one last wary look around, he crouched down out of sight.

Rothausen and his goddamn beans. The bean diet was playing havoc with his regularity.

He'd been down out of sight for some time when he heard the bear's roar, quite loud and close, it seemed. He cursed elaborately, but stayed hidden. He wasn't sure he wanted to know how close the beast was.

But then Mary's scream brought his head and longjohned shoulders shooting up out of the shrubs.

He looked around wildly. He didn't see anything to the south, up in the gap, or uphill—the trees weren't too far away—or downhill, where he'd climbed up from the trail. It had to have come from the only remaining direction, north, but the slope was uneven and he had no clear line of sight.

He burst from the thicket, fumbling with his buttons and suspenders. A few strides south along the slope brought him to a slightly different vantage point and he saw the girl, Mary . . . and the grizzly, standing erect some hundred yards below her!

He was as far from the grizzly as he was from Mary. He moved forward slowly, his hands reaching for his guns—

Damn! They were back in the thicket.

He was about to turn and run back for them when he saw the grizzly drop to all fours and start up the hill for Mary.

Mary staggered backward.

Ben Cohen started running.

He was dimly aware that the men from camp had come into view and were beginning to shoot, but they were way out of range. All they could do was make the grizzly madder. Or worse yet, hit Mary with a stray bullet.

Ben closed in, heavy legs pumping, determined to reach the bear before it got Mary. And after that?

Ben Cohen's strength, his awesome skill and power in unarmed combat, were the stuff from which legends were made, but grizzlies had a few legends of their own.

Just as Ben was taking his last few pumping strides, he was conscious of a rider. . . .

And yes, a rider, copper-skinned and clinging to a pony with his knees, had ridden out of the trees above and was swooping down. And as Ben Cohen rammed his shoulder into the grizzly, the Indian reached down and gathered Mary Bainbridge up and carried her out of harm's way.

Ben had managed to ram the grizzly off its feet, but he'd gone tumbling too. And now, as he righted himself, the grizzly did likewise, turning toward him and rising to its full height.

Ben could have reached out and touched it if he'd wanted to. Which he didn't. But—

Ben froze, his mind a turmoil of sounds, thoughts, and instincts. He knew Mary was safe, heard the men getting closer, and gave some thought to turning and running. But he knew the bear, that close to start with, would catch him easily. From behind. Better to face the bastard.

Ben sucked in breath and tensed himself. The grizzly roared and he imagined he could feel its breath.

But then a hundred and ten pounds of shaggy, brindle-hued hound hit the grizzly, traveling at about forty miles an hour.

It staggered the bear and shook Ben free of his glorious death wish. He turned and began lumbering downhill as fast as gravity and his aching legs could manage.

He heard the sounds of George Armstrong taking on the grizzly, and he heard himself sounding like an overworked steam engine.

The sounds of battle died away.

He glanced over his shoulder.

The bear was on all fours, heading up toward the trees. There was no sign of George.

Ben Cohen began to sound like that same steam engine

pulling into a station and letting off steam. He slowed and tried to reassemble his wits.

The men were still charging uphill toward him, their guns out. He blinked the sweat from his eyes and saw Windy riding up behind the men, waving his arms.

Cohen interpreted the arm-waving correctly and roared, or gasped real loud, "Hold your fire, goddammit, *hold it!*"

The charging men came to a stuttering halt, except for Malone, Dobbs, and Holzer. And as Cohen got to the waiting men, the three privates ran right by him, on up the hill.

Windy arrived.

"Windy," Cohen gasped.

"That's Mama Grizzly," said Windy. "The girl was between her and her cubs. Them cubs is up in the trees."

That was all the explanation the men needed. Anyone dumb enough to get between a mother bear and her cubs . . .

"You might've gotten away anyway," said Windy, grinning, "even if George hadn't got there. Grizzlies don't like runnin' downhill."

"I don't either," growled Ben. "I was gettin' set to fight her . . ."

Ben saw he'd lost his audience. They were looking up the slope toward where the three privates ran toward them, Dobbs carrying George Armstrong easily, as though he didn't weigh anything.

They arrived, and didn't even break stride. "He's hurt real bad," shouted Malone, as he rushed by. "Matt'll kill us if we don't get him fixed."

Cohen watched the three privates rush back toward the camp. No, Matt wouldn't, he thought, but he'd sure be sick at heart. And so would Ben Cohen. That hound had probably saved his life.

"Ben!" Maggie Cohen, wild-eyed and in disarray, burst upon the scene. "Goddammit, Ben, goddamn you, goddammit all to hell . . ." and so on and so forth as she fell upon Ben, pounding him about the shoulders for all she was worth in anger and relief. "Why did you do such a crazy thing? You could have been killed, you . . . you . . ."

"Aw hell, woman," said Ben, "you know I didn't have no choice. Besides, that there grizzly's lucky I let her get away. She interrupted the finest dump I've taken since we left home."

The men roared with laughter, and Maggie flushed.

As for Charles Bainbridge, he was nervously watching the Indian guide his pony slowly and carefully toward them, giving his swollen cargo an easy ride.

"Mary?" Charles cried. "Are you all right?"

She was speechless, still, but nodded, trying to smile.

"And the . . . ?"

She smiled tightly and nodded, indicating that the baby was all right.

The Indian lowered Mary into Charles Bainbridge's arms.

He clutched her, and that seemed to signal a release of tension. Everyone started talking at once.

After a while, Cohen gave Windy a sign and Windy spoke to the Indian.

Windy then listened to the Indian's verbose reply.

"He's Ute, Sarge. He says this is their land, their hunting grounds, but if the Americans help his people fight the Arapaho, they'll let the Americans stay in peace."

Sergeant Cohen screwed up his face to give the impression that he was seriously pondering the matter, giving the Ute's proposals weighty consideration. "Cocky gent, ain't he?" he muttered.

He finally raised his head and gave the Ute the full wisdom-of-Solomon treatment. "First thank him very much for saving the girl. Tell him he will always be our friend. And his people will be our friends, if they wish to be. But tell him that this land belongs to the Great White Father and that it is sacred, not to be used by *anyone*. Tell him that he and his people can *visit* some, to hunt—God, I hope this clears with the Captain— but that they must always return to their reservations and stay there."

"I'll see if I can get that across," said Windy unhappily.

"And give me an accurate translation, goddammit. Matt told me what you been doin' to him."

Windy, even more unhappy, complained, "I ain't said that much to an Indian, all at once, in years."

"Not even when you married Matt off?"

"Not even then. That was a real short ceremony."

"How about those maidens in the friendlies' village?"

"Oh, *them* . . . that's different. All right, listen up, Little Hawk—" He then switched to Uto-Aztec for a long stretch of conversation, back and forth.

"He ain't happy," Windy finally said. "This 'park' stuff

bothers him. He knows about sacred grounds, but what about the Americans with the cattle, and the one building square tipis, and the trappers and the hunters."

"They're all goin', goddammit, they're all goin'. Tell 'im that."

Windy told him, and Little Hawk looked as if he'd believe it when it happened. He told Windy he was still unhappy, but that he was a good warrior, a peaceful warrior—

"Ain't that a contradiction, Windy?"

"Not in his language."

—but that, Little Hawk enlarged, there were other warriors not as nice as he was.

"Well," said Cohen, "I reckon we'll just have to take it as it comes. I can't promise nothin' more. I already told 'em he could hunt and the captain will prob'ly have my ass for that."

The Indian abruptly turned his pony around and rode away.

"He wants you to wait, Sarge."

"What for?"

Little Hawk came riding back, carrying Ben's shirt, harness, and guns.

"Dammit, that bastard was spyin' on me."

"Be glad, Ben," murmured Maggie at his side. "Be glad."

Cohen nodded, gave Little Hawk a smile and a peace sign, and turned to go down the hill. "Let's go see how poor George is comin' along. I owe *him* a hell of a lot, too."

Later, on the way back down to camp, Private Malone said to Private Dobbs, "Y'know, Dobbsy, runnin' up this here hill, so soon after grub, I never heard so much fartin' in all my born days."

"A-men, buddy, a-men. Ol' Dutch's gotta quit with them beans. I about choked."

eleven ─────────────

The Union Pacific train had pulled out of Laramie at about noon, and by midafternoon was pulling into just about the sorriest excuse for a town that Sam Adams had ever seen. Not even a proper station, just two buildings and a water tank.

He got off the train carrying a large piece of luggage and a small satchel. He was dressed neatly in dark-colored, richly textured civilian clothes. There was a brand-new Colt tucked away in his luggage, but on his person he carried no weapon.

One of the two buildings was a saloon, the other a store. He went into the store, but there was no one there. He went into the saloon.

A man came out of a back room. "Howdy, friend. Whatcha want?"

"Good afternoon, my good man," said Captain Sam Adams, on leave from the Surgeon General's headquarters just outside of Washington. "Can you tell me how the hell to get to some place called Outpost Nine?"

The man smiled. "Got a horse?"

"Oh sure, in my bag." So far it had been a long, not very interesting trip and he was cross. He smiled nastily. "I gather it's not within walking distance."

"No one's walked it yet."

"I need a horse."

"Well"—the smile broadened—"horses ain't cheap these days."

Sam Adams wondered what had possessed him to make this trip. A life of cold, calculating, sober reason . . . and now this wild adventure.

He eyed his man. "That's a nasty-looking growth on your neck there. Ever had it looked at?"

"No. Why? Is it something bad?"

Sam Adams reached for his satchel.

Captain Conway, heading west with the surveyors, was making slow progress. Every outstanding land feature required reference to several maps and lengthy conferences among Captain Forsythe and his aides.

"Are we still in the park?" asked Captain Conway.

"Oh yes," replied Captain Forsythe, "as far as I know."

"You're not certain?"

"As far as where we're standing right now, I'm certain, but some discrepancies between what we see and what's on the map have arisen. Minor, I assure you, but—"

"Can't you move any faster?"

"No. Each step depends on the previous step. We can't go running ahead and expect to draw an accurate map . . . or to know exactly where we are."

"I see." They might get to this so-called hotel by the following week. "I'll tell you what, Bryce. I'll take two men and ride ahead, and leave the rest of the squad with you. It's getting late and I want to see this Peckinpah."

"I thought you wanted to know if he was inside the park."

"I do, but it doesn't appear as if you're going to get there today, and if I don't see him it'll just be a wasted day for me." As if he had anything better to do the next day, or the day after that. But Flora did; she had plans.

So Captain Conway rode on, accompanied by two privates from Corporal Wojensky's third squad of First Platoon, Hazlett and Murtha.

•   •   •

A few miles farther along, on a rise overlooking a multitiered complex of sulfurous springs, a small house had been built. Captain Conway stopped and looked inside.

Nothing. Just the shell. But enough space for anything—living, sleeping, eating, especially eating. With tables placed properly by windows, a visitor could simultaneously dine and scan the scene below.

Conway shook his head. If this was Peckinpah's doing, he was getting himself firmly entrenched. The captain didn't need to be a surveyor to know that the trail he'd been following was perfect for a road. And this building, right beside that "road," was two-thirds complete. If Peckinpah was allowed to continue, it was going to take a hell of a lot of work and/or money to get him out.

The trouble was, this park idea was still too new. No firm policy had been established or, if established, published and understood by all. This Peckinpah person could say, "I didn't know, the park is for the public, I'm the public, and I spent one hell of a lot of money getting all this built." Of course, he would double or triple the amount he'd actually spent.

The thing to do would be to stop him now, root him out before he had a chance to get really established.

In which case he'd probably yammer, "What about the Rocking K, how come they get to graze?"

It was turning into one hell of a dilemma. Captain Conway began to lust for the simpler routine of Outpost Nine. There, it seemed, the issues were more clearly drawn, and if there was violence you at least knew who you were supposed to be fighting. But up here? What the hell was he supposed to do about white men honestly trying to make a living? Blast them out?

He had a hunch, though, that at least one white man, Peckinpah, wasn't all that honest and knew exactly what he was doing.

The captain rode on, nursing his hunches.

Meanwhile, somewhat to the southwest, Kreutzer and his foreman, Sam Billings, were still trying to figure out who the dead man was, the one the cavalry had dumped on them.

"Stackpole says he heard shooting, and a lot of it. Him and Benny checked later and said there was some kinda shootout over by Granny's Gash. Apparently—"

"Granny's Gash? Where the hell is that? And Sam, I want to know who's naming these places. Whoever it is has a despicable turn of phrase."

"I think it's Turnbull, boss. He bids fair t' be useless at anything 'cept killin' and thinkin' up names."

"Well," said Kreutzer, "the killing may come in handy, but the names—"

"*Despicable.* I guess that ain't very good."

"Not very."

"Anyhow, there seems to have been a fight and it seems the army thinks we was the ones."

"They would. Rigid, unimaginative, military minds."

There he went, thought Sam. Every time he got sore, he started slinging those two-bit words around.

"The very idea," Kreutzer went on. "We find this land, scour it clean of vermin, render it safe for raising beef, safe for hunting and trapping and even sightseeing, and what happens? The federals think they're going to evict us."

"Yeah. Who the hell do they think they is, callin' this a *park*? It's free land, for free Americans, right?"

"Right," agreed Kreutzer, though not with a lot of heart.

"An' who the hell ever heard of a park, anyways. It don't make sense. There's plenty of land for everybody."

Actually, it made a great deal of sense to an educated man like Kreutzer. And he'd be all in favor of a National Park. Somewhere else. Just south of Yellowstone were the Tetons. They were perfect. Those incredible mountains weren't good for anything but staring at, anyway. Why didn't the government go down there and leave hard-working folk be?

"Well," said Kreutzer, "the problem they have is that they can't kick us off until they have the place properly surveyed, and they're not going to find that an easy thing to do." He smiled coldly. "Or until they receive a top-level ruling from back East, and it'll be winter by then. Besides which, I have some friends back East."

"Peckinpah?" said Billings.

"Eh? He's no friend."

"I'll bet that feller come from Peckinpah's place. There've been some mighty unpleasant-lookin' fellers hangin' around that hotel of his."

"Oh? Why didn't you think of that before we . . . disposed of the body?"

"I thought you'd think of it."

"Aha. What are these 'fellers' doing there?"

"Dunno. Helpin' him out, I 'spect."

"And taking on the cavalry on the side? Seems like an unlikely recreation. Of course, I imagine Peckinpah isn't any happier at having the army around than we are."

"Dunno, boss. He seems like an awful happy feller to me."

Kreutzer reflected that conversations with Sam were sometimes unrewarding. "He may be, Sam, he may be. But that's not our concern. You just keep an eye out for those surveyors and if you get a chance, turn those cattle loose again. But—"

"That last one was close."

"I was about to say, give them a bit more warning next time. I don't want to kill them, just impede their progress."

"Impede..."

"Slow them down, Sam."

Along about four o'clock that afternoon, as Captain Conway was beginning to think he was lost and as Red Adair was trying to round up some cattle to run at the surveyors, a twelve-team, four-wagon mule train drew up alongside the almost-finished stockade and stopped.

First Sergeants Ben Cohen and Jack Faulkner, wed by circumstances and equal disdain for all junior officers, came out of the stockade and appeared to surround the wagons.

"You goin' someplace?" asked Sergeant Faulkner.

"There ain't nowhere to go," said Sergeant Cohen.

"You can turn it around over there," said Faulkner.

"Take it easy goin' downhill," said Cohen.

The man handling the reins, and apparently the train's complete crew, seemed to find their repartee vastly amusing. His bright, beady eyes danced. "This *is* the detachment with the surveyors, is it not?"

The sergeants' eyes narrowed; the surveying expedition wasn't exactly public knowledge.

"Yeah? So?"

"I'm down from Fort Ellis. I'm J. B. Lathrop, your sutler."

"That's tough," said Sergeant Cohen. "We brought our own stores."

"*We* didn't," said Sergeant Faulkner. "We've been buying yours."

110

Cohen eyed his brother top kick. Poor planning, that. No wonder Sergeant Wilson said he was running low.

"I was overruled," explained Faulkner.

That figures, thought Cohen. It also figured that they'd soon be out of beer and tobacco and sweets. "Well . . ."

"I've got beer."

"Three-pernt-two?"

"No. No one said anything . . ." His voice died away.

"Well, what the hell, Ben," said Faulkner. "There's no town around to shoot up, and who's gonna know."

Cohen dug in his ear for wax. "There *are* a few essentials we've run a bit short of."

"Whiskey. I've got that. And some brandies."

Faulkner eyed Cohen. "That sounds essential to me."

"Canned vegetables," the sutler went on. "Canned fruit—"

"Beans!" squawked Ben Cohen.

"No. Fruit. Real fruit. Beans aren't fruit."

"Licorice?" demanded Faulkner.

"Yessirree."

That clinched it, as far as Sergeant Faulkner was concerned.

"And," said the sutler, readying his most telling argument, "items for the ladies."

"What?"

"How'd you know we had ladies?"

"Trade secret."

"What kind of items?"

"That's between me and the women. I really don't think you'd be interested, Sergeant."

"Hell no. Jesus. What would I be interested in them for?" Faulkner managed to look outraged.

"All right, Lathrop," said Sergeant Cohen, "park your wagons here. Unload if you want or work outa the wagons, don't make no difference to us."

"Not inside?"

"Nope. You can sleep inside, set up in a corner maybe, with a few of your wares, but there ain't room for your whole goddamn load. Too damn cluttered as it is, with all the tents and workin'. And don't get in no one's way, ya hear?"

"Gotcha, Sergeant. I'll let them find me."

"And no beer till I give the word, got that?"

"Right. Till you give the word."

"Or till Sergeant Faulkner does, you got that, Lathrop?"

"Goodness, yes. And please, call me J. B. . . . or Jellybean."

"Jellybean?" Cohen's mouth began to water.

Jellybeans weren't cheap, though, as Cohen soon found out. Nor was the licorice. Nor were any of J. B. Lathrop's wares.

The number of crooked post traders, or sutler's, had declined with the passing of the Grant administration. But they hadn't disappeared.

The problem stemmed from the fact that army personnel, including officers, were obliged to buy everything from the post trader. That, in itself, was not bad. But, under Grant, Secretary of War Belknap had sold those traderships to the highest bidders, and then, after permitting those traders to hike prices far above a fair market level, had received royal kickbacks. Investigations, in which George Armstrong Custer had played a large role, had uncovered the frontier swindling known as Belknap's Anaconda, forced Belknap's resignation, blackened Grant's reputation, and presumably marked the beginning of a new era as far as post trading was concerned. Pop Evans, back at Outpost Nine, was a shrewd dealer, but fair and honest. Lathrop, though, appeared to be cut from the traditional cloth. His prices were well above those to be found in Helena, Bozeman, or even gold-rich Virginia City.

"Those goods didn't get hauled this far for nothing, remember," was Lathrop's defense.

Sergeants Cohen and Faulkner, with their jellybeans and licorice, huddled to discuss the situation. Something had to be done about this robber.

"I dunno, Ben, he's got the proper government licenses. Don't know how he got them. Probably got pull with the territorial government."

"Traders are federal."

"I know, but one hand washes the other, and they don't send them wagons rollin' outa Washington. Someone out here's gotta vouch for 'im, so legally he's straight."

"But we've gotta do somethin', short of beatin' the son of a bitch up. Show him the error of his ways."

"You come up with something and I'll go along," said Faulkner. "How're them jellybeans?"

"Dee-licious . . . 'cept I gotta chew 'em so slow. The way they cost, I feel like I'm chewin' pearls."

112

"Wal, leastways we're fixed for sweets. You hear him tell how much honey he's got? 'Bout enough to float a raft. Dunno where he got the idea we got such sweet tooths." Faulkner chewed on a strand of licorice.

"Just a wild guess, Jack, just a wild guess." He popped a jellybean home. "Damn, do I want to get that bastard."

twelve =====================

Captain Conway, accompanied by Privates Hazlett and Murtha, finally arrived at the site of Peckinpah's construction.

It turned out to be larger than Conway had expected, and was well on its way to being completed.

Peckinpah emerged, smiling, and Conway recognized him.

"Long time no see," he said.

"Eh?"

"We stood beside each other some years ago, in Washington, admiring Thomas Moran's painting."

Astonishment washed over Hiram Peckinpah as he remembered the occasion and the painting, which had inspired his present venture. "Well, I'll be durned, I'll be *gol*-durned."

He sounded pretty Western, thought Conway. "What have you got here, Peckinpah?"

"Gateway to Paradise, I'm thinking of calling it. Run some tours into the park from here, provide guides—"

"This is public land," Conway interrupted.

"That's me, the public."

"I mean it's government land, a federal park. You—"

"The hell it is. This ain't parkland. And I got permission

from the governor to be here, got friends in the governor's office."

That could very well be true. Honest government was hard enough to come by back in the civilized East, and considerably harder west of the Missouri. "You're not inside the park?"

"Nosirree. Been right careful about that."

"Which governor are you talking about?"

"Montana. You're in Montana, Captain." He smiled. "Didn't know that, did you? This here's Montana. The Continental Dee-vide, just south o' here, that's the border between Montana and Idaho."

"I'm aware of that. But it's not that border that concerns me. Where's the Montana-*Wyoming* border? The park overlaps into Montana, north and west, and if the border's close—"

"It ain't. It do indeed overlap, but not this far."

"Aha. Well, I guess I'll just have to wait for the surveyors to confirm that."

"You got surveyors?" It appeared to be news to him. "Well, that's just dandy. You go right ahead, Captain, I'd sure appreciate knowin' exactly where I am." He smiled suddenly. "Now don't go getting your hopes up, Captain. I know I'm off the park. I just want to be able to tell my guests, 'You are *now* entering the great Yellowstone National Park.'"

"You expect to have guests, do you?"

"Expect? Got 'em already."

He led Captain Conway into the lodge.

They entered a large lobby in which the appointments were rather modern and comfortable-looking, if not luxurious. Several doors opened onto the lobby from all three sides.

"This way," said Peckinpah, leading him toward some open double doors to the left. Beyond lay the dining room.

About a dozen people, male and female, were distributed among several tables. Peckinpah addressed Conway brightly. "Late afternoon tea, Guv'nor."

Two of the men, well-dressed, looked as if they might appreciate tea. Another man had a studious appearance. The three other men, though, had the flashy look of adventurers. Conway wondered what kind of adventuring they were up to.

Of the five women, three looked rather gamy, the kind that went where the men were, who weren't apt to do much touring. The two others . . . Conway couldn't get a fair reading.

Back outside, Captain Conway noticed a number of men

115

lounging about. They kept their distance, but were watching him and the two privates.

"Who are they?"

"The luck of the roll, Captain. Here I was, wanting to build and hard up for labor, and along come these fellers, some of them anyway, ridin' along the Dee-vide, heading south. Itinerant cowpokes, seemed. About had their fill of north-country winters, up to Idaho and thereabouts. I told 'em they could work for me and ride south this fall with a hefty stake. It's worked out pretty good. I'll tell you, though, punchin' cows doesn't prepare a man for construction work."

Nor does outlawry, thought Conway. The half-dozen he could see had neither the smell nor the look of law-abiding cowhands. "How much do you know about them?" asked Captain Conway confidentially.

Peckinpah's brow puckered with concern. "Not a damn thing," he whispered. "You think something's wrong with them? That one there, he's got a couple brothers that aren't here now. I agree he don't look pretty, but hell, Captain..."

Captain Conway realized that if he dressed several of his own men in civilian clothes, they too would make him edgy. "Well, it's your show, Peckinpah, for the time being, anyway, until we get the surveying done."

"I'm not worried, Captain."

"Tell me, are those your shacks being built in the park?"

Peckinpah frowned hard for a while. But finally he nodded. "Aw hell, Captain, folks gotta have someplace to stop, get outa the rain maybe, get a bite to eat, take a leak, or—"

Captain Conway held up a hand. He could do without a rundown of toilet needs. "That," he said, "will be settled in due course. Now, however, I have to get back to camp. Possibly we'll see each other in the days or weeks to come."

"Weeks?"

And Captain Conway rode away, leaving Peckinpah vaguely unhappy.

A bullet whined by Captain Bryce Forsythe's head and he pressed his body closer to the earth.

He turned his head. Ten feet away from him lay the body of Lieutenant Peters, eyes wide open and staring back at him.

The attack had come without warning. The surveyors had

116

been working their way along the banks of a westward-flowing stream. Captain Forsythe had studied the conifer forests flanking the stream some fifty yards distant, and he'd decided that a road could probably run up along the trees. It would afford a good view of the terrain and, if continued, might provide access to the park from the west, depending on the Idaho terrain . . . or was that Montana up ahead?

He'd taken his map out and was studying it through reading glasses when the first shots came from the trees.

Forsythe had hit the ground almost as fast as Lieutenant Peters. He'd admired Peters' reactions until he realized why Peters had gone down so fast.

He'd groaned loudly. Peters had a wife back East somewhere.

He'd looked to the trees but had seen only a blur.

Cursing, he'd whipped the reading glasses off and looked again, but had seen nothing, nothing but muzzle flashes. He'd realized he was exposed before the gunmen did, and scrambled to the safety afforded by a large round mound of lava.

He'd thanked God they hadn't been attacked from both sides of the stream. They'd have died in a crossfire, most certainly, or drowned trying to hide.

Which was just about what Corporal Wojensky was thinking, lying on the bank, sighting over his Scoff and firing at the bursts of fire and smoke from the trees.

Wojensky was as expert a sharpshooter as Holzer, but he and his men had all been dismounted when the attack came, and their horses had taken off with their rifles. Unlike the cavalry's mounts, Easy's had not been trained to sacrifice their lives in battle.

All the same, the horses had barely escaped. Wojensky later realized that they owed their lives to the hidden gunmen trying to get the scattering horses first. Thank God the beasts *didn't* lie down. There'd be nary a one left alive.

Wojensky tried to figure the strength of the enemy, also who they might be.

No more than six or seven was the number he arrived at. And too disciplined for hostiles. They were probably those effin' punchers.

Wojensky had been among those riding to the cavalry's rescue two days before, and he knew of the cavalry's conclusion, that it had been elements of the Rocking K that had waylaid them. Undoubtedly that had influenced Wojensky's present judgment.

"Jes' take it easy, men," he called softly during a lull in the firing. "Dig in and don't do nothin' foolish. And you on the flanks, keep an eye out that they don't get around us."

Their one hole card was that Captain Conway, Hazlett, and Murtha were out there somewhere. Unless—the thought wasn't pleasant but had to be faced—unless they were already dead.

Fortunately they weren't. At that moment they were on foot about a quarter-mile downstream, hunkered down in the trees.

"All right," said Captain Conway, "you two work your way closer. Not too close, though. Make them think you're at good rifle range. Stay hidden and open up with your handguns."

"What's the point in that, sir?"

"You probably won't see anything you hit anyway. But if you waste time loading those Springfields each time, they'll know there're only a couple. Crawl around fast and fire the handguns, and they'll think it's a whole crowd."

"How many you figger are there, sir?"

"Enough to keep Wojensky and the others pinned down, not enough to wipe them out. Half-dozen, likely."

"You gonna stay here, sir?" Murtha realized he might be casting aspersions. "Back us up?"

Conway grinned. "Hell no. I'm going around back, catch 'em getting away."

"You'll get killed, sir!"

"Not unless they've got bullets that can go through trees. You've got the wrong hero, Private." He took his Scoff out and checked the loads.

"Now as soon as you figure they've pulled out, you charge along the trees and wave Corporal Wojensky after 'em. I can keep them busy for a while but I don't figure to stand off the whole bunch, just slow them down. But give me about five minutes before you start shooting. Got that? Five minutes."

"Yessir," said Hazlett, and he and Murtha exchanged looks as the captain disappeared into the trees, starting to work his way around.

It took Hazlett and Murtha a couple of minutes to get within good rifle range. Another thirty seconds passed.

"Aw hell, Murth, if we wait any longer, the captain's sure as hell gonna get his ass blowed off."

"You ain't jes' whistlin' Dixie, buddy."

And with that, the two raised their Scoffs and opened fire.

Corporal Wojensky, who'd been hoping for something like that, grinned fiercely as he heard the shots and gathered his feet under him.

Warner Conway, however, cursed a blue streak.

He picked up his pace, dashing through the trees, losing his campaign hat. Slender, nasty tree branches left red marks on his face. He squinted. He could hardly afford to let himself be blinded.

At last he heard horses shuffling and snorting and stamping somewhere up ahead of him.

He heard an animal scream—was that a horse?

Then he heard the pounding of hooves, diminishing in the distance.

"Damn!"

He raced along, the pine-needled forest floor springy underfoot. He angled to his left. He still might get a shot at them.

He suddenly burst into a small clearing and had to jump to clear a fallen, thrashing horse.

A man, about to step into the trees at the far side of the clearing, heard the gasping grunts of his exertion and spun, his Colt searching for a target.

Fortunately for Captain Conway, he presented a stumbling, careening, erratic target, and the shot missed.

Conway had been running with his gun in hand, and he whipped a shot at the gunman, spoiling the man's follow-up shot.

By which time Conway had steadied himself and sent a .45 slug crashing into the man's breastbone.

The man was slammed back into the trees.

Captain Conway heard noises behind him and he turned, freeing his second gun—maybe there were more.

Corporal Wojensky burst into view and sudden astonishment washed over his face. He struggled to find his voice. "Sir!" he finally gasped.

And then others began to arrive.

Captain Conway holstered his guns. "I got one," he said

evenly, "lying over there. But the rest got away."

Murtha and Hazlett arrived.

"Goddammit," said Captain Conway, "why'd you start shooting so soon?"

"You said five minutes, sir," protested Hazlett.

"Yes, soldier, I did," growled Conway, but then he gave up. How the hell could he prove they knew they were shooting early? And besides, he guessed why they'd done it.

"You all right, sir?" asked Murtha.

The captain's knees were suddenly shaky. "Yes, of course. Just haven't had to run like that for a while."

They searched the dead man, but he carried nothing that might identify him.

"Probably one of them damn cowpunchers," said Corporal Wojensky. "I think it's about time we wiped them out, sir. They got one of the surveyors this time."

"They did?" Captain Conway seemed to sag. "Did they get anyone else?"

Wojensky shook his head. "We gonna go after 'em, sir?"

Go after them where? wondered the captain. He looked back down at the dead man. He might have guessed that he was a cowpuncher too, but since he'd seen the slimy bunch hanging around Peckinpah's . . .

Captain Conway shook his head. "Just put that poor horse out of his misery. Strip the gear off. We'll pack this body back with us."

"Hell, sir, leave 'im for the wolves and grizzlies."

"I might . . . if I wasn't afraid he might poison them. Let's get 'em going, Corporal." Captain Conway was suddenly very tired.

"Hey, sutler."

J. B. Lathrop turned at the sound and watched a mountainous form approach. A sergeant. "Just call me J. B."

"Sure thing, J. B., pard," said Sergeant Rothausen, smiling warmly.

Lathrop's eyes had narrowed at the word "pard."

"Can we confer in private, J. B.? Got me a little deal I wanta talk over with you."

"Deal? Business?"

"You got it, pard."

J. B. suffered the "pard" nobly. Men twice his size could call him anything.

They were outside the stockade, by the wagons. Lathrop had most of his goods off the wagons and piled against the stockade wall. He'd considered setting up a store inside, as had been offered, but that would have meant leaving his supplies untended. And the way these men had reacted to his prices, anything could happen. So he kept everything together, did his dealing right there, and even slept in the first wagon.

They stepped around between the wagons and the wall.

"I understand you've got honey and lots of it, that right?"

Lathrop's eyes brightened. He'd counted on the military sweet tooth and so far he hadn't been disappointed. "Yes."

"Well, I'll tell you what, pard. I guess you got suckered into carrying that much, and I don't figure you'll sell it all. Hell, what're these men gonna do with jugs of honey, I ask you?"

Lathrop was preparing a number of answers when Dutch resumed.

"So I'll tell you what. I'll take them all off your hands. Not at cost, of course, but at a fair price. Then I can give the men a treat with their flapjacks, come mornin'. They been workin' hard and I haven't been able to do them right like I usually do back at the post—you followin' me so far, pard?"

Not at all. Lathrop was too busy doing figures in his head.

"I usually lay out a pretty good spread for my men, but up here . . . those damn beans are about to drive me nuts, me and everyone else. We been gettin' some meat, true, but still . . ."

Lathrop gave him a price.

Rothausen blinked. "Now look here, *pard*, this is the army *command* you're dealin' with, in charge of feeding the men, not one of these recruits. Hell, you can charge them anything you like, I don't care, but for *me* . . . we're friends, aren't we? We're kinda in the food business together, the way I see it."

Lathrop didn't see it that way, but he gave a little. Not much, but a little.

Dutch, encouraged, went through his song and dance again. But Lathrop wouldn't be budged.

"All right," Rothausen finally said, "it's a deal. I'll draw you up a letter and you can get the money at Fort Ellis, from the—"

121

"Cash."

"Aw c'mon, J. B. The army's good for it, you know that."

"Cash. *You* can get the money back from the quartermaster. I've dealt with those stingy bastards before."

Stingy is right, thought Rothausen, and if this had been *his* idea . . .

But it wasn't. And he counted out the money.

"Are you going to get some men to help you carry it?"

"No, no! I told you, this is a surprise."

And Sergeant Rothausen had to make numerous casual trips to get all the honey stored away in his mess tent without anyone becoming the wiser.

Where the hell was this Outpost Nine? wondered Captain Sam Adams, staring at the northwest horizon.

The sun was touching the tops of the distant mountains, and the hitherto bright yellow plains had turned amber, with shadows revealing what appeared to be an endless parade of swells stretching out ahead. Earlier he'd wondered why, when it looked so flat, he was either riding down an incline or up one. Now he knew. It wasn't flat.

He got his nag going. It wasn't much of a horse. But then he hadn't performed much of an operation on the gent at the station. Cut out a harmless mole.

If I don't get there by dark, he thought, it's going to get real hairy.

He felt for the weapon. In dividing up his suitcase into two carpetbags of equal weight, which were now hanging on either side of his horse's rump, he'd kept the Colt out. Just in case.

God. What a man would do for the woman he loved, for a woman he'd never met, for crying out loud. What was her name? Isabelle? He wondered about her last name. It couldn't be Conway.

He searched the empty plains. Maybe if he fired the gun, that might alert someone out there.

He fired it.

At first he heard nothing . . . but then he thought he sensed a slight rumble, as of horses' hooves.

He smiled. What a clever bastard you are, Sam.

He didn't feel so clever, though, a minute later, when he saw a large group of brightly painted rascals lining up atop a

122

nearby swell. The much-maligned red man. They'd been drawn by the shot.

Maybe they're peaceful, thought Sam Adams, but he'd heard some disquieting rumors regarding the significance of paint on the face and he wondered—

He didn't have to wonder anymore. The hostiles came down off the hill toward him, screaming.

Sam Adams got his horse running as fast as it could. Which wasn't very fast. If he'd known this was going to happen, he would have cut out the bastard's heart along with the mole.

The hostiles closed fast, shooting as they rode. They were shooting wildly, though, and the only slug that might have nailed Sam plowed instead into one of the carpetbags that was bouncing all over his horse's rump.

Sam leaned over the horse's neck, closing his eyes, clutching its neck, and mumbling Hail Marys.

Unknown to him, the hostiles were suddenly throwing on the brakes, turning their ponies, and hightailing it the other way.

Corporal Hicks and his squad had suddenly come on the scene, also drawn by the shot.

They chased the hostiles for a while but then stopped, turned, and rode after Sam Adams.

At length they caught him. "Slow it down, fella," cried Corporal Hicks.

Sam Adams, his prayers interrupted, was astonished. English-speaking savages.

He opened his eyes.

Corporal Hicks led Sam Adams to the orderly room.

Lieutenant Carpenter, sitting behind Sergeant Cohen's desk, listened to Corporal Hicks' report and then lent an attentive ear to Captain Sam Adams' woeful tale of hard travelin'.

"Well, you're out of luck, Captain. The CO's up by Yellowstone. I don't know when he'll be back."

Sam Adams smiled broadly. "Well, I'll just wait for him, then. He shouldn't be gone too long." He checked his nails. "Would you tell his wife, Flora, that I'm here? We're old friends."

"I'm sorry. Flora went up there too."

"What? Who's here, then? Anybody? Flora's sister?"

123

"Flora's . . ." Mr. Carpenter squinted at Sam Adams.

"This is terrible. Warner knew I was coming. We wrote each other."

"Maybe he didn't get your letter."

"Of course, I *am* a little early."

Carpenter nodded. He was a bright young man. "Why don't I take a look?"

"A look?"

"He usually keeps his mail in his desk." They went into Captain Conway's office. "If you don't tell him I went through his mail . . ."

"My lips are sealed."

Carpenter took out a sheaf of variously colored sheets of paper and shuffled through them.

"My letter was on army stationery. Hospital stationery."

Mr. Carpenter's look sharpened considerably. He pulled a letter out, scanned it quickly, and said, "This is it. You're a month early."

"I told you I—"

"You're with the Hospital Corps?"

"Yes. Surgeon General's staff."

"And what did Captain Conway say in his letter to you . . . unless it's too personal."

"Well, it was . . . somewhat . . . but I don't mind." Sam Adams tried his best to remember. He ended up with the jist if not the exact wording.

Carpenter rubbed his chin as he listened. The more he felt like laughing, the harder he rubbed it. When Adams had concluded he kept on rubbing.

"Is something wrong with your chin?"

"Hm? Oh no, I was just thinking. You know, before I went to the Point I gave some serious thought to medical school—"

"Our loss," said Adams dryly.

"What is your particular discipline, Captain, if I may ask?"

"Obstetrics. Birth and death, the only sure things. I'll always have a job."

"I wouldn't have thought the Surgeon General—"

"That's not *all* I do. But that will be my civilian specialty . . . someday."

"Aha. Well, getting back to the subject, I think, from what you've told me, and from the captain's letter . . . I think I'd best send you up there."

"What? Where?"

"Yellowstone."

"My God. How far is that?"

"Figure two hundred miles."

"Two hun— That's a week's traveling!"

Carpenter shook his head. "Three days. You'll be taking spare horses, practically ride straight through."

Adams paled.

"I'll send two men with you. Three days will get you there." Half dead, maybe, but there. "You can leave in the morning."

"That's . . . that's absurd."

"I agree. It would be a terrible strain. I'm sorry I suggested it. But now that I think about it, I do recall Flora and her sister talking about you. They'll hate to have missed you, and I shouldn't think you have that much leave."

"Well, no. But I can get an extension."

"Oh good. As long as you don't mind sitting around here for a month."

"Here? A month?"

"It's not terribly exciting, I grant you. Those hostiles you encountered are about the only thing going on around here. And we've been after those renegades for a while. As soon as we catch them— Now there's an idea, sir. You can go on a patrol."

Which was worse, a month's boredom or the very real risk of getting scalped?

"As a surgeon I think you might be interested in various scalping patterns."

Captain Sam Adams clenched his buttocks, testing for soreness. "How early in the morning did you think I might leave?"

"Leave?"

"For *Yellowstone*, you idiot!"

Captain Conway rode into camp with the surveyors, Corporal Wojensky's squad, and the bodies of Lieutenant Peters and the gunman.

Flora almost fainted when she heard what had happened, which only made Captain Conway stand a little taller. But just for a while. A man fighting a mid-forties sag could only posture for so long. And Captain Conway was visibly relieved when Matt Kincaid dragged him out of the limelight and into the dim, cool confines of the HQ tent.

Sergeant Olsen watched the two men disappear into the tent, and then he congratulated Hazlett and Murtha for their premature attack.

"Sergeant." Clara Mills was at Olsen's elbow. "Have you seen Captain Forsythe?"

"He was just here, ma'am—I mean Clara. Try the mess tent."

Clara Mills went off to corner Captain Forsythe.

In the meantime, Captain Conway, between sips of brandy, had described the action to Matt Kincaid, and told also of Peckinpah's establishment.

"I'll tell you, Matt, I would've been dead game to go after those goddamn punchers if it wasn't for the men I saw hanging around Peckinpah's. A shady lot if ever I saw any."

"Is that gent you hauled in any example, sir?" wondered Matt.

"Now that you mention it, yes."

Matt gave it some thought. "Hang on a second, sir," he said, and left the tent.

He walked to his own tent and ducked inside.

George looked up from his bed of blankets and made a noise. He petted the hound. George looked like he was going to recover. Matt then rummaged through the saddlebags that had belonged to the recently deceased deputy marshal, Cal Murphy. He came out with a packet of handbills.

He returned to the HQ tent and handed the circulars to Captain Conway. "Any of these look familiar, sir?"

Warner Conway went through them as Matt looked over his shoulder.

Captain Conway wasn't certain about two of the first three, and the third was a total stranger, but when he flipped to the fourth, both he and Matt suddenly exclaimed, "That's him!"

It was the dead man Conway had just brought back to camp.

A while later they came to one that reminded Matt of the gent Holzer had killed. But he'd only seen him that once, and not for very long. He couldn't be sure.

But then Captain Conway stared hard at a likeness. "He was at Peckinpah's, I'm certain."

Matt read the name. Jack Rafferty.

"Peckinpah said he had some brothers. . . ." Warner Conway flipped through the rest and extracted handbills featuring a Tom and a Jim Rafferty.

126

"They must be using this place as a hideout," said Conway, "and Peckinpah as a cover. Anybody official happening by would be more concerned with what Peckinpah was doing there than with who his help was."

"Yeah, it could happen that way. Unless you were a U.S. marshal."

"And anything Peckinpah's help did would get blamed on the Rocking K."

"Now just a minute, sir," said Matt. "From what I've heard, those cowpokes sound like they can hold their own with any outlaws."

"Not in the same class, Matt," said the captain. "Not nearly. Damn that Peckinpah anyway. The trouble he's causing."

"What do you mean, sir?"

"If it wasn't for him, it'd be cut and dried."

"We'll move them all out anyway."

"Can't. Not if Peckinpah's legal. We've got no jurisdiction. And besides, the man's just a good businessman. We can't penalize him for that."

"What if he knows he's inside the park? What if he's just trying to keep the surveyors from establishing that?"

"You've never met him, Matt, you just don't know him. He's a straightforward hustler. A convoluted scheme of that nature . . ."

"What's convoluted about running a hotel and guiding tours?"

"Nothing. But if he knew he was in the park and was holding up the surveying until he could get established, knowing that the government would have to buy him out at a big profit, that takes a special kind of mind, a rare level of deceit."

"Which is not impossible."

"No, Matt. Knowing the man makes all the difference. He's short, stout, effervescent, full of ambition and energy, the kind of salesman who can sell you what you don't want and make you like it. He'd not your highwayman, your bank robber, your cattle baron. Those are ambitious men too, but of a different stripe."

Matt made a grunting sound that could have been interpreted as agreement. But he wasn't about to turn loose either the Rocking K or Peckinpah. He was being asked to pass judgment on men he'd never met.

He was going to have to meet them.

Later that evening, Charles Bainbridge entered the tent he shared with his wife. A bemused expression was on his face.

"What's wrong, Charles?"

"Wrong? Nothing's wrong. Captain Forsythe's requested that I be allowed to help the surveyors. Apparently Miss Mills told him I'd studied surveying."

"That's marvelous, Charles. For how long?"

"Oh, just as long as we're up here, I guess. All the surveyors are either officers or civilians. I haven't heard tell of any privates being surveyors."

"You are."

"It's just temporary duty, honey. They need me. How're you feeling?"

"Fine." But the hope that had suddenly appeared was now gone. "What's that book?"

"Surveying." He made a face. "I think I'd better do a little reviewing."

Just then, Sergeant Breckenridge stuck his head into the tent. "Y'all better batten everything down, Charlie. Windy says there's a storm headed this way."

"A storm? This time of year?"

"These are the mountains, Private, and Colter's Hell to boot. Anything can happen."

thirteen _____

At about ten o'clock, Lieutenant Grady got back with the stolen horses, having recovered them in the southeast portion of Yellowstone, on the far side of the Lake. He might have returned earlier, if he and his man hadn't experienced considerable trouble herding the normally docile animals. Even the cavalry's own mounts had behaved unusually, prancing nervously, rolling their eyes wildly.

"There's a storm coming, sir," explained Sergeant Fletcher.

"I figured that. But they've been through storms before."

Not like this, though.

Around midnight the storm hit, sheets of rain driven by gale-force winds. Had the stockade walls not been there to break the wind, the tents would have been blown to the other side of the park.

At 1:00 A.M., encroaching water and irritable NCOs rousted the men from their sacks to dig drainage ditches.

"Didn't know we was building a *dam*," groused Sergeant Cohen, referring to the solid stockade with its one exit.

Fortunately, due to Captain Conway's foresight, the ground

outside that one exit sloped away. If it had been sloping toward the stockade, or even just level . . .

"Were you figgerin' on this when you laid it out?" asked Sergeant Fletcher.

"Hell no. Besides, I didn't lay it out, the captain did."

Captain Conway slogged about the square enclosure, satisfying himself that the drainage system was going to work.

True, he'd had melting snow and spring rains in mind, but surely any freak storm was implied. Runoff was runoff. Yet, in his tour of the enclosure, he'd overheard more than one man remark that it was lucky the stockade faced the way it did.

Lucky!

If only he'd gone on record, loud and clear, before the storm.

It was a petty gripe on his part, but it did illustrate the loneliness of command.

"What's that, sir? The loneliness of command?"

Captain Conway looked up at Matt, aghast. Had he been talking to himself? "Pay attention, Matt," he said testily. "I was remarking that this was going to be a lonely command up here."

"Oh," said Matt, and he grinned. He knew that Captain Conway had had no idea his adjutant was there. And in the same spirit he remarked, "Lucky we've got such good runoff." He imagined he could see smoke shooting from Captain Conway's ears, but he didn't have to imagine the look he got. "Sure is wet, isn't it, sir?"

Conway scowled. "Comments like that, Matt, I expect from Mr. Branch."

Sergeant Faulkner and Sergeant Cohen watched the two dark shapes slogging around the enclosure. "How come them two ain't doin' nothin'?" wondered Faulkner.

"'Cause that's Matt and the CO," explained Sergeant Cohen. "They like to get out with the men when it's rough. Now about that honey . . ."

"Ain't no good in weather like this."

"I know. But Rothausen still thinks he got it for the men. You and me, we're gonna have to keep an eye on it till this storm passes."

Faulkner nodded. "How long you think it's gonna last?"

"Dunno. You know these mountains better'n me. We get

summer rains down on the Plains, but never nothin' like this. Can't count on nothin' up here."

It rained through the night and through the next day. And the following night was lit by lightning.

Lieutenant Kincaid, Captain Conway, and Sergeants Cohen and Faulkner were sitting around the HQ tent. A small stove was going, its chimney sticking out the side of the tent. A pot of coffee sat on the stove. And several pairs of socks were draped about the stove and the stovepipe.

"Wonder how the sutler's doin' out there in his wagons?"

"Least he's not robbin' no one," said Sergeant Cohen. "A man could drown gettin' out to his wagons."

"Understand the horses are getting proddier and proddier."

"Is that so?" said Matt. "George has been pretty restless too. Seems unusually apprehensive."

"Maybe the storm's going to get worse."

Windy stuck his head in the tent flap, his black hair plastered down around his swarthy face.

"Windy!" cried Matt. "Have you heard of any Indian gods being mad at us? Don't they want us here?"

Matt was joking, but Windy seemed to take the question seriously. "I'll ask around."

"Around? Around where?" Matt studied Windy's typically impassive face. Besides Lieutenant Grady's scout, Spotted Calf, and the few Delawares, who was there to ask? "You mean there've been Indians hanging around?"

"They come, they go," said Windy. He gestured upward at the raging elements. "This is big medicine. They're lookin' for answers too, I 'spect."

A split second later there were a hell of a lot more questions to be answered as the tent suddenly seemed to shift and Matt found himself clinging to one of the support poles. But the pole hadn't leaned toward him; rather he had lurched into the pole. And Windy had shot back out the tent flap. And Captain Conway, Sergeant Cohen, and Sergeant Faulkner were lying on the damp ground.

There was a tremendous rumbling sound, above the wind, and a pot rattled on the stove, and the stovepipe shook.

"What the bloody hell!"

Matt let go of the pole, but had trouble standing.

131

The men on the ground made it to their knees, but stayed there, wobbling.

No one said anything, though all were certain that the end of the world was upon them.

The rumbling slowly died away, the earth calmed, and the continuing sound of wind and rain was, comparatively, like dead silence.

But the silence only lasted for about ten seconds. Then a great clamor arose throughout the compound, joined by squeals from the animals tethered outside, other squeals from J. B. Lathrop, also outside, and soaring above all was a lugubrious howling, courtesy of George Armstrong.

The officers and NCOs within the HQ tent stared at each other, still speechless.

Windy regained the tent, impassiveness replaced by confusion.

And then Captain Bryce Forsythe entered, beaming, despite the water pouring off him. "Wasn't that *incredible*?"

They regarded him as if he were a madman.

"What the hell was it?" Matt asked.

"An earthquake."

"Holy smokes," said Matt. "Windy, check with those gods again."

Windy smiled cautiously, wondering what his Indian friends were thinking just then.

Captain Forsythe stood just inside the entrance, the air of a connoisseur about him, speculating. "Of course, it wasn't much of one. Could have been a lot worse. This ground we're standing on could have split right open. I wouldn't be surprised if all the springs and geysers are right where they were before."

The assembled men stared at him. Conway muttered to Matt, "Why the hell shouldn't they be?"

"We thought there was something freakish about this place," Forsythe went on, "that this was once a volcano, or a volcanic thrust through the earth's surface. And not that long ago, either, as such things are measured. That would account for the hot springs and whatnot, active lava not too far down. Things boil and shift down there and these earthquakes should be pretty common, small ones anyway, like this one. We'd guessed as much." He smiled. "It's grand to have such confirmation."

"Hey, Matt," said Windy, "do you suppose that was why

Grady had such trouble with them horses, that the horses sensed it comin'?"

"Now that, Mr. Mandalian," said Captain Forsythe, "is a really interesting thought. It's quite possible, isn't it? These relatively wild creatures, they're quite instinctive, they just might sense something like that, mightn't they?"

Windy stared at him. "That's why I said it."

"Come on, Sergeant," said Matt to Sergeant Faulkner. "Let's go settle the men down."

Captain Forsythe followed them out, saying, "Tell them to expect some more shocks. It's typical. They'll be smaller, however."

Did Matt detect disappointment? "They'll like hearing that," he muttered.

It kept on raining and blowing, and sporadically shaking, through that night.

The next day the shaking quit, but the rain and the wind didn't.

Matt Kincaid began to get damned bored.

The man dismounted before Peckinpah's lodge, tied up his horse and unsaddled it, and strode through the rain and wind to the front door. He opened it and quickly stepped inside, dropping his saddle, removing his hat, and shaking water from it and his slicker.

He then removed the slicker to reveal fringed buckskins, darkened by dirt, oil, and time, and a brace of ivory-handled six-shooters low on his hips.

He was a tall, ruggedly handsome, gray-eyed man with a few days' growth of beard on his face.

He put the hat back on his head, looked around, and didn't see anyone. He heard a low murmur, though, and strolled toward some double doors that stood open.

Halting in the doorway, he looked the dining room over.

Several people, including Hiram Peckinpah, looked up at him and were surprised. They'd thought it was one of the guests or hired hands they'd heard enter the lobby. Peckinpah rose to his feet. "Good Lord, man, you must be drenched."

"Yep."

"And hungry."

"Yep."

Peckinpah readied a table for him. "I reckon you'll be eating?"

"Yep."

Peckinpah smiled uncomfortably. "Whereabouts y'all coming from?"

The gent fixed him with a basilisklike stare, and Peckinpah's smile froze.

"Camped north of here, tried to stick it out...headed south..." He gave his gunbelt a hitch and Peckinpah twitched. "What the hell kinda place you got here? This a ho-*tel*?"

"It sure is, mister. Serving those that are bent on seeing the wondrous sights of Yellowstone."

"Of what?" The gent's eyes narrowed suspiciously.

Peckinpah waved to the east. "Yellowstone...or perhaps you know it as Colter's Hell."

"Oh. Is *that* where I is? Goddamn, musta made a wrong turn somewheres." He grinned, but no one felt like laughing.

"Now you just make yourself comfortable," said Peckinpah, "and I'll whip you up some grub." His eyes glittered. "You care for a nice slab of venison?"

"Aw hell, right about now ah'd eat the ass end of Sittin' Bull's mammy...iffen it was cooked right."

"You just wait, mister, you just wait."

And he did, right there in the doorway, his eyes moving slowly about the room, pausing frequently.

Seven men, five women. Five of the men were grouped together, dirty and forbidding; the other two men were clean but nondescript.

Two of the women were interesting. All five were at least fair-looking, but two weren't as gamy as the others. One gal was pushing thirty from one side or the other, the second one was younger and sweet lookin', but with old eyes.

Peckinpah returned and slapped a platter down on a table along with a knife and fork. A steak lay on the platter. "Prob'ly won't even need the knife," gurgled Peckinpah, "but just in case..." he kind of whinnied.

The tall gent walked to the table, picked up the plate and utensils, and strode on to where the young woman with the old eyes sat. "Mind if I join ya?"

The young woman, flustered, indicated that it was all right with her.

The tall gent sat, twisted around to look back at Peckinpah, and patting his guns lightly, he said, "I'd 'preciate not bein' bothered."

He wasn't, at least not by Peckinpah. But he'd barely gotten through finding out where the girl came from—Virginia City—when he found a man standing by his elbow.

He froze.

"Don't get excited, fella," said Jack Rafferty, "you're covered."

The gent slowly twisted around again and stared past Rafferty across the room to where the table of toughs stared back, some grinning inanely. Two of them showed him their guns.

The gent also glanced at the two nondescript men. They were staring hard at their plates, evidently petrified.

Peckinpah looked uneasy, but not overly so.

"I never git excited," drawled the gent.

"What's your name?"

"Ain't none of your business."

"Thought I mighta heard it, that's all," Rafferty said.

"You mighta," the gent replied.

Jack Rafferty nodded knowingly. "You lookin' for work?"

"For *him*?" He gestured toward Peckinpah, seated several tables away.

"For me."

"Not for neither one of ya. I got me a job. South. It's gonna be short and sweet and worthwhile."

Jack Rafferty nodded. "You'll be riding on in the morning."

The gent eyed the girl, overpowering her.

"I said, you'll be—"

"I heard ya. Dint know if you was askin' or tellin'." The gent glanced at Rafferty and the far table of toughs, weighing his reply. "Like as not I will. Ain't nothin' keepin' me here."

He spent the night with the girl at whose table he'd sat, during which time, between couplings, she talked about her companions at the hotel. All of the women, appearances notwithstanding, had come as a group from Virginia City. Their purpose? Well, what did shady women do in a resort?

"Peckinpah told us this was a resort," the girl said, "that it was gonna be swarmin' with tourists an' drinkin' an' gamblin' an' all that good stuff. But all there is so far is a few drummers scared half to death, some kind of professor from somewhere, and that goddamn Rafferty bunch. Hell, you'd think Peckinpah brung us up here just for them. Pheeew! Them lizards gimme the willies."

"Ah'll take care of them," the man said laconically.

"The hell you will, Pony Jackson. You had your chance to take care of them downstairs, and that was only a third of what's here, if even that many." She smiled to show she didn't mean he was a coward. "Pony. No wonder you dint wanta tell 'im your name. Howja get a silly name like that?"

"Had a silly ma an' pa, that's how."

"Stallion's more like it," she said, and grinned.

By morning the rain had finally stopped and the wind had died down.

Pony and the girl slept late. When they did get downstairs, they found steaks and hardtack and coffee awaiting them. Pony thought it wasn't a bad life and that maybe he'd hang around for a while.

When Pony got outside, though, he found his horse all ready, saddled and waiting. The Rafferty gang stood around waiting, too.

"This horse's from Bozeman," said Jack Rafferty. "I know the livery mark. How come?"

Pony was in no hurry to answer. But finally he said coldly, "I know where the goddamn horse comes from. I tol' ya, I made a wrong turn. I'm headed for Utah."

"Well then, let's see how fast you kin make it."

The threat was there, and it sorely rankled Pony, but the odds were heavily with Jack Rafferty.

Pony mounted quickly and rode west.

Jack glared at the girl and she quickly told him Pony's name. Which got a good laugh.

Matt Kincaid, alias Pony Jackson, waited until he was certain he was out of sight, and then doubled back.

The riding was pleasant. The skies had cleared. The sun was shining. The air was crisp. The horse, a gelding Clara Mills had chosen from a Bozeman livery, had a nice, easy gait. And the saddle, borrowed from Windy, was the kind one could settle onto without fear. Matt's thoughts, though, were not quite so pleasant and comfortable.

The Raffertys were formidable opponents, them and their

136

gang. A pack of killers. The army had them outnumbered, but wouldn't be able to handle them piecemeal; an all-out war, with total involvement on both sides, would have to be arranged. Trying to take them on, squad by squad, would spell disaster. Unless, of course, it was First Platoon's first squad.

Matt smiled.

But then he frowned, thinking of Peckinpah. He wasn't sure what to make of him. He was just as gregarious as Captain Conway had described him, and bouncy and pushy, and probably being taken advantage of by the Raffertys, although he wasn't stupid and must know what the Raffertys were. But it didn't seem to bother him.

But what did the Raffertys hope to gain? Let Peckinpah get it set up and then take it away from him and force the government to buy *them* out?

Did they really think the feds would deal with them?

Maybe they had an intermediary ready to step in, one whose face wasn't spread on handbills all over the frontier. Perhaps one of those weak-looking men he saw. They looked like they might be accountants, or something similar.

It was a puzzle, and a problem. What kind of problem depended on solving the puzzle.

He thought of the girl with whom he'd spent the night, her warm, comfortable body. She didn't seem bad, considering her profession, and she'd been unusually clean. It was probably due to her youth; she was new to the game. How long had she said she'd been in Virginia City, in the business?

One month. Which had to be a lie. She was no beginner. But even if it was a year, she was still new to the game, compared to those three other war horses. They'd probably been real good-looking once upon a time, but were now a mite long in the tooth and worn down to gristle.

If he'd selected one of them, he probably would have come down with one of Stretch Dobbs's "manly" diseases. But he also might have come away with a bit more information; when it came to knowing what was really going on, the girl was something of a cipher.

But damn, she was pretty.

About an hour later a thought slowly surfaced in Matt's mind. What if it was Peckinpah himself who was running the entire operation, running the Raffertys? Was it possible? Was Peckinpah that deep, that deceitful, that ambitious? Enough to kill?

But then the thought sank back beneath the surface, disappearing with no apparent trace.

fourteen _____

Matt Kincaid got back to the camp to find most of the army's clothes and equipment spread out to dry. They wouldn't be getting back to work until the next morning.

"Where were you, Matt?" asked Captain Conway. "We were worried. Almost sent a boat out after you."

"Spent the night at Peckinpah's, sir. Met a nice girl . . ."

The two men retired to the HQ tent and discussed Peckinpah and the Rafferty gang.

"They're a mean bunch, sir. Put them and the Rocking K together and we've got a problem."

"I agree. But we can't ignore it, and delaying will only make things worse. We'd best establish immediately whether Peckinpah's inside the park or not."

"If he is, he probably won't let the surveyors near, or the Raffertys won't."

"Which will be a partial answer in itself."

"But inconclusive."

"We'll send the surveyors out in the morning. You can go with them, take a couple of squads."

"That's asking for more trouble, sir," Matt broke in. "The

cavalry's awful touchy, and for the moment they've got the patrolling duty. If I took a detachment out, they'd take it as an insult."

"You're dead right, Matt. I'd feel better about it with you out there, but . . ." He ran his hand through his hair. "But now that the stockade's up, maybe it's time to sit down and redistribute duties."

"Good idea, sir, but afterward."

"Let's get Grady in here, and Forsythe as well, if he's done admiring earthquakes."

Fifteen minutes later, Lieutenant Grady and Captain Forsythe joined them.

"I'm sending Captain Forsythe out tomorrow, Lieutenant," Conway said, "to determine once and for all whether Peckinpah's inside park boundaries. There may be trouble. You'll be escorting him. Take all your men. And if you run into trouble, send for us. We'll be ready."

Grady nodded, but didn't say anything.

"After tomorrow I'm going to want to discuss dividing the duties up differently. The stockade's up, but the rest of the buildings are your concern. My men didn't join the army to be carpenters any more than yours did."

Grady nodded again, but a little more slowly.

"All right then," Conway concluded. "Prepare your men, Lieutenant, and you get your surveyors ready, Captain, and let's be ready to get cracking at first light."

The moon showed up late that night, less than half full. Its light filtered down on Colter's Hell, and if the place wasn't spooky enough already, with its sulfurous springs and geysers and sinister lava formations, the pale light made it spookier. And, appropriately enough, strange doings commenced.

Up in the gap south of the army camp, where Mary Bainbridge and Sergeant Cohen had had their close call, dark forms began to lumber down out of the trees.

They were mostly medium-sized forms, belonging to the brown bears, a few larger, grizzly-sized forms, and a lot of small cub-forms.

They began to work their way down the hill, noses to the ground, growling back and forth, following a trail of honey north.

Sergeants Cohen and Fletcher had, earlier that night, insisted that the remuda of army mounts be held north of the stockade for a change, and consequently the horses were not alarmed by the approaching army of bears.

That seething mass of fur, barely distinguishable in the weak moonlight, slowly but steadily approached the stockade, like a dark wave rolling leisurely toward shore.

The south picket guard, walking his post some fifty yards from the stockade walls, sensed that the terrain south of him was steadily changing shape. A dark mass was approaching him. And it was making noise!

He backed away, scarcely believing his senses. But when he did finally believe them, he wasn't sure what to do.

At the same time that the first sergeants were having the horses moved, they departed from the routine in yet another way, reminding the guard mount that under none but the most drastic circumstances were any park animals to be shot or harmed. It had seemed an odd warning at the time, unexpected and seemingly unjustified, but it was fresh in the south picket's mind as the bears shuffled his way.

He didn't shout or discharge his weapon. They seemed peaceful enough, so far. No sense getting them excited.

Eventually, of course, he backed into the stockade walls.

"Who's that?" called a jumpy guard overhead. "Sing out, or I'll—"

"It's me," he whispered.

"Who the hell's *me*?"

"Hannah, goddammit."

The guard's voice dropped to a conversational level. "What the hell you doin' there?"

"We got company."

"What? Where— Holy Christ! What is that?"

"Quiet! Them's bears, a whole platoon. Don't excite 'em. And help me up."

"How the hell am I gonna do that? My arms ain't *that* long."

"Goddammit, Merkin, you got a ladder in there. Lemme have it."

Merkin hustled off, got the ladder, and brought it back, throwing it over the side.

"Jesus, Merk, you almost hit one of them."

Hannah leaned the ladder in place and scrambled up it. A

141

few moments later a large bear, the biggest thing the guards had ever seen, stood at the base of the ladder and looked up at them.

They grabbed hold of the ladder and hauled it up.

The bear opened its mouth wide and uttered an ear-splitting roar.

"Don't guess we gotta whisper no more."

The bear appeared to lose interest then, and dropped back down on all fours, following its nose and joining the rest in a mass movement toward the sutler's wagons.

The sutler had cleared out his first wagon, making comfortable living space for himself, and, with the advent of the rain, packed everything into the other three wagons. Not surprisingly, the trail of honey had skipped his personal wagon, but the other three had been liberally doused.

J. B. Lathrop, dreaming contentedly of two-hundred-percent profits, had been awakened from that dream by the grizzly's roar. By the time he was fully awake, though, there was naught but the sound of shuffling—probably that damned wind—and a distant but unintelligible sound of voices. He had no idea what had awakened him.

"Goddammit," he muttered, "why don't they keep the noise down?" He pounded his pillow and then settled back down.

It wasn't until then that he really woke up and came bolt upright. That shuffling noise. It could be someone trying to steal his supplies. Those soldiers were so pissed at him, he wouldn't put it past them. But they'd have to be a damn sight slicker to put one over on ol' J. B.

He rolled from his sack. No harm in checking.

Just then there came a crash from one of the wagons, accompanied by a grunting sound.

Goddamn, they weren't even trying to be quiet about it! Christ, they sounded like pigs, sounded just like the swine they were.

He leaped to the back of the wagon and threw open the canvas. Not five feet away from him a large, dark shape was trying to get into the second wagon. "You thievin', effin' swine!" he cried.

The grizzly, on his hind legs, cocked an ear. Then he swung his half-ton of bone and muscle around, rested his forelegs on

142

Lathrop's wagon and peered at the man. That close, there was no mistaking what he was. *Ursus horribilis,* without a doubt. Lathrop's eyes bulged. And then the bear roared and almost blew him out of the wagon.

Lathrop frantically clawed his way to the other end of the wagon. He thrust his head out that end, looking around wildly. Nothing. No dark, furry mounds, nothing. It was all clear.

He leaped from the wagon, scrambled a safe distance, found his voice, and started screaming, "Shoot 'em, shoot 'em, goddammit, they're destroying everything!"

Indeed they were. In their ruthless search for tasty edibles, the bears were rapidly devaluing Lathrop's merchandise.

"Why don't you *shoot* them?" squealed Lathrop.

"Can't do it, Lathrop," came Matt Kincaid's steady voice. "The animals in this park are under federal protection. We're here to see that they *aren't* shot. Sorry."

"That's . . . that's insane!"

"Maybe so, maybe not," replied Matt, "but it's the law. If I were you I'd hurry around front and get inside. You don't have to worry about the brown bears, but there are a couple of grizzlies mixed in, and they might decide you're something to eat. And they can move pretty fast when they've a mind to. A lot faster than you, at any rate."

A full realization of his perilous situation finally intruded upon Lathrop's sense of outrage. And he fainted.

"Oh, for crying out loud. Hannah? You got a ladder over there? Go down and get that silly bastard."

There was no sign of movement anywhere.

"Hannah?"

"Me, sir?"

Matt almost laughed. "Where's the ladder? Give it here."

Matt Kincaid climbed down, picked up the sutler, and hauled him back up the ladder.

He dumped Lathrop on the four-foot-wide catwalk. "Heavier than I figured."

"Loaded down with all our money," someone grumbled.

"Probably. All right, let's wait until they look like they're done with the food and then we'll start shooting over their heads, maybe scare 'em off. Wheeler?"

"Sir?"

"You and Fritsch head around to the horses, mount up, and

be ready to herd 'em out, just in case."

The privates went hopping.

"Windy?"

"Yep. I'm here."

"Any danger of them trying to get in here?"

"Nope. They're way off their usual range, 'specially them monsters. Musta been somethin' powerful special to bring 'em this far."

Matt Kincaid had an idea what it was.

And sure enough, down in the HQ tent, Sergeants Ben Cohen and Jack Faulkner, wearing only longjohns, were laughing their heads off.

Captain Conway stuck his puffy-eyed head into the tent. "What the hell's going on?"

Cohen leaped to his feet and roared, "Thought there was an emergency, sir. Repaired here, sir, to conduct the defense, *sir!*"

Captain Conway blinked rapidly.

"False alarm, sir!"

Conway eyed Cohen's and Faulkner's longjohns, nodded wearily, and plodded back to bed.

Cohen sat back down. "Wish these officers didn't think they had to know *everything*."

"At least he showed up," said Sergeant Faulkner. "Grady's prob'ly still sleepin', he even slept through that earthquake. An' Foster's probably shit a brick."

"I thought he was pretty fierce."

"Yeah, he'd like to think that, too."

There came the sound of gunfire.

"Drivin' them off. Wonder if the sutler's got anything left?" More gales of laughter.

The firing died down.

A while later, Matt Kincaid stuck his head in. "Someone could have been hurt, Sergeants. There's not much light. A sentry could have been mauled."

"Gee, sir, that's right. But he woulda had to've been sleepin'."

It seemed to Matt a severe penalty for dozing off on duty. But he didn't say anything, simply withdrew his head.

"Someone could have been hurt, Jack," said Ben Cohen, his manner somber.

144

"Sure could, Ben. Damn, who woulda done such a thing?"

Cohen reached down beside him and came up with a paper sack, into which he reached.

"What's that?"

"Jellybeans," said Cohen, grinning. "I saved me some."

"Really? Damn."

"Lemme see now, what else have I got?" Cohen reached down again, eyes twinkling. "Whaddya know, licorice!"

The next morning, after the cavalry and surveyors had pulled out, Sergeant Rothausen was having a heated discussion with Sergeant Cohen when J. B. Lathrop marched up. Lathrop had been inspecting his ruined wares fairly closely.

"Sergeant Rothausen! Where is that goddamn honey you bought?"

Rothausen glared at Sergeant Cohen, but the face he then showed Lathrop was innocently genial. "Well, lemme tell you, J. B., when the men found that honey on the table with their flapjacks this mornin', well, the expressions on their faces woulda made you proud t' be an American, proud to have done your part in making these men happy and combat-ready."

Lathrop was no college man, but he knew when he was hip-deep in horse manure. "Are you tellin' me you used it all up? This morning?"

"Every last drop. Damn, that stuff was good."

Lathrop stomped off in a fury.

"Or woulda been good," growled Dutch. "Dammit, Ben, why'n't you lemme know? We could've at least had a taste."

"Couldn't do it, Dutch. This was a top-secret operation. Top level, if you know what I mean."

"You mean . . . the old man?"

"Here—"

"What's this?"

"—have a jellybean."

Lathrop was shaking his head. Was it possible that they'd eaten all that honey? And that the bears had simply blundered onto his supplies? "Hey, soldier," he called to a passing private.

Private Merkin quit yawning long enough to stare at him. "Oh. You. Finally woke up from yer beauty snooze, huh?"

"How did you like that honey?" Lathrop asked.

145

"What honey?"

"This morning," said Lathrop, his heart heading toward his toes. "With the flapjacks."

"What flapjacks? We had effin' shit on a shingle, same as always."

Captain Conway and Flora had breakfast in their tent. Sergeant Rothausen himself brought them their morning fare.

"I was planning flapjacks and honey, sir, 'cept I ran short," and he gave the captain a grotesquely broad wink.

After Dutch had lumbered off, Flora wondered aloud, "Was there something wrong with his eye?"

Warner Conway stared at his wife as he tried to make sense of things. It had been one hell of a strange night.

Right about then, in another part of the park, Lieutenant Grady's cavalry and Captain Forsythe's surveyors were running into trouble. Or trouble was running into them, in the form of the Rocking K herd and its wranglers.

The cavalry and the surveyors had ridden through the gap and turned west to head for Peckinpah's place. They hadn't gone far, though, not more than four or five miles, when they ran into the Rocking K herd. It blocked them.

Grady stood in his stirrups and looked for wranglers.

He spotted some at the far side of the herd, a good ways off. "Get these damned cows out of here!" he yelled.

Either he wasn't heard or he was ignored.

"To hell with it," he muttered, "we'll go around." He started to his right, followed by Foster, Forsythe, and the rest.

But the herd moved right along with them. They'd have to gallop like mad for the trees and then pick their way through the forest to get around. And the forest was just dense enough, with nasty, low branches, to make that an unpleasant experience. And humiliating besides.

"Goddammit," he suddenly cursed, reining his horse in. "Sergeant Fuller, stay here with your men and the surveyors. The rest of you, Mr. Foster, Sergeant Boatwright, come with me."

He sent his mount into the herd, bucking the tide of horned flesh. Twenty men followed.

It took them a while to get to the far side of the herd, and when they finally did so they found that the few wranglers had multiplied. There were now some fifteen, including Kreutzer.

Sam Billings sat on his horse beside Kreutzer, and next to him was Whitey Turnbull, the puncher who was only good for making up crude names and for killing.

Kreutzer and his men hadn't been far off when word of the approaching cavalry reached them. Kreutzer, in fact, had been waiting for the army to make some kind of move, thought this was it, and had ordered the blockade.

Still, he and the cavalry might still have had an intelligent discussion, despite Kreutzer's mistaking the cavalry's true purpose, had not Lieutenant Grady been so damn mad.

"Get these goddamn cows out of here," ordered Lieutenant Grady.

Kreutzer snapped at the bait. "Says who? By what authority?"

"Goddammit, you ain't got the brains of a buffalo, mister. This is a park. A National effin' *Park*. And I say so. *I'm* the goddamned law up here."

Kreutzer wasted maybe half a second considering Grady's ungentlemanly language, and another half studying Grady's reddened face, and then he started yelling too. "The hell you are, soldier. This is public land. It's for the public and we're the bloody public. We found this bloody land and we're bloody grazin' it and you can stay the bloody hell clear! If you and your *boys* want to push us off, well, you can just bloody well try."

Damned sudden for a showdown, thought Grady, besides being unexpected. And damned if he understood all the ramifications of this "public park" business. And driving Indians out and stopping hunting and trapping was one thing, but shooting up white men, shooting up ranchers who were only trying to make a living...

Yet these bastards were pushing awfully hard. They should have a lesson taught them. You don't push the U.S. Cavalry around any old time you feel like it....

Grady was rapidly working up another full head of steam when he noticed a slight movement among the punchers.

Whitey Turnbull had shifted his weight in his saddle so that his right sixgun was sticking out clear. And his right hand was hanging down alongside it.

Grady suddenly realized they might be facing a collection of fast-drawing gunfighters, and it gave him pause.

No one had ever questioned Lieutenant Grady's courage or his expertise in waging battle, cavalry-style, but gunslinging was something else again. He'd never practiced getting his gun out extra fast. He'd never had to. No one did. If a cavalryman knew what he was doing, he had his gun out well before he actually needed it.

Grady swallowed hard.

"How about it, Lieutenant?" asked Whitey Turnbull with an especially offensive nasal intonation. "Y'all wanta have it out, here an' now, jes' you an' me? Huh? You ain't chicken, is you?"

Kreutzer didn't like the way things were going, but was powerless to stop it now. One or the other had to back down, thanks to Turnbull. They could have slid clear before, but now . . .

Grady didn't trust himself to try to speak. He glared at Turnbull and wondered if, just that once, God might make him fast on the draw.

Might have helped if he'd been to church recently.

Turnbull suddenly made a move and Grady flinched, but when Turnbull's gun flashed up and boomed, it was Lieutenant Foster, down the line, who suddenly twisted in his saddle and sagged, the gun he clutched still half in its holster.

"All right!" roared Kreutzer. "That's it. Soldier"—he nodded toward Grady—"you take your men and get the hell out. Consider yourselves lucky. That's just a taste of what's in store if you give us any trouble."

Lieutenant Grady bit back on his anger, turned his horse around, and plowed back through the cattle. His men, furious but helpless, followed. One trooper tried to give Lieutenant Foster a hand, but Foster angrily shook him off, holding his side with one hand and clinging to the saddle with the other.

Kreutzer, teeth clenched, jaw muscles throbbing, watched them go. "I don't like it," he grated. "I don't like it one bit."

"Aw hell, boss," said Turnbull, "we can take 'em."

"We can't take on the whole goddamn army, you blundering idiot. Who told you to poke in where you weren't wanted?"

"Jesus Christ, boss. That's what you brung us out here fer, wasn't it?"

Yes, he had to admit, it was. But he'd just been trying to raise the ante. He'd never thought . . .

"An' if that feller's hoss hadn't moved I woulda nailed him square. I ain't *that* turrible a shot."

Kreutzer hoped like hell that soldier recovered. "Who was that man you shot? Some private?"

"Naw, jes' one of them loo-tents. Had one of them little gold bars—"

"Christ!"

"An' he tried to draw on me, you saw 'im."

Kreutzer didn't bother answering him. Instead he leaned down close to Sam Billings and said quietly, "First chance you get, get rid of him."

Billings' eyes widened.

Kreutzer groaned. "I mean *fire* him, not kill him. Jesus, what kind of outfit do you think we're running here?" He sagged in his saddle. "Another bloody James gang."

But then he pulled himself together. He was a tough man. "Well," he said briskly, "maybe it will work out for the best. And we're still not going to let ourselves get pushed out."

fifteen _____

"I'm not a gunfighter, Captain," said Lieutenant Grady.

Upon arriving back at the stockade, he'd seen that Lieutenant Foster had some kind of medical attention from Dutch Rothausen, and then had reported straightaway to Captain Conway.

He'd spoken in a soft voice, but Captain Conway, without being told, knew how it must be tearing him apart. "Don't be too hard on yourself, Marcus, there wasn't much you could have done."

"He really wanted me to try to draw on him. He wanted to kill me. And if Foster's horse hadn't moved, he'd be dead."

"I wish the situation were clearer, more black and white," Conway said. "Grazing rights... Indians hunting..." He rubbed his chin. "I understand Sergeant Cohen gave the Utes permission to hunt." He shook his head very slowly.

His fingers, though, were drumming the top of the table he was using as a desk, fast and furiously.

"I don't know how clear you want it, sir," said Lieutenant Grady. He didn't want to sound like a fire-eater, having quit the battlefield, but some points had to be made. "It was a clear case of provocation. True, I didn't help matters by yelling at them, but they'd run the cattle at us first."

Captain Conway nodded.

"But once you got back with the rest of your men," said Lieutenant Branch, "why didn't you lay into them? You—"

"Branch!" barked Conway, half rising.

"—you could have taken them," finished Branch, and then he looked at the captain. His eyes widened and he managed a weak, "Sir?"

"Nobody asked you your goddamn opinion and it's not your prerogative to question the actions of a senior officer. I'll talk to you later."

Branch turned to leave.

"Stay right where you are, mister." Captain Conway was boiling, and since Grady had already been through enough, Branch was now the target. "And if you keep chewing on that lip of yours, I'll rip it off."

Branch was astonished. He'd never seen the captain like this. And in truth, few had.

"May I say something, sir?" Grady asked.

Conway nodded, and Grady turned toward Branch.

"I didn't do what you suggested, Mr. Branch," said Lieutenant Grady evenly, "because I'd spoken rashly and already let myself get sucked into a bad situation. And once I backed down . . . You simply can't just ride off a safe distance and start shooting."

"You may respond, Mr. Branch, if you'd care to," Conway said.

"Well, sir, I know what he's saying, and maybe he thinks the cavalry has a reputation he has to uphold—"

"We all have a reputation, Mr. Branch," said Conway.

"Yessir, but he's gonna get shot dead one of these days while he's giving some bastard a fair shake."

"That may be realistic, Mr. Branch, I'll give you that much," said the captain, "and from that *ordinary* standpoint you may be right. But don't downgrade honor. Don't lower yourself to the level of your enemy."

"Yessir," said Mr. Branch.

"Now go find Lieutenant Kincaid and ask him to step in here."

Matt had been in the mess when the troop rode in, and had lent a hand when Dutch dug the bullet out of Foster. He was listening to Foster's biased and colorful account of the confrontation when Mr. Branch found him.

"Have you heard?" asked Captain Conway as Matt ducked into the tent.

"Got a version from Mr. Foster." He glanced at Lieutenant Grady. "This fellow went first?"

Grady shook his head. "Just his mouth. He was . . . he was spittin' on us."

Matt nodded.

"What do you think, Lieutenant Kincaid?" asked the captain.

"Do you have any orders, sir?" Matt's manner and voice were unnaturally calm.

"No."

"Good. Mr. Grady, let's go."

"I don't think—"

"I said let's go!"

Quite aside from time-in-grade, Matt's fierce look was downright scary. His eyes seared Grady. "You've got satisfaction coming."

Grady hustled out of the tent after Matt.

Once outside, Matt roared, "Olsen! Let me have the first squad and Claiborne, Daggs, and Crawford."

"What about me, sir?" asked Olsen, who didn't have to round up anybody; the first squad and the three other men were racing to get horses.

"Sorry, Sergeant," said Matt, "you're too slow. Can't risk you."

Olsen took it well. Matt's answer told him what was up and it was true, he wasn't very fast getting his Scoff clear. He also knew the first squad was something else again. Those meatheads spent half their free time having fast-draw contests. As for Crawford, Sleepy Jim Crawford, he could spot anyone a split second and still beat him. Except for Matt Kincaid.

Two men advanced on Kincaid, leading horses. Two cavalry troopers. "Permission to go along, sir," requested one.

"We was out there before, with the lieutenant, sir," explained the other, his voice tight.

Matt looked askance.

"We been foolin' around with your men, sir," said the first.

"And?" prompted Matt.

"Wal, Crawford ain't human, but the rest, we can hold our own."

Matt eyed them. They had the look, all right. "Mount up," he said. "But remember, you're covering me. You'll get action only if they're dumber than they sound."

"We can always hope," muttered one of the troopers.

Matt glanced at Grady.

"They would have shot it out if I'd told them to," explained Grady. "I didn't tell 'em."

Matt nodded. That was what he'd wanted to hear.

"And I told Captain Conway before you got there, I'm no gunslinger."

"No one'll notice," growled Matt.

"And that puncher's fast."

Matt just gave him a look.

And then Corporal Miller, Lance Corporal Weatherby, and eleven privates were there, hanging on to eager, impatient mounts—the horses had sensed the urgency.

Matt said, "Hope you boys have got 'em oiled," and then he led them from the stockade.

A little while after Kincaid had left, Mary Bainbridge poked her head into HQ.

"Mary," said Sergeant Cohen, "what's wrong?"

"Nothing, I hope. I was just looking for Charles. I can't find him."

"Wasn't he with the surveyors?"

"I thought so. But Captain Forsythe says he wasn't. No one seems to know where he is." She looked around the tent as if Bainbridge might be hiding there.

"It's . . . it's just that I'm not feeling too well and . . ."

Captain Conway's head rose where he sat at his makeshift desk.

"Sergeant," he said, "send someone for Flora and Maggie. Mary, you just come in here and sit down."

She did so.

"And Sergeant," continued the captain, "see if Windy's around. If he is, tell him to go find Private Bainbridge."

Private Bainbridge, armed with surveying equipment, books, and maps as well as his Springfield and Scoff, had trailed out

153

that morning on the heels of Lieutenant Grady and the surveyors. But long before Grady encountered the Rocking K, he'd turned south, heading for the three geyser basins. He wanted to put his reawakened interest in geology to the test, see how much he remembered, and as long as he was the odd man out, with no particular assignment that day...

By the time Grady was being backed down, Bainbridge was watching Old Faithful shoot up. Excited by what he saw, he decided to explore further. Maybe he'd stumble on some freak of nature that no one else had found. He worked his way west.

A few hours later he stood on a rise, alternately consulting his map and looking around. Some distance to the north he saw the roof of a building. Must be that hotel he'd heard talk about; it was too big to be anything else.

He'd also heard there was some question as to whether it was inside the park's boundaries or not.

He started looking around some more, while consulting his map, this time looking for distinctive topographical features, a number of which were clearly identified on his maps.

A couple of hours later he'd located enough to determine that Peckinpah's hotel was well within park limits.

Granted, the park's boundaries were not yet firmly plotted, but unless the government planned to shrink the park considerably, Peckinpah was not only inside the park, he was inside Wyoming. Bainbridge had been told that the park overlapped a bit into Idaho and Montana.

Bainbridge smiled. This Peckinpah had made one big mistake.

Private Bainbridge's attention was then drawn to a curious rock formation. Forgetting the whole matter of Peckinpah's hotel, he headed off that way, doubling back to the east.

He got to the rocks and found them uninteresting, but then he smelled something and thought he saw smoke, or steam, rising some distance farther along. He rode off that way, now several miles from the hotel.

What he found were some hot sulfur springs that had created several descending and unworldly terraces, the whole thing surrounded by acres of lush, yellow-green grass. Stupendous, and it wasn't marked on his maps.

Unfortunately his concentration was so complete that he didn't notice a large band of Indians, Utes, as they emerged from some trees far to his left.

They saw him, though, and ducked back out of sight. Theirs was a hunting party, but it didn't take much to change a hunting party into a war party. Especially with an easy coup at hand.

The Rocking K, once rid of the cavalry, had drawn their cattle back to the west. They weren't running, though, just looking for different graze and moving slow. As a result, it didn't take Matt and his men very long to catch up.

The riders of the Rocking K saw them coming and pulled closer together. Kreutzer watched them as they approached. He was a little mystified; if they weren't ready to fight, what did they hope to accomplish?

As the army drew yet nearer, Kreutzer spotted Lieutenant Grady and was surprised that he'd apparently come back for more of the same. But then he noticed that while Grady wore a yellow cavalry bandanna, the rest of the army riders wore light blue ones. Kreutzer frowned as he realized that these weren't exactly the same troops he'd sent packing earlier, but he didn't know what to make of this development.

Whitey Turnbull smiled tightly and shifted around to get his gun handy.

Matt and his men rode up. Grady leaned toward Matt and told him something.

"You fellows forget something?" asked Kreutzer.

Matt Kincaid ignored him and stared straight at Whitey.

"You're the gent that gunned an army officer."

"He tried to draw on me," drawled Whitey. "Shouldna tried t' do a dumb thing like that."

"You can hand over your guns," Matt told him.

Whitey almost laughed. "I tol' ya, he tried to draw on me." His lips curled as he sneered, "You got that, asshole? Too bad the stupid bastard wasn't faster."

In a curious way, Matt felt relieved. This shit wasn't worth the clothes he was wearing.

"Yeah, too bad," said Matt. "But I *am* faster, and I'm waiting on you, you slimy, yellow-bellied son of a bitch."

Whitey's hand blurred to his gun. . . .

And then an expression of disbelief whipped across his face as three slugs in rapid succession lifted him clear of his saddle and left him lying on the ground.

155

Shock froze the Rocking K riders for an instant, and then the realization that Matt's men were also leveling guns their way froze them longer.

If Lieutenant Grady, eyes bulging, had had any less self-control, he might have started babbling. As it was, his head was still ringing so loud he could hardly think. He'd still been leaning toward Matt when Matt had gone into action.

Kreutzer was blinking hard, wondering first if he was seeing things and then wondering where the army had come up with this trigger-happy bunch. He finally found his voice.

"You *are* U.S. Army Infantry, aren't you?"

Matt slid his guns home, but still stayed on edge. His men followed suit.

"You want some more, mister?" growled Matt.

The men of the Rocking K were rapidly reassessing the opposing force, and didn't care for what they saw. And Sleepy Jim Crawford looked like he was about to go to sleep.

Sam Billings, who'd happened to be looking Crawford's way when Matt's guns went off, thought at first that Crawford was shooting, Crawford's draw being slower by just a flicker than Matt's.

"Now jes' one goddamn minute," squawked Billings. "I ramrod this here outfit. Billings is my handle, and this here's the owner, Roman Kreutzer. Who're you?"

"Kincaid. First lieutenant, mounted infantry, U.S. Army."

"Well now," said Billings, a wry grin twisting his mouth as he glanced at his shaken boss, "him an' me, we're pleased to make your acquaintance."

Matt recognized the man, or the breed. Tougher than baling wire, but straight.

"We ain't excusin' nothin'," Billings went on, "an' we ain't admittin' we're wrong or anything like that . . . but you oughta know that after Turnbull here shot your man, Roman told me to get ridda him." He looked back down at the man who was leaking blood onto the plateau. "Didn't have this partickler method in mind, exackly, but . . ." Billings took a deep breath. "Reckon you kinda got us by the short hairs."

Matt Kincaid was still breathing shallowly, wound tight and poised. "You mean you've got no more hardcases wanting to test us?"

"Hardcases? You've got the wrong outfit." He suddenly leaned forward and looked down the line at Red Adair. "And that means you, Red. I don't gotta lose no more men to learn me a lesson."

A barely audible, "Shhooot," slid from between Sleepy Jim Crawford's lips.

Billings, who was onto Crawford, and Crawford's craft, swallowed hard. Then he looked back at Matt Kincaid. "So... what's the word?"

Matt hadn't thought it through that far. And he wasn't about to make any rash decisions. He said to his men, "Watch 'em," and he turned his horse and rode off some thirty yards.

He sat there on his horse for a while, looking east over the park. It was going to be a real fine place someday.

He rode back.

"For now," he said, "you just tend to your business. I'll discuss it with my captain, and with Lieutenant Grady and the government surveyors, and we'll make a decision. We'll tell you what it is and you'll do it."

Roman Kreutzer had gotten a lot of his color back. He nodded. He wouldn't like losing the Yellowstone graze, but he'd like losing his life even less.

At that moment there came the distant, echoing sound of gunfire, from the south.

Matt's eyes narrowed at Kreutzer.

"We got nobody there," said Billings, answering the look.

"Then it's the Raffertys... or hostiles... or God knows what," said Matt.

A rider came from the south, punishing his horse.

Matt and his men started out to meet him. The Rocking K followed.

"That's Benny!" cried Stackpole.

"What was he doing?" demanded Billings.

"Jes' chasin' strays, far's I know," said Red Adair.

Benny whirled up to them. "Injuns! Got one of them effin' sojers pinned down." Then he realized he was talking right at some "effin' sojers," and his heart paused—

But the word "sojer" had no sooner left Benny's mouth than Matt was laying leather to his horse.

Private Charles Bainbridge had finally realized there were Indians around when three of the Utes burst from cover and ran at him yipping, war axes raised high.

He'd been leading his horse as he skirted a network of

157

smoking holes and hot, foaming water. Now he snatched his rifle from the saddle's spider hook and, without waiting to aim, fired at the Utes. Then he grabbed his Scoff. But by then the Utes, still some distance off, had come to a skidding halt, turned, and scrambled away. Bainbridge smiled, watching them scamper, until a shot from the trees took his hat off.

The horse bolted and he bent down, searching for cover. There was a large piece of mineral compound jutting up no more than five feet from the edge of the scalding water, and he lurched toward it. Another shot took the heel of a boot off. He crawled behind the odd formation, hoping it was solid, muttering, "Nice try."

He knew a little something about Indians and realized that he owed his life to the Indians' reluctance to count coup from a distance. A coup that was counted in hand-to-hand combat was always better. But the subsequent shot told Bainbridge that these hostiles, deprived of the most honored coup, were willing to take it any way they could.

He peeked out from behind his rock. He'd heard that hostiles often fired so fast and frantically that they weren't very accurate. He hoped that was true.

A slug hummed by and, typically, Bainbridge's mind wandered. He'd heard stories of the way Indians on horseback could, in the days of the muzzle-loader, double and triple army firepower, given equal odds. They'd ride in circles, their mouths full of bullets, throwing random amounts of powder in the breech, spitting bullets down the barrel, ramming them home. They'd get off two or three shots while some trooper was loading a single round. But the Indian rarely hit his target. Or if he did, the chances were he'd used too little powder and the ball would just bounce off the intended victim.

Another slug hummed by, and Bainbridge felt like cursing the invention of cartridges. These slugs were whipping by with plenty of zip and power.

Bainbridge gave his situation some thought. The outlook was bleak.

He had nowhere to go without getting scalded. And while the hostiles shooting from the trees weren't apt to get him, or not from there anyway, the grass between him and the trees was tall enough so that they could creep down real close. Even a cross-eyed hostile wouldn't miss from the nearby grass.

He wondered what Mary was doing just then . . .

And he sort of hoped she did miscarry. That way, with him dead, she'd be free and clear of any tiny, squalling encumbrances, free to make a new life for herself.

Mary . . .

Well hell, he wasn't going to make it easy for them. He reloaded his Springfield, poked the rifle around the lump of mineral, and searched for a painted face.

He caught a glint of sun on steel, and fired. . . .

Nothing.

Even if he hit him, the lousy, stoic bastard probably wouldn't give him the satisfaction of a scream.

His mind wandered again.

He wondered how Indian children, who were notoriously noisy, unruly, wild, and pestiferous, could ever grow up to be such quiet, disciplined warriors.

Well, they didn't, he answered himself, but after the painful ordeal of something like the Sun Dance, a mere bullet wound was hardly worth noticing.

Hell, he thought, it didn't take much more than a hangnail to start him squawking.

He wondered about childbirth, how it must feel. Probably awful.

Now the hostiles were really firing in earnest.

And Charles had to laugh. Blind sons of bitches, they weren't even coming close.

But then he heard a pounding sound. Hoofbeats. The hostiles were *charging* him.

He poked his head around the outcropping, prepared to go down fighting . . . and didn't see a single damn horse.

But suddenly there were Utes rising from the tall grass, running away for a few strides and then turning and ducking back down. And bullets whistled out of the grass.

Bainbridge looked the other way and saw Matt leading his men around one side of the springs, and some cowboys coming around the other side.

Bainbridge had a front-row seat.

Matt broke the charge off as soon as he realized that the tall grass hid a whole mess of hostiles. If they rode right over them, even a hostile couldn't miss. So he hit the ground, crouched, and moved forward a lot more slowly. His men followed suit.

Red Adair's horse took a slug in the chest, and the cowboy himself caught one on the lower leg before Sam Billings's bunch did the same.

The creeping attack wasn't nearly as exciting, thought Bainbridge. He almost came out from cover and charged himself, just to set an example. But fortunately he didn't.

Matt and his soldiers moved forward efficiently. The Utes fell back before them, and might have escaped if Sam Billings's men hadn't gotten behind them first.

There were some guttural sounds, and suddenly all the remaining Utes stood up, dropping their weapons.

Matt's men and the punchers surrounded them.

"Holzer, Rottweiler, Medwick!" called Matt.

"Yohhh," came a chorused reply.

"What?"

"Yohhh, *sir!*"

"That's better. Gather up all the guns, and look for wounded."

"What're you gonna do, Lieutenant?" asked Billings.

"I don't know yet, so you just hang around. First I want to know who that soldier was...or is." He looked down the gentle slope and saw Bainbridge carefully gathering all his equipment that had gone flying. "Bainbridge!!"

Bainbridge looked up the slope, and then came trotting on up it. "Hello, sir," he said, throwing up a feeble salute. "Nice that you all could get by. I just about had 'em on the run, though."

General hilarity coursed through the assemblage.

"What the hell are you doing out here, Bainbridge?"

"Surveying, checking maps, boundaries, topographical formations. You know, sir, my *job.*"

"Your job?" Matt hadn't heard about the new assignment. Bainbridge explained.

A light came into Matt's eyes. "Did you, by any chance, get west of here, northwest a ways, and see a building?"

"That Peckinpah place? Just the roof, sir, but I don't imagine there are too many like that around. I saw it."

"And do you happen to know if it's inside or outside the park?"

"Oh, hell, sir, it's *miles* inside. It's even inside Wyoming."

Matt had to be sure. "It's not just a little bit inside? Like an honest mistake?"

"I don't know about honest, sir, but it's not just a little bit, not according to my maps."

"You're sure you can read a map properly?"

Bainbridge appeared grievously offended. "I'm a *surveyor*, sir."

Matt nodded, but his face showed doubt.

"Look at that pool down there, sir. See all those colors in the rock formations? Seems like about fifty of them, doesn't it? Well, each one has a name, and I know each goddamn name. Want me to name them, sir?"

Matt shook his head. "No."

"Well," Bainbridge said, "I can read a map just as well as name all those minerals. A lot easier, as a matter of fact. Maps are child's play."

"Windy says the maps have got the Wyoming boundaries wrong."

Bainbridge looked stumped for a second. "Oh. That's right. The *published* maps do. Captain Forsythe told me that was probably true. But this one's from the '71 Hayden Survey, and it's got Yellowstone smack-dab where it's supposed to—"

"All right, enough. I believe you." And he did. He knew Bainbridge well enough to know he couldn't be that certain and that wrong at the same time.

"Then let's get moving. We'll take these Utes back with us. Malone, you haul ass back to camp and tell Windy to go round up some Arapaho and some Shoshone, if he can find any."

"What are you planning, Matt?" asked Grady.

"An old-fashioned powwow. Get a few things settled and out of the way. You, Billings, go get Kreutzer and bring him along."

"What for?"

"What for? Before the day's out, you're going to know exactly what you can and cannot do."

"You seem to be in a big hurry."

"Just clearing the decks."

Sam Billings's eyes narrowed. "Peckinpah? An' that crowd of toughs an' lowlifes?"

"You got it, mister."

sixteen _____

"Windy said he knew where to go for the Arapaho," said Sergeant Cohen, as Matt ducked into the HQ tent. "Said he'd be back real quick."

"Good."

"What happened?"

"Didn't Malone say? Most times you can't shut him up."

"He told everyone else, I guess, but he didn't tell us." Meaning himself and Captain Conway, who was trying to pretend that letting his first officer go gunning for a puncher was all in a day's work. "Besides, Malone exaggerates."

Matt told them, with neither exaggeration nor false modesty.

"There won't be any problems, will there?" asked the captain. Army men who wielded their guns "out of season," so to speak, could anticipate disciplinary action.

"Nope. Unless it comes from you. Far as I could tell, the Rocking K was glad to be rid of that firecracker. And incidentally, Billings and Kreutzer should be here soon. Let's decide what we're going to tell them. This latest scrape gave me some ideas."

The two men called for Lieutenant Grady and Captain Forsythe, and the four sat around discussing the matter.

They'd just about finished when Maggie Cohen burst in. "Ben, do you know where Bainbridge is?"

"He's back, I know that," said Ben, "and he's around here somewhere. Why?"

"Mary's giving signs. It may be time." Maggie looked worried.

"It's too soon!" exclaimed Captain Conway.

"Maybe so, but the baby might not know that."

Warner Conway cursed roundly.

"Try the surveyor's tent, Maggie," said Ben, "he's probably there. Seems to think he's a surveyor now."

Maggie ducked back out.

"Now ain't that a hell of a note, sir?" said Cohen.

"Goddamn," groaned Warner Conway, "a month early. You don't know how much of a hell of a note."

A half-hour later, Windy rode in leading a small group of Arapaho. The Arapaho were sent to one end of the compound, where they stood eyeing their "favorite enemies," the Utes, who were at the other end.

Matt and Captain Conway took up a position in the center.

"You men keep them all covered," ordered the captain, and the Indians rolled their eyes apprehensively at the sound of guns being cocked.

Windy sauntered up to the captain.

"Bring them together, Windy, peacefully."

"I gotta warn you, Captain, these Arapaho and Utes might agree with you, but they don't represent no one but themselves. Howling Wolf over there, he's about as close to a chief as these Arapaho got, but he can say, 'Peace forever, white man,' and every single Arapaho's got the right to tell him to go sodomize hisself."

Captain Conway nodded, then asked, "What is the Indian expression for that particular activity?"

"You don't wanta hear it, Captain."

"Indeed. Well, yes, I am familiar with that leaderless aspect of Indian culture. As it pertains to warlike activities, it's been at the root of much trouble."

"The Indians never made no secret of it, Captain."

"I know, I know. The white man's always believed what he wanted to believe. In this particular case, we can only hope that word gets around. Now call them together."

Windy did so, and the captain told the assembled Indians that though this land, this park, was sacred to the Great White Father, he would permit them to continue to hunt there, but only to a strictly limited degree. They would be allowed to enter the park and, with the permission of the Americans, hunt, but they would have to register their kill with the Americans and then return immediately to their reservations. If they abided by those rules and did not hunt too often, or kill too much, then they and the Americans could live together in peace. But should they abuse their hunting rights or behave in anything other than a peaceful manner, the Great White Father's wrath would be terrible.

It was obviously something of a repetition or confirmation of what Sergeant Cohen had told Little Hawk. And Sergeant Cohen, standing just outside HQ, was greatly relieved. He did not know that because of his promises, the captain had been more generous than he might otherwise have been.

As Windy translated, Matt and Captain Conway watched the faces of the Indians. But that didn't tell them much.

When Windy had finished, Howling Wolf made a fiery speech, and one of the Utes made a similar speech.

"They say all right," said Windy, "and a lot of other things at each other."

Captain Conway nodded. "Let us smoke the peace pipe," he said solemnly.

But nothing happened, aside from Cohen suddenly disappearing.

The captain turned and yelled back at the HQ tent, "Sergeant, hurry, before they start shooting each other."

Cohen rushed from the tent, clutching a pipe. "Hope you got the right stuff, Windy," he said to their chief scout, the last word on Indian lore. "I tasted it. Tastes like dog droppings."

"Ahhh," said Windy, as Captain Conway paled slightly.

"Take a real short puff, sir," Cohen whispered to his CO.

"You can count on that, Sergeant," said the captain.

The pipe was passed around. It had to be relit five times, and Windy had to repack it once.

Conway thought Cohen had hit the nail on the head.

The ceremony finished, a few gifts were exchanged and the Arapaho were allowed to file out and be on their way.

The Utes were held for a while, and then given their weapons and released.

No sooner had they departed than Cohen came out of the HQ tent asking, "Who's been eating my jellybeans?"

"Sergeant," said Captain Conway sadly, "I had to give them *something*."

"Them? You gave *them* my jellybeans . . . sir?"

It was ludicrous, thought Conway. The toughest noncom he'd ever known was getting excited over a bag of candy. He stepped close and said confidentially, "I will replace those jellybeans you stole, Sergeant, as soon as we get back to post. I'll steal you some more."

Five minutes later, gunfire erupted in the hills to the south.

"I have a feeling," said Matt, "that the Arapaho didn't go very far."

"What should we do?" asked Lieutenant Grady.

Conway shrugged and said, "Let 'em fight. I hope your Kreutzer and Billings aren't in the middle of it."

"I think Billings is a little sharper than that," said Matt.

He was. He and Roman Kreutzer showed up a half-hour later. "We had to wait until them fellers was through shootin' at each other."

"Anyone killed?"

"Nawww. You know them, they fight an' fight and one man gets hurt, just one, an' they all pack up and head home." Billings grinned. "Them fellers woulda lasted forever out here if it wasn't for us."

"Us?"

"Us white men. First we diseased 'em, then we shot up all their food, and then we shot *them* up."

"You sound like a friend of the Indian."

"Hell no," declared Billings, "but facts is facts."

"Speaking of facts . . ." began Captain Conway. "But first let's go inside."

Captain Conway, Lieutenants Kincaid and Grady, Sergeant Cohen, Sergeant Faulkner, and the two Rocking K men crowded into the HQ tent.

"Now," said Conway, "the irrefutable fact is that this is federal land, by act of Congress. It's public land, but by that is meant that it's owned by the public and open to visitation by anyone, but is not open for *use* by the public, not to hunt or trap . . . or graze cattle. . . ."

Kreutzer and Billings had known that was coming.

"Except by special permit."

"Hm?" Kreutzer's ears twitched.

"Special grazing permits make sense," said Captain Conway, "and we're confident the Department of the Interior, or whoever handles the park, will agree. I intend to make a report on the matter, as does Lieutenant Grady."

"I don't understand," said Kreutzer.

"Well, for one thing," said Conway, "the grass is too long. If the army's going to patrol this land, they don't want grass that's so long it can hide entire villages or large gangs or hunters or . . . you name it. This came to Lieutenant Kincaid's attention earlier today when he tried to charge some hostiles and they all vanished into the grass."

Sam Billings said, "That ain't no joke. They was up an' down like goddamn prairie dogs."

"And the army's not going to detail any men to cut the grass. There's a concept known as 'convenience to the service,' which means we make exceptions to general rules when it's to the army's advantage."

Kreutzer and Billings were beginning to smile.

"But it must be done under some kind of licensing procedure," Conway went on. "You'll have to apply in writing for a permit. We'll issue you a temporary one. We'll also have to work out some regulations pertaining to areas to be grazed, and how much grazing. You know what overgrazing can do. And all of this will be subject to review by higher authorities.

"So whenever you want to sit down with Lieutenant Grady and Lieutenant Foster, who's bedridden thanks to you, and Captain Forsythe of the surveyors, whose expertise seems to extend to farming and such, to work out the details, we'll get an agreement drawn up."

"What the hell?" said Kreutzer. "Why not right now?"

"Because for the next day or two we'll be tied up—"

"Foster and Forsythe won't, sir," Matt pointed out.

"That's true." He looked at the Rocking K men. "If you want to get together with Captain Forsythe and Mr. Foster right now . . ."

It seemed they would. And Kreutzer and Billings went looking for the two men before Conway changed his mind.

But Conway's mind was already elsewhere. He eyed Matt. "That leaves Peckinpah."

"I was thinking of the Raffertys."

"They may not figure in this, Matt. If Peckinpah simply

made a mistake in his haste, well, we'll just ease him on out and handle the Raffertys separately...that's if the Raffertys don't just fade away."

Matt couldn't see the Raffertys doing that. "But if Peckinpah hasn't made a mistake," he said, "it'll mean he and the Raffertys are in cahoots, most likely, and we'll have us a little war getting Peckinpah moved."

"Or locked up," added Sergeant Cohen, "since that'd probably make him guilty of a whole lot more than trespassin'."

"Well," said Captain Conway. He just couldn't see Hiram Peckinpah as an outlaw. The man was too soft. And he said as much.

"I've seen bears what looked soft too, sir," said Sergeant Cohen, the bear expert.

Flora burst in just then. "Warner. That girl, Mary, she's going into labor. Maggie's with her."

"Damn!" Conway exploded. "I was afraid of this. Sergeant, get Dutch over there, let's see what we can do."

They all rushed from the tent, Flora in the lead.

No sooner had they started across the compound, though, with Flora leading, than a cry sounded.

"Flora! Or are you her lovely sister?"

Three bedraggled-looking men stood just inside the stockade gate, leading horses.

Flora stopped, staring at them, and the men behind collided as they sloshed to a muddy halt.

"Who?..." ventured Flora as Warner Conway uttered a noise that sounded like a compound of misery and ecstasy.

"Captain Samuel Adams, Flora," said Adams, sweeping his hat off. "Somewhat the worse for wear after one hell of a trip, damned near drowned getting here, but still alive. Warner! Is this the wife or her twin sister? You must tell me quickly before I blunder."

All eyes turned to Warner Conway, who struggled to find his voice. "It's Flora," he finally croaked.

"Flora. I should have known." Adams advanced on her. "But Warner did write me of your sister, your twin sister, and if I'd had to *walk* these thousands of miles to get here, well, I would have done just that."

Poor Flora looked as though she were on the point of becoming completely addled.

Conway was beginning to see the possible consequences of

what, in a moment of mad inspiration, he had done. And since his goose was already as good as cooked, he might as well follow it through to the end.

"You specialize in children, don't you, Sam?" he said.

"Children?"

"Babies."

"Yes . . ." Sam Adams suddenly didn't like Conway's look. He reminded himself that they'd never been particular friends, joined only by a common lust for Flora.

"We've got a woman in labor."

"What about the letter?"

"She's had several miscarriages. . . ."

"What about Flora's sister? Isabelle?"

Conway shrugged and smiled. "We can discuss all this later."

"Conway!" Adams seemed about ready to kill. "Don't tell me you got me here just to take care of some ba—"

"Are you a doctor, Adams, or not?" Conway cut in.

"Well, I sure as hell am not going to be bilked into traveling this distance, seduced by a goddamn out-and-out lie, and then, to top it off, do you a favor by helping some stupid, miserable army *cow* have a goddamn *baby!* No sirree bob, not on your life—"

Adams might have gone on at greater length had not a cry of pain and suffering reached them all.

Adams's mouth opened and closed several times as he tried to carry on with his condemnation, but in the end he asked, "Was that her? She's in labor now?"

"Yes."

"She's on time?"

"Premature. By a month or two."

"Well, which? One or two?"

"They're not too certain," said Flora.

"They're not certain? These *are* humans, aren't they, two competent, reasonably intelligent people we're dealing with? I'm not a vet, you know, I don't handle animals."

"They're humans," confirmed Warner Conway wearily. He knew the worst was yet to come.

Sam Adams gave his situation a quick review. "Shit!" he said with heartfelt force. Then he said thinly, "Well, Captain Warner Conway, you royal son of a bitch, it's lucky I happened to come by, isn't it?"

168

"I'd watch my tongue, Captain," said Matt Kincaid in his most metallic of voices.

"Oh. Watch my tongue, you say. Well, young man, I don't know what charges can be brought, but to lure a member of the Surgeon General's staff two thousand miles at grievous expense, to deliver a *baby* . . . I believe my headquarters might have something to say about that, and *do* about that."

"My understanding, sir," rejoined Matt mildly, "is that you were lured two thousand miles with the promise of a woman. Your headquarters might have something to say about that too."

Sam Adams fumed, but finally he cocked an eye at Kincaid and almost smiled.

"All right!" he suddenly shouted. "Get the water boiling, and wherever that poor creature is, I want that place *clean*, in case I have to cut."

Flora Conway started chewing her lip.

Maggie Cohen emerged from a tent and sloshed toward them. She was the only one in on Conway's ruse. "Is this him?" she asked the captain, and he nodded.

"Let's go," Maggie said brusquely and, getting a strong grip on Adams's sleeve, led him forcibly away.

Private Charles Bainbridge, holding his wife's hand, looked up as Maggie and Sam Adams entered.

"Who's this?" asked Bainbridge.

"A doctor," said Maggie.

"Another *cook*?"

"A real doctor."

Bainbridge glanced at the medical bag Adams carried, but neither his voice nor his expression changed. "It's no use. This is what's happened before."

Adams saw the effect Bainbridge's words had on his wife, and snapped, "Shut up, son, and stay shut up. Or get the hell out of here." He leaned over Mary Bainbridge. "You're going to be all right, honey. I'm with the Surgeon General. Everything's going to be just fine."

Mary relaxed a wee bit.

"Now I'm going to examine you, honey—"

"Her name's Mary," murmured Maggie.

"Mary. So just relax and let Doctor Adams handle everything."

He began to lay hands on Mary.

His examination became so close that Charles Bainbridge began to get embarrassed, and even Maggie began to question the propriety. Adams caught their expressions.

"Now come on, you two," he said softly. "Mary's going to need your help. Don't start acting like a couple of old ladies."

"What about *him*?" muttered Bainbridge, meaning Dutch Rothausen.

"I don't think Mary minds who's watching," said Adams, stroking Mary's forehead. "She just wants to have her baby."

Mary's eyes signaled assent. Adams's gentle, certain, professional touch was winning her over.

"Now you stay with your wife for a few minutes, son, and comfort her, you hear? You two"—Maggie and Dutch—"come with me."

They stepped outside the tent. Captain Conway, Matt, and a score of men, mostly from Easy, stood in a circle around the tent entrance. "She's never gone this far before, has she?"

"No," said Maggie. "Why?"

"Because unless she'd had good care, she'd likely be dead." He paused long enough to shoot Warner Conway a baleful look, just for practice, and then said to Maggie, "I assume you've done some midwifing?" Maggie nodded. "And you, Sergeant?"

"Field surgeon. Basic repair. Cuttin', settin', sewin'..."

"Schooling?"

"Penn State."

"Indeed?"

"But nothing medical. Got to doin' some medic work in the War, but that's it."

"It should be enough." Adams paused then, his chin in his hand, thinking. Then he looked up at Maggie and Dutch, and at the others. "How tough is this girl?"

"Tough enough," said Ben Cohen. "She ran from a bear a while ago and came through all right. Why?"

"The baby's all wrong inside. It's alive, but it'll never come out the way it is. I'll reach in, try to shift it around—"

"Reach *in*?" echoed Mr. Branch.

"Hey!" yelped Dobbs. "Jes' like birthin' a cow when the calf's set up wrong."

"Exactly," said Adams. "It's not that difficult, given a hospital, that is, and an operating room. But here... well, I've got the tools, but we're going to need a lot of light, and that place is going to have to be clean."

"I can take care of that," said Dutch Rothausen.

"And I'm going to need some steady hands."

"How many?"

"Room for another couple of men...or women. We're going to have to tie off a lot of loose ends, and do it clean and fast, if I do have to operate."

"Why not wait until you're sure you have to do it?"

"Better to be ready to go right away. Won't hurt to be ready."

"All right," said Captain Conway, "who have we got that can give a hand? A *steady* hand?"

There was a moment's silence.

Then Malone asked, "Ever see Holzer build a house of cards?"

At the mention of cards, Conway thought of the women-folks' weekly card games. They were friendly games for very small stakes, but it was uncanny the way Sergeant Brecken-ridge's wife always walked off with everyone's money. "Matt. Have you ever seen Amy Breckenridge handle a deck of cards?"

"Seen? I've *played* that woman. And if she's doing any-thing, I can't see it."

"Think she's just lucky?"

Matt smiled. "Don't think it matters, sir. Luck or skill, Mary could do with either one."

"Someone run get Amy, the girl with the magic hands."

"No one's gotta run," said Amy, stepping into view. "I knew it was comin'." She fixed Conway with a look. "Magic hands, huh, Captain? Why don't we play us a round real soon, just you and me? Soon's we get Mary squared away."

Conway swallowed, smiled weakly, and—when Amy didn't look away—nodded. There went another month's pay.

A half-hour later the four "surgeons" emerged from the mess tent, with lobster-red hands and forearms raised before them.

Silently they entered the makeshift operating room.

Lieutenant Grady and Sergeant Faulkner had wandered outside the compound. The bears had spared the sutler's beer and hard liquor, and the two cavalry men thought the time appropriate to bend an elbow.

The sutler sullenly sold them a bottle, and Grady suspected that J. B. Lathrop was trying to make up all his losses with that one sale.

"He doesn't learn easy, does he, Sergeant?"

"Whaddaya mean, sir?" asked Faulkner innocently.

Grady grinned at him.

Then the two men fell to discussing the prospects for the next day. Grady filled Faulkner in on the discussions with the Rocking K and the subsequent speculations regarding Peckinpah and the Raffertys.

"You'll be riding in the morning, sir? Gonna clean out that rats' nest?"

"Sure looks that way, unless this birthing drags on all night. No one's going to get any rest until that's done with."

"You hear how Captain Conway suckered this here doctor into coming all the way out here?"

"Mmmm. But this doctor's a captain too, and being with the Surgeon General and all, I suspect he may have time-in-grade on Conway. Old Warner may have to pay the piper. But I'll be damned if I can figure out how."

"He can always lend Flora to the doc for a night."

Grady nearly choked on his whiskey. Then he smiled but said, "You'd better not let Conway hear you say that."

"Well, I surely don't intend to let *that* happen."

"Tell you what, Sergeant, let's get a couple more bottles and let the men have a drink. It may be the last night for some of them."

"It's gonna be that serious, sir?"

"I've got a feeling it might."

They looked around for J. B. Lathrop, but couldn't find him.

"Maybe he's gone inside to see what's happening, sir."

"Probably. Grab a couple of bottles. We'll pay him when we see him."

"Ain't like that cheap bastard to leave things unguarded like this. Serve him right if he got cleaned out."

They reentered the compound, and while Sergeant Faulkner headed off to give his men a treat, Grady looked for the sutler.

But he couldn't find him.

He finally ended up cornering Matt Kincaid in the HQ tent. Matt looked up quickly. "The baby—"

"What baby?" Grady frowned. "Oh, *that* baby. No, Matt, it's not that. Something funny's happened. The sutler seems to have taken off."

"So?"

"He's left everything behind, unguarded."

Why should that get Grady worked up, wondered Matt.

"Sergeant Faulkner and I were out there having a drink. I was filling Faulkner in on our discussions. . . ."

"Which discussions?"

Grady took a deep breath. "About hitting Peckinpah and the Raffertys in the morning."

Matt groaned.

"That's what I was thinking too," said Grady dispiritedly.

"The captain thinks Peckinpah's got some kind of clout up in Helena. And this sutler, Lathrop, just shows up, appointed by someone, somewhere. He's got to have some kind of clout himself."

"You think Lathrop and Peckinpah are partners?" Grady asked.

"Who knows? It always helps to have a spy in the enemy camp, or it may be that Lathrop's so pissed he'd warn them out of spite. Either way, I'll bet he headed there."

Grady hung his head. "So much for a surprise attack. Sorry, Matt."

"Don't blame yourself. I might have done the same. It just never occurred to me to go get a drink." He smiled grimly. "And *now*, goddammit, I think I need one."

The air was suddenly rent by a tumultuous cheer.

Matt shot to his feet, grinning. The cheer could only mean one thing.

And sure enough, standing outside the operating tent was Maggie Cohen, holding a bundle in her arms. As Matt approached, he heard her say, "He's small, but he's healthy. And Mary's just fine."

Captain Sam Adams emerged then, and another cheer went up.

He smiled, basking in the applause, but eventually his eyes began to search for Warner Conway.

Everybody seemed to know the story of Adams's trip, and they all grinned broadly. "Hey, Captain, sir," cried Private Parker, "if things don't work out, I got me a sister."

"She look like you, Park?" asked another private.

"She ain't as pretty, but she's stronger."

Adams eyed the six-two, two-hundred-pound Parker. He grinned goodnaturedly. "I may let that opportunity pass, Private, but thank you anyway. Now has anyone seen—"

Conway elbowed his way through the gathering, Flora right behind. The captain looked sheepish. "Darn it, Sam, I feel just terrible. Isabelle *swore* she was going to visit."

"Ah. So that's it. Well, maybe I'll drop in on Isabelle when I get back to Maryland. You'll let her know I'm coming, won't you?" Boy, was he going to make Warner Conway crawl.

Conway laughed nervously. "How about a drink, Sam? You look like you need one."

I need one? thought Sam Adams. He smiled. This was going to be delicious.

seventeen ————————

"Ready to mount!" cried Matt Kincaid, at first light the next morning.

"Ready to mount," echoed Lieutenant Grady.

"Mount up!" cried Matt, and again Grady echoed him.

"Did your man and Spotted Calf get off on schedule?" Grady asked.

"Windy left a half-hour ago," said Matt. "I guess Spotted Calf went with him."

A couple of weeks earlier, Grady might have argued about who went with whom, but they'd left that rivalry far behind.

Captain Conway emerged from his tent and, determined not to show his age, vaulted into the saddle.

"Ouch!" muttered Matt.

Grady and his troopers rode out of the stockade, then stopped and waited for Easy.

Conway asked Matt, "Who've I got?"

"Mr. Weaver, Sergeant Breckenridge and two of his squads. I've got Mr. Branch, Olsen, and two squads. We're leaving two squads with Cohen, and Grady's leaving a squad too."

"I count that as you with twenty, me with twenty, and Grady with thirty."

"In round numbers, yes, sir."

"You don't think we should leave any more?"

"It's all we can spare, sir. And as long as those left behind don't go wandering off...And besides, Captain Adams can keep a close eye on Mrs. Conway."

Warner Conway made a strangling sound.

"So if you're ready, sir, we'll—" Matt suddenly broke off. "Mr. Weaver. Who the hell's that back there?"

"Where?"

"There!"

"Bainbridge?"

"Come here, Private Bainbridge," called Matt.

Bainbridge rode forward.

Matt and Conway exchanged looks.

"What are you doing here, Private?" asked the captain.

"Sergeant Breckenridge told me to stay behind, sir, but it's my squad that's riding and...well, it just wouldn't be right for me to stay behind."

"Breckenridge!" Conway called.

Sergeant Breckenridge heeled his horse over. "Suh?"

"Didn't you tell him why he was staying?"

"Didn't figger I had to, sir, what with his wife laid up."

Captain Conway fumed. There was always someone who didn't get the word; it was an honored army tradition. But he didn't have time to waste finding out why. "You're not going, Bainbridge, because you've been transferred, effective as of midnight last night."

"What?"

"You're being transferred to the surveyors. You're going with the Corps of Engineers."

"Topographical Engineers, sir," said Matt.

"That's right, them. So get off your horse, Private, and get out of the way."

"How...?"

"Goddamn 'convenience of the service,' Private, that's how. You've heard of that, haven't you? We've been beating you over the head with it for the past few months. Now are you going to sit there and argue?"

He sounded pissed, but if he hadn't wrenched his horse around just then, Bainbridge would have seen the captain's grin.

Bainbridge jumped off his horse, but then had to scramble

as some forty horses went pounding by.

Lieutenant Grady and the cavalry fell in with them as they came out of the stockade, and the army force, some seventy strong, rode south up into the gap.

Matt Kincaid leaned toward the captain and yelled, "Another ten men and we could take on the whole Sioux Nation."

Conway was perplexed for a moment, but then remembered. Some eleven years earlier one Captain Fetterman, who'd boasted that he could whip the entire Sioux Nation with just eighty men, had ridden out of Fort Kearney with exactly eighty men. He'd encountered Red Cloud and Crazy Horse, and not one of his men had survived. Captain Conway laughed. "It's lucky Mr. Foster's laid up. He's the type to try it."

A couple of hours later they were nearing Peckinpah's and had begun to assume their combat formation.

Conway slowed, dropping to the rear with his twenty men to make up a reserve force, available where needed. Matt Kincaid, to whom Conway sometimes referred as his "war chief," prepared to take the right side, while Grady began to string his men out to the left.

Suddenly two riders came out of the trees ahead and rode toward them. Windy and Spotted Calf.

"There's a fight goin' on," said Windy, without preamble, as they met. He turned his horse and rode beside Matt. Grady came over to listen.

"What kind of fight?" asked Matt.

"Peckinpah's under attack."

"By whom, the Rocking K?"

Windy shook his head. "'Pears to be that gang."

Matt chewed on that for a while. Then he said, "It's got to be that sutler. He told 'em we were comin'. Peckinpah finally realized what was going on, and he tried to get rid of the Raffertys. Guess we forced their hand."

"I reckon that's as good a guess as any," said Grady.

The only thing was, it made Peckinpah out to be about the most innocent lamb that ever crossed the Missouri. And Matt hadn't read him quite that way. As a matter of fact, Matt hadn't really read him at all. He'd have to keep an open mind.

And hell, who did Peckinpah have that could fight off the Raffertys? It was sure one hell of a situation. "Head on back to the captain, Windy. Tell him what's happening."

They rode into a sparse growth of trees, and when they came out the other side, they slowed.

Peckinpah's place lay dead ahead about a mile and a half. The attack was coming from the rise to the south of the hotel.

"Well, sure looks like someone's attacking someone," said Matt. "We'd better split up, Marcus." The moment he said it, he didn't like it. It wasn't a good idea to divide your forces before you knew exactly what was happening, but the setup did look awfully cut and dried. "Branch and I'll go straight in, Marcus. You head for the high ground and hit 'em from the side. Once we secure the hotel, we'll come up the slope."

They picked up the pace again, Matt leading Branch and Easy straight for the hotel, Grady sliding off to the left with the cavalry.

"McBride!" yelled Matt. "Sound the charge. Let 'em know we're coming." Matt figured it would draw all the attention and mask Grady's flanking movement.

The sound of the bugle overrode the noise of the battle, and the gunmen on the rise began to split their attention between the hotel and Matt's charging score of men.

"Find cover!" yelled Matt as they arrived at the large, solid building. "Some of you come with me."

Matt left his horse on the run, as slugs hummed by, and hit the hotel door with his shoulder as he grabbed the handle.

He burst inside with Corporal Wojensky and privates Fritsch, Daggs, and Sleepy Jim Crawford on his heels.

Matt waved his men toward the dining room's double doors, and was about to head that way himself when a shape in the corner of the lobby caught his eye. He paused to look closer.

It was the girl he'd spent the night with here, huddling, scared silly.

She saw Matt and stood up, and her eyes grew large. She gasped, "Pony!"

But then her alarm appeared to grow instead of diminish.

Her eyes skidded off to the side, to the right and rear of Matt.

There was an explosion of gunfire from the dining room, sounding like a close-up gunfight, and the answer flashed through Matt's brain—a trap!

He lurched to the side, turning as he went, hands flashing for his guns. It was instinct, pure self-preservation.

By the time he was turned, his guns, the ivory-handled Scoff and Peacemaker, were finding their targets and starting to dance.

He found himself recognizing the enemy moments after he'd killed them.

Jack Rafferty, his face a mask of disbelief, blood gushing from the hole in his throat.

Another man, his gun going off, blowing holes in Peckinpah's floor.

And Peckinpah himself, his shotgun kicking high after blasting a hole where Matt had just been, a dent suddenly appearing in his gut where the heavy slug entered, and then blood splattering the wall behind him.

Matt spun back around. There was silence from the dining room. God, he'd waved his men on into a trap.

He advanced toward the gaping double doors, guns level. . . .

He edged into the doorway. . . .

And stared down the barrels of two pairs of Scoffs.

They were held by privates Fritsch and Daggs.

Beyond them, Matt saw five men lined up against the wall, between windows, two clutching their shoulders.

Corporal Wojensky covered the five men.

Four more lay on the floor, still.

"He's all right, Corp," said Daggs.

Wojensky glanced back at Matt and croaked, "Did you know what you was sendin' us into, sir?"

"Jesus, Corporal, I didn't. This was about as neat a trap as— Where's Crawford?"

"Ovuh here, sir."

Matt turned. Crawford was pouring himself a cup of coffee. He smiled pleasantly. "Care for some, sir? Sounded like you had yuhself some fun coverin' our asses."

Matt was temporarily speechless. Then he started to redden.

"Hold yer hosses, sir," said Wojensky. "Them four on the floor belong to Sleepy Jim. He earned himself a cup."

Matt began to smile.

"And iffen you don't mind, sir," said Daggs, "how about sendin' Crawford somewheres else next time? I hardly got me a chance to shoot anyone. One goddamn shoulder, that's all I got."

"Whaddaya mean, *you* got?" cried Fritsch. "*I* got him!"

"Which one?"

"*Both*! I got both the shoulders!"

"The hell you did!"

The distant rattle of gunfire reminded Matt that the fight was only half over. He went to a window and looked up the rise.

Easy's men, under Olsen and Breckenridge, were already starting up the slope.

Lieutenant Grady and his men did not have the benefit of surprise. The Raffertys, in fact, had hoped the army would split and try to flank them, and they were waiting.

Only discipline and a keen fighting edge saved the cavalry. With the first shots they were off their horses, and those who found cover lay down a blanket of fire until the rest could crawl to safety.

Those first shots had killed two troopers and wounded two more, but the Rafferty gang had needed a pulverizing first strike to win, and they hadn't gotten it. From that point on, the game was lost. The numerically superior cavalry slowly chewed them up. And those that they didn't get, Easy did.

Captain Conway rode up with the reserves, dismounted, and went into Peckinpah's building.

Matt inclined his head toward where Peckinpah lay.

"Is he dead?"

"Pretty near."

"The Raffertys get him?"

"No, I did."

Captain Conway, after the slightest delay, said, "A trap?"

Matt nodded.

"You know, that thought crossed my mind."

"You could have said something, sir."

"You weren't around to say it to. You shouldn't be in such a hurry."

Captain Conway went over and looked down at Hiram Peckinpah.

The man's eyes were open, but Captain Conway wasn't sure whether he could see anything or not. "I guess you never figured that Moran's painting could bring you to this."

Peckinpah's eyes closed.

eighteen _____

No trace was ever found of J. B. Lathrop.

The surveying resumed.

Private Bainbridge tried to adjust to his new duties, and did adjust quite easily. He never made any direct show of gratitude to anyone involved in the changeover. But he did name his son Samuel Warner Bryce Bainbridge.

Captain Sam Adams insisted on being given a guided tour of Yellowstone, by *Flora*, and Captain Conway gritted his teeth and acceded. Further discomfiting him was the evident fact that Flora and Sam Adams got along famously.

Lieutenants Cliff Branch and Pete Foster, the latter walking with a cane and cutting a very cavalier figure, were both seen in constant attendance on Miss Clara Mills.

And Matt Kincaid spent an inordinate amount of time seeing to arrangements to transport the five women and four legitimate male tourists from Peckinpah's back down to Virginia City.

"If you want to take a break, Matt," said Mr. Weaver, "I'd

be happy to see to arrangements."

Matt just smiled and declined the offer.

Two days after the big shootout, Captain Conway was sitting in the HQ tent, paring his nails and trading silences with Sergeant Cohen—Sam Adams and Flora were off somewhere again—when Lieutenant Grady entered.

"Morning, Captain."

"Morning, Lieutenant." Captain Conway then smiled and said, "Thought you were off patrolling the north forty."

Cohen groaned. The captain was getting humorous again.

"No, sir. I've been conferring with your relief."

"What's that? Relief? Well, it's about time. Where are they?"

"They're, ummmm, camped down the river a piece. They'll be coming in when you leave."

Conway studied his nails. "Tell me, Lieutenant," he asked quietly, "who's commanding this troop?"

"Washburn, sir. Captain Thomas Washburn."

"Oh Jesus. *That* asshole."

Grady tried not to smile. "Yessir. If you say so, sir."

"I do. And you may quote me, Lieutenant, if it suits your fancy. Captain Washburn and I may have graduated from the Point in the same class, but I have time-in-grade on him."

"I understand he was ranked third in his class, sir," said Grady, for want of anything better to say.

"I know that. Everybody knows that, thanks to blabbermouth Washburn. Tells you something about class ranking, doesn't it?"

Conway addressed Sergeant Cohen. "So, Sergeant, Captain Washburn and his crack troops are camped down the river. Can't be too comfortable. . . . I'll tell you what, Sergeant. Let's give the men a few days off to sightsee properly. We'll plan to pull out by the end of the week."

He turned back to Lieutenant Grady. "He's not going to make you camp down there too, is he?"

Grady smiled. "Not yet, sir. When he hears this, though, he may change his mind. But I shouldn't worry about it."

"Thank you, Lieutenant."

A few hours later, though, the situation changed.

Sergeant Fuller returned from patrol with disquieting news.

182

The Indians were up to their old tricks, hunting all over the park and taking potshots at troopers; there were signs of poachers; and more cattle were being pushed in.

Captain Conway, listening as Fuller reported to Lieutenant Grady, said, "But they have permission to bring more cattle in."

"These ain't Rocking K, sir."

"Ah," said Grady. "Aha. Well, perhaps I'd better get word to Captain Washburn."

"I already sent word on down to him, sir," said Sergeant Fuller. "Run into one of his men." He saw the look on Grady's face. "I thought you'd be wantin' to, sir."

"Yes. Very good, Sergeant."

"Lieutenant Grady," said Captain Conway, "if you could use any help..."

Grady smiled and shook his head slowly. "Thank you, sir, but I—"

"From effin' blue legs?" sounded a booming voice as the tent flap was thrown open and a spare, ruddy-faced man entered. "Not on your bloody life."

Conway had always wondered how so much hot air could issue from such a slight person.

"Captain Washburn," said Captain Conway sharply.

Washburn stared at Warner Conway, his face clouding.

"Stuff it, Washburn," completed the captain.

Washburn trembled in place for a few moments, then turned and stomped out.

"Good luck, Lieutenant," said the captain to Grady as the cavalry officer unhappily followed his captain.

Sergeant Cohen and Captain Conway exchanged bemused looks. "That few days' vacation still go, sir?"

"Hell yes. For all I care, Washburn can camp out till hell freezes over. Colter's Hell, that is."

There was the sound of a horse pulling up outside the tent. Moments later a dispatch rider entered.

The private threw up a salute and said, "Message from Fort Ellis, sir."

"You've got the wrong outfit, soldier. That'll be the cavalry. You should have passed them, camped down the river."

"Are you Captain Conway, sir?"

"Why, yes..."

"Then it's for you, sir."

Conway ripped open the dispatch and read.

"This is from Mr. Carpenter, Sergeant. There's trouble brewing back at the post."

"Why didn't he just send a rider?"

"Faster this way. Wired Regiment, Regiment wired Fort Ellis. There's a note here that Regiment added. Says as soon as the cavalry relief gets here . . ." the sentence finished itself. "Well, I guess that takes care of that few days' vacation. Get the men packed up, Sergeant, we'll leave immediately." He studied the message again, musing, "If Mr. Carpenter was in this much of a hurry, it must be worrisome."

"Is there anyone not present and accounted for, Sergeant, that you know of?"

"Just Matt, sir, though I guess you could say he's accounted for."

Matt Kincaid had seized Peckinpah's private quarters for his own. They had the biggest and best bed.

He stood at the window that overlooked the eastern approach. Wagons were drawn up beneath the window and were being loaded.

The girl came to stand by his side.

He put an arm around her shoulder. He'd be sorry to see her go. The last couple of days had been very pleasant.

In the distance a rider appeared. Matt wondered passingly who it might be, but then concentrated on matters at hand.

"I'm declaring martial law," he said.

"Not *again*?" cried the girl in mock dismay.

"'Fraid so. These are perilous times. And we can't let those clothes of yours fall into enemy hands. You'd better take them off."

"I guess there's no point in resisting."

"None."

She let her clothes fall to the floor and sought safety on the bed.

Matt also approached the bed, letting his own clothes drop to the floor. "You must be brave," he told her.

"Death before dishonor!" she cried.

"No. I told you, that's death *after* dishonor."

"Oh. Be patient. I'll get it right."

And Matt was poised over her, about to penetrate her feeble defenses and secure the moment.

There was the sound of a horse clattering up out front.

"Lieutenant Kincaid!" The shout seared across his consciousness. "Sir? You gotta come, sir. We're pullin' out."

The girl giggled as Matt groaned.

"Hurry, hurry," she said.

SPECIAL PREVIEW

Here are some scenes
from

*EASY COMPANY AND
THE HEADLINE HUNTER*

the next novel in Jove's exciting
High Plains adventure series

EASY COMPANY

coming in November!

It was Windy Mandalian who circled out wide, checking the sad heap of ashes, blackened timbers, and scorched iron that had been a prairie schooner. The patrol saw Windy step down and circle the wagon, his rifle across his arm.

Lieutenant Taylor sat his bay rigidly. The horse bowed its head to pull at the rain-freshened grama grass. It was a time before Windy came back in and reported. Taylor had read it on his face already, however, and the scout's words only reinforced what he already knew.

"Civilians," Windy said, his dark eyes fixed on Taylor's. "Man, woman, and boy child. Man had his fingers trimmed, scalp lifted. The old lady had her skirt up over her face. The kid had his skull bashed in. They'd went through their trunk; clothes and linen's scattered around."

"Elk Tooth?"

Windy shrugged. "I can't read him by that, but he's the only Cheyenne I know of that's kicking up his heels right now."

"Where's he heading, Windy?" Taylor's eyes swept the far horizons. He watched the grass quiver in the wind that blew in gusts, following the storm. It gave the illusion of a sea, of a trembling earth.

"Maybe to the mountains. Camus meadows?" Windy shrugged. "I can't figure him, Mr. Taylor. He's runnin' crazy, seems like. But whatever path he chooses—" Windy nodded toward the burned-out wagon—"it'll be a bloody trail."

"I'll need a burial detail," Taylor said to Corporal Wilson, who sat his horse beside him.

"Yessir."

Taylor watched as they rode toward the wagon, the wind in his face, the horse shuddering beneath him. Then he lifted his eyes again to the far horizon.

"I hope to Christ there's nobody else in Elk Tooth's path," Taylor said. Windy looked up, his dark face nodding agreement, but they both knew there would be folks in Elk Tooth's path. That was the way the Cheyenne wanted it.

Taylor's eyes swept the plains. It would seem that across all that vast flatness a man could be seen for miles, but it was all illusion. The plains were cut by deep, sudden gulleys where a hundred Cheyenne could hide unseen until it was too late for the unwary. He sat his horse without moving until the burial detail had returned. Then they formed up again and swung north and west, the cold wind in their faces.

Windy drifted over beside Taylor and asked, "What the hell do you suppose that is?"

Taylor shifted in his saddle to squint back into the sun. He saw them now too, but couldn't quite make them out, even with his field glasses.

"Wagon train. Seems they got some stock."

"Want to swing back?" Mandalian asked.

"No. They're heading into Outpost Nine, looks like. They'll get the word there, if they haven't already. Most likely they've heard that Mr. Lo is kicking up and have decided to shelter up at Outpost Nine."

Windy nodded. Taylor was undoubtedly right. There was something funny about that wagon train, though. Windy gave it one last hard look, then, having no luck, he shrugged and swung northeast, taking the point as they tracked over Elk Tooth's path.

Taylor had made the right decision. Swinging back to check on that wagon train probably would have cost him some men. Not to combat, however.

That wagon train was a special one, an incongruity rolling

across the country that had been stained with the blood of Custer's men not a year earlier. It was big, colorful, bizarre. The wagons were bright, festooned, illustrated. Their stock, shambling along behind the wagons, or locked in cages, was most unusual.

Grimaldi's Spectacular Continental Circus rolled through Wyoming, and Taylor's boys would have found that fascinating. What would have been irresistible to the Easy Company forces, however, were the three young ladies who sat on the tailgate of the last wagon, dressed only in their chemises, which they had hiked up well above the knees at the urging of a warm sun.

Six feminine, nicely turned, and firmly fleshed legs flashed in the sunlight as the Grimaldi Circus rolled and lurched across the High Plains.

The girl in the middle was long-legged, with full, pouting lips and a lot of rich dark hair that tumbled free in the sunlight just now. She had those slashing, dark eyes that warned of a temper, and a tempting, full-breasted figure that caused such warnings to be ignored by men. This was Carla Bramante, palm reader, veiled dancer, hellion.

She was flanked by two identical blondes: Ava and Anna Boles, twin sisters, magician's assistants, sideshow team. They each possessed the same lush figure. Perhaps they could now look back and see their prime, but it wasn't far behind. Their mouths were small and dabbed with red. They had flawless white skin that flowed evenly across their dumpling breasts, down across their wide, vigorous-looking hips and slightly full thighs.

Ahead of this wagon rolled three cage wagons containing a genuine Siberian tiger, a tired, ancient African lion, and a black bear. Beside and between the wagons, three camels plodded along, their rubbery, outsized lips flecked with foam. There were seven beautiful white geldings, three chimpanzees, and a nine-year-old female Indian elephant named Jumbo, gender and originality aside.

There were probably half a hundred elephants named Jumbo working in circuses in America. With the publicity the original had gotten as the largest animal walking the earth, the name drew them in. Originality be damned; it was those ticket sales that mattered to old man Grimaldi.

They rumbled on, the wagons listing and screeching. The

animals lifted their weary heads from time to time, sniffing for water while the men watched the horizon, wary of Indians. Mostly they stumbled on, one foot before the next. The prairie had that way about it. It smothered a man, strapping the senses, blinding thought with stultifying sameness.

But that was not the case with Arturo Mercator.

Grimaldi's wagon went first, followed by the tiger cage. Behind these were the various living-quarters wagons, then the lion and bear, the spurious Jumbo, and finally the wagon that carried Carla and the Boles twins.

Yet that was not the very tail of the party. Behind the last wagon marched Arturo Mercator, pleading, cursing, threatening.

He was not blinded by the prairie, but by the face and form of Carla.

"Please. Put down your skirt! Such a shame. I'm afraid the men will see you. Have you no decency?"

Carla tossed her head and looked out across the grasslands, disdaining reply.

"I'm sorry," Arturo shouted. "I thought he was putting hands all over you. I went crazy. I'm sorry I stuck him with my knife."

Carla whispered something to Anna Boles, who began giggling hysterically. She lifted her legs, holding her chemise just above her knees, and turned them, looking at them. It was enough to drive Arturo to the edge of madness.

"I love you. Marry me!" The wagon hit a rut and lurched, bouncing the three women into the air a few inches. "I'll tame my temper for you, Carla!"

Then, since he wasn't looking where he walked, but only at the long limbs, the sun-bright hair and limpid eyes of Carla Bramante, Arturo hit a fresh, warm elephant turd with his foot and sank to his ankle.

Arturo cursed, Carla laughed, and the wagon rolled on.

Milo Grimaldi was not laughing or smiling, or even managing a decent deadpan. The sweat dribbled down his coarse face, the sun was hot on the backs of his hands. The wind was cold, and the seat of his wagon was blistering his butt.

Mrs. Grimaldi sat beside him. The missus had been bitching for the last fifty miles, but finally the prairie had worn even her sharp tongue to a blunt edge.

"You'd think there had to be a town. Something. What kind

of a place is this?" Milo grumbled to himself, repeating his befuddlement endlessly, as if in some way that chanted repetition could banish the prairie.

"Why did we leave the railroad?" he asked himself. The missus had formerly jumped in here with both feet. Now she was exhausted, and Milo had to perform both parts himself.

"Sure, we do a little damage, and the money runs out. With no hay for the animals, we have no choice but to detrain. All this grass." He waved a hand. "All free."

Someone had told Milo that Montana was booming, with the mines in full gear, the miners ready to throw their gold at anything resembling a woman, at any entertainment after months in the cold, empty hills.

But Milo hadn't really understood how far apart things were in this country. In Europe it was different, settled, civilized.

"When we reach the army fort?"

Milo's head came around. The voice was so small and hoarse, so different from the missus' usual rasping, shutter-rattling voice, that he wasn't sure someone had spoken at first.

She repeated the question. "How far the army fort?"

"Tomorrow we'll be in there," Milo said with a lack of confidence. A passing party of buffalo skinners had told them of Outpost Nine. There they could rest, refill their water barrels, and most importantly, perform. If these American soldiers were anything like those Milo Grimaldi had known in Europe and South America, they were every bit as starved for entertainment and women as those miners in Montana could possibly be.

Milo found that thought momentarily cheering, and he broke into a tuneful whistling. That whistling would have been strangled in his throat if he had glanced toward the low, oak-studded knoll to the north at that moment. There, watching with narrowed eyes and intense interest, was a party of mounted Cheyenne braves.

The sentry on the south wall saw the dust pluming into the windy skies, to be torn apart and drifted across the prairie. The coach was running hard, and judging by the way the driver sat the box, it was Gus McCrae driving.

The sentry called down, "Coach coming in!"

A runner took the word to the orderly room, and Ben Cohen rose, tapping at the captain's door.

"Coach coming in, sir," the first sergeant said.

Captain Conway stood with a touch of weariness, and crossed to the hat rack, where he put on and carefully positioned his hat before following his sergeant out into the clear, crisp afternoon.

Matt Kincaid had also gotten the word, and was coming toward the flagpole to join them. Flora Conway, in that new blue satin dress, and Maggie Cohen watched from the door of the Conways' quarters.

"You have a recruit on this stage, Ben?" Captain Conway asked.

"Yessir."

"I think it'd be best if you indoctrinate him after I have ushered Mr. DeQueen off parade."

"Yessir."

They waited in edgy silence, watching as the gates were slowly opened and Gus McCrae, looking like the devil had chased him up from Cheyenne, rolled that Concord stage into Outpost Number Nine.

The captain, with Kincaid at his shoulder, stood waiting as the dust swirled and settled. That rain had kept the dust down for approximately three hours, no more. Now every movement, every puff of wind, set it to drifting across the parade.

There were a few curious soldiers watching the stage, perhaps hoping for a woman passenger, Wolfgang Holzer and Cutter Grimes among them. Cohen glared at them, but without a direct order they weren't likely to move along.

It was then that the crash of metal against stone and metal against metal sounded from the mess hall, and all heads snapped that way. Conway shot one quick, meaningful glance at Cohen, sending him at a run toward Rothausen's kitchen.

The stage rocked to a stop, swaying on the springs. Cohen dashed past Holzer, grimacing as another bang echoed from the kitchen.

"You!" Ben panted, leveling a finger at Holzer. "Have someone meet the new recruit and read him out. Anybody," Ben said over his shoulder, "just so it's not you!"

Then Cohen was gone and Holzer stood there, touching his chest. Something about a new recruit. His face twisted with puzzlement, then brightened.

Bates DeQueen stepped down from the coach and stood dusting off his hat. A narrow-faced man with dark, thinning hair, he wore a brown twill suit and a brown derby. He lifted his eyes to Captain Conway and Matt Kincaid, who approached him with warm smiles and wary eyes.

"Welcome to Outpost Nine, sir," Captain Conway said. He offered his hand to DeQueen and the newspaperman took it, measuring the man before him. Tall, competent-looking, a Southern gentleman apparently. He had the manner, DeQueen decided.

He was also army through and through. Yet he appeared a trifle old for his grade, and that gave DeQueen pause to wonder. It was early to be making guesses, premature to be judging a man, but Bates DeQueen believed he had a talent for reading character, and he thought himself, if not infallible, to be ninety percent accurate. His instincts had served him well in the past, and he had no reason to doubt they would now.

That instinct was what had made him the reporter he was. After all, we do not live in a world where a man admits to his failings, where the truth is spoken regardless of personal considerations.

"Would you like to come inside, sir? I am sure you have had a long and dry trip."

"I appreciate it, thanks," DeQueen said.

His eyes narrowed slightly as the two women on the porch came forward to meet them. That taller, elegant lady, a woman of breeding with a smile at once genuine and facile. Was she the captain's lady?

DeQueen smiled warmly as he was introduced to Flora Conway, who took his hand with genuine welcome. Maggie Cohen, he was told, was the first sergeant's wife. A sturdy Irishwoman with snapping blue eyes and the roses of good health blooming on her cheeks.

The tea was set out for them, and the men went into the captain's quarters, followed by the ladies. Bates DeQueen was weary. Dust clogged his ears, stiffened his hair, and had lightened the color of his dark brown suit by two shades.

Still he was alert, his sharp mind evaluating all he saw and heard. This was a man who never relaxed. Captain Conway saw it and he glanced at Flora, but his wife had already read the same danger signals in DeQueen's dark eyes.

This was a man to be wary of. Most wary.

After DeQueen had stepped down and been escorted to the captain's quarters, the stage driver had handed down the baggage and mail he was carrying, then slowly walked his hot horses toward the paddock area, where he could switch teams.

Only then, as the coach rolled away, did the other disembarking passenger come into Wolfgang Holzer's view. He stood on the far side of the coach, his massive shoulders hunched, his round, open face vaguely amiable.

Big! Jesus!

He was as tall as Stretch Dobbs and as thick as Dutch Rothausen, without the belly. Holzer tightened his belt and strode over toward him. The recruit grew bigger with each step, and Wolfgang swallowed hard as he drew nearer. It was enough to give a man second thoughts, but he had promised Ben Cohen.

Wolfgang Holzer had only half an understanding of Ben Cohen's speech, but he had heard this welcoming ritual repeated so many times that he had it memorized exactly. He therefore stepped in front of Lumpy Torkleson and, with an iron-heavy accent, told the recruit:

"Velcome to Easy Company. If you keep your mout' shut and your ears open, you'll find us firm but fair. If you fuck up, you can give your soul to Jesus, because your ass vill belong to *me*! I am Sergeant Cohen and I am the first soldier."

Torkleson cocked his head like some mammoth, puzzled puppy and gawked at this stiff-spined, gesturing private who announced himself as the first shirt. The guttural welcome went on.

"Ven I say froggy I expect you to jump. If you tink you can vhip me . . ." Wolfie hesitated here. He did know what that part meant and he shuddered as he looked up at the towering recruit before him. "I'll be glad to take off my stripes and show you the error of your vays. If you're ready, soldier, go ofer to the kitchen and tell dem I said to coffee and grub you before you report to your squad leader."

"Well, thank you very kindly, Sarge," Lumpy Torkleson said with genuine friendliness. "I could use a bite to eat."

"Vell, tank you," Wolfgang answered, clicking his heels. "I could use a bite to eat, too."

"Where is the mess hall?" Lumpy asked, squinting into the brilliant sunlight.

"Vell," Wolfgang Holzer replied, "vhere is the mess hall too."

"Are you funnin' me?"

"Vell, I am funnin' you."

196

"That's what I thought." Torkleson grinned and thumped Holzer on the chest. "You're a joker, Sarge. Come on, I think my nose has just located that mess hall."

Wolfgang Holzer walked along with Torkleson. Entering the mess hall, they heard one muffled thud and then a sigh. They glanced at each other and peered in through the kitchen door.

Cohen was there, rolling his sleeves down, and Dutch Rothausen was cutting a buffalo steak for the red welt under his eye, which would be a first-rate shiner by morning.

Sergeant Cohen glanced up, ready to chew Wolfie out for entering the kitchen. But there was little point in chewing out Holzer's butt. He simply nodded, cocking his head, as if by listening intently he would come to understand the language.

"Enough," Ben told Rothausen. "And this time I'm not kidding." He waved his hands in a gesture of finality. "No more of this crap."

"Ben..." Rothausen was frustrated, angry, lost for words. "I need some help!"

"Nobody can work for you, Dutch!"

Cohen sighed again, and then his eyes settled on the man behind Holzer. An affable-looking hulk of a man. Cohen crooked a finger. "Come here."

"Me?"

"Yes, you, goddammit! You think I'm talking to that Sioux behind you?"

Torkleson turned his head, his eyes puzzled. There was no Indian there. "You were funnin'," he said with a wide grin.

"Jesus God!" Ben Cohen breathed. He wiped his hand across his face. Dutch was leaning against the cutting block, a steak draped over his face. Holzer was nodding, understanding nothing.

"You know who I am, soldier?" Ben Cohen asked, stepping forward.

"No I don't, Sergeant."

"You're the new man—Torkleson?"

"That's right."

"Welcome to Easy Company," Ben Cohen said heavily. "If you keep your mouth shut and your ears open, you'll find us firm but fair. If you fuck up, you can give your soul to Jesus, because your ass will belong to me! I am Sergeant Cohen, and I—"

"Beg pardon," Torkleson interrupted, his face a model of puzzlement, "I thought *he* was Sergeant Cohen." He nodded toward Holzer, who clicked his heels and nodded, and Ben Cohen just gave it up.

"Your squad leader will be Corporal Wojensky. You're temporarily assigned KP. Dutch!"

"What?" Rothausen answered from behind that huge slab of red meat.

"He's yours for now."

"Mmfh," Rothausen answered, and Torkleson peeled off his tunic, rolling up his sleeves.

"Holzer," Ben Cohen said, "you may as well stick around and help for a while."

"Yes, certainly!" Holzer said. He bowed sharply. Ben Cohen turned then and, shaking his head, walked toward the mess hall door. When he glanced back, Holzer was following him.

LONGARM

He's a man's man, a ladies' man—the fastest lawman around. Follow Longarm through all his shoot-'em-up adventures as he takes on the outlaws—and the ladies—of the Wild, Wild West!

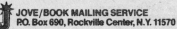